BIP= no newer 12/08

Carol F. Schroeder, MS, MBA
Gloria G. Roberson, MLS, MEd
Editors

Guide to Publishing Opportunities for Librarians

*Pre-publication
REVIEWS,
COMMENTARIES,
EVALUATIONS . . .*

"**T**his is just the publication for those librarians who want to write or who have to 'publish or perish' for tenure reasons. Written in directory format, this book supplies much valuable information for both the beginning professional and the seasoned librarian.

This book provides a comprehensive listing of library-related serial publications. Arranged alphabetically, each entry describes the purpose and scope of the publication, and gives the name of the editor, the business address, the editorial policy, the acceptance rate, manuscript requirements, and telecommunications.

Most significant for me as an academic librarian is the information about refereed journals provided throughout the directory, as well as the peer-reviewed titles listed in the appendix. Highly recommended for academic and larger public libraries."

Vivian Wood, MA, MLS
*Collection Development Librarian;
Assistant Professor of Library Services,
Hofstra University,
Hempstead, NY*

More pre-publication
REVIEWS, COMMENTARIES, EVALUATIONS . . .

"**S** chroeder and Roberson's *Guide to Publishing Opportunities for Librarians* is an excellent compilation of the purposes and policies of more than two hundred periodicals devoted to information on librarianship. It presents in a consistent format everything an author would need to know about a journal before submitting an article or paper, including editorial and review policy, manuscript length and format guidelines, and the addresses for mailing or E-mailing manuscripts. The acceptance rate for manuscripts and the copyright ownership policy are two especially interesting features of each entry.

The description of each publication's scope and content should make the *Guide* an invaluable tool for authors to select the best journal for their work to reach its intended audience. The wealth of detail provided by Schroeder and Roberson to help authors should be especially welcome in tenure-granting institutions where scholarly publication is obligatory, but any thoughtful individuals writing about library theory or practice will profit from this volume."

Jerome Yavarkovsky
Director, New York State Library,
Albany

"**C** arol Schroeder and Gloria Roberson have compiled a unique reference source in this *Guide to Publishing Opportunities for Librarians*. Some of the most asked questions are answered for each periodical, such as the scope covered, if it is indexed, publication lag time, publication restrictions, format in which to submit articles, etc.

The book has an excellent format of presentation. It is concise and to the point, with listings of a large number of publications in library science and related fields. Both English language and foreign journals are included, giving the potential author a wide range of journals in which to submit articles.

The list of refereed journals is extremely useful since tenure depends on publishing in refereed journals, as is the list of state library associations with contact persons.

This is an excellent source book for librarians and others in related fields who are interested in publishing opportunities."

Janet Sims-Wood, MLS
Assistant Chief Librarian,
Reference/Reader Services Department,
Moorland-Spingarn Research Center,
Howard University,
Washington, DC

The Haworth Press, Inc.

Guide to Publishing Opportunities for Librarians

HAWORTH Library and Information Science
Peter Gellatly, Editor in Chief

New, Recent, and Forthcoming Titles:

The In-House Option: Professional Issues of Library Automation by T. D. Webb

British University Libraries by Toby Burrows

Women Online: Perspectives on Women's Studies in Online Databases edited by Steven D. Atkinson and Judith Hudson

Buyers and Borrowers: The Application of Consumer Theory to the Study of Library Use by Charles D. Emery

Broadway's Prize-Winning Musicals: An Annotated Guide for Libraries and Audio Collectors by Leo N. Miletich

Academic Libraries in Greece: The Present Situation and Future Prospects edited by Dean H. Keller

Introductory CD ROM Searching: The Key to Effective Ondisc Searching by Joseph Meloche

Guide to Publishing Opportunities for Librarians edited by Carol F. Schroeder and Gloria G. Roberson

Guide to Publishing Opportunities for Librarians

Carol F. Schroeder, MS, MBA
Gloria G. Roberson, MLS, MEd
Editors

The Haworth Press
New York • London • Norwood (Australia)

© 1995 by The Haworth Press, Inc. All rights reserved. No part of this work may be reproduced or utilized in any form or by any means, electronic or mechanical, including photocopying, microfilm and recording, or by any information storage and retrieval system, without permission in writing from the publisher. Printed in the United States of America.

The Haworth Press, Inc., 10 Alice Street, Binghamton, NY 13904-1580

Library of Congress Cataloging-in-Publication Data

Schroeder, Carol (Carol F.)
    Guide to publishing opportunities for librarians / Carol Schroeder, Gloria Roberson.
       p.   cm.
    Includes bibliographical references (p.) and index.
    ISBN 1-56024-348-1 (acid-free).
    1. Library science–United States–Periodicals–Directories. 2. Library Science–Periodicals–Directories. 3. Library science literature–Publishing–United States–Directories. 4. Library science literature–Publishing–Directories. 5. Library science literature–Marketing–Directories. I. Roberson, Gloria.
II. Title.
Z665.2.U6S37   1994
020'.973'05–dc20   93-27250
                                                 CIP

CONTENTS

ABOUT THE EDITORS

Carol F. Schroeder, MS, MBA, is Reference Librarian at Adelphi University in Garden City, Long Island, New York. She is a member of the Library's Faculty Development Committee, which provides guidance and mentoring for scholarly work such as the preparation and submission of manuscripts for publication.

Gloria Grant Roberson, MLS, MEd, is Reference Librarian at Adelphi University and an adjunct member of the faculty at Hofstra University, New York. A published author, she is currently chairperson of the Adelphi Library's Faculty Development Committee.

Acknowledgments

Once our idea for this publication found acceptance with Peter Gellatly, Editor in Chief (Library Science), we were spurred in our work by the support of Eugene T. Neely, Dean of Libraries, of Adelphi University, and the cooperation of colleagues and staff of the Adelphi Libraries. We gratefully acknowledge their technical assistance, suggestions, and encouragement. A special thanks to Tanya Duvivier, student assistant, and Sarah Iannacone who typed the manuscript. Our sincere thanks to the journal editors and their staff who took the time to complete the questionnaire upon which this book is based, and the journal publishers who supplied additional information.

Introduction

RATIONALE

Today's librarian is more interested in publishing than ever before. This is evident by the number of publications in library and information science, and the value placed on them by librarians. The medium most often selected by writers is the journal or the magazine article. Regardless of its type, whether comprehensive or brief, scholarly or informal, descriptive or analytical, the article remains a popular source of current communication for the library professional.

For the writer, the process of publishing an article can be a long one. Once the nature of the topic has been decided upon, and before or during the initial phase of planning, the writer should target potential journals or magazines willing to accept the final product. All too often, writers tend to earmark a small, select group of periodicals as appropriate for their needs. These are the publications of which the writer has some awareness, usually because they are considered nationally eminent or locally important. In some instances, the nationally eminent periodicals accept few unsolicited manuscripts. However, the range of other library science publications available to the writer comes as a heady revelation. There are over 200 English-language publications covering every kind of article imaginable to satisfy the aspirations of writers seeking to promote their ideas, advance their research or contribute generally to the professional literature. This *Guide* comprises detailed descriptions of publications in library and information science to assist the writer in selecting appropriate journals of interest.

SCOPE OF THE GUIDE

Our purpose in compiling this *Guide* is to familiarize the reader with a comprehensive listing of library-related publications, mostly periodicals, that will serve the needs of both the novice and experienced writer. Since the needs of these two groups vary greatly, each with different levels of writing skills, interests, and aims, it seemed appropriate to include a wide variety of publications to meet their demand. For this reason, we have included regional publications, newsletters, bulletins, scholarly journals, interdisciplinary and general periodicals, subject-specific publications, electronic journals and newsletters, as well as many of the more familiar organs of national library associations, societies, and library schools.

Although this is not an exhaustive listing, it does include many international publications that enjoy a well-deserved reputation, as well as other foreign journals written in the English language that may not be as familiar to readers. Together they form an additional group of potential sources for the writer to pursue. It is indeed germane to explore these sources since many of these publications share areas of interest and concerns which, while not identical to those in the United States, are surprisingly congruent. However, in some areas, disparity exists. One region of the world, for example, may be addressing a methodological topic that has little relevance elsewhere. However, other topics, well documented in the United States library press through exhaustive series of articles, might well fill a need and close a substantive gap in the literature in a foreign publication.

CONTENTS OF THE GUIDE

After identifying approximately 300 publications for possible inclusion in the *Guide*, in March 1992 questionnaires were distributed to the editors. They were requested to respond with the following information about their publication: (1) its name, address, price, frequency, circulation, and affiliation, (2) the name and address of the editor for submitting manuscripts, (3) the names of indexing and abstracting services which include their publication, (4) the editorial aim and policies, (5) scope and content, (6) intended audience, (7) manuscript style and format requirements, (8) acceptance rate, (9) review procedures for submitted articles, and (10) telecommunications (electronic addresses, telephone and fax numbers). These categories are fully explained in Table I. The information provided by the editors was, in some instances, augmented by the publishers. Based on the above information, the *Guide* provides a detailed and extensive description of each publication to aid the writer in identifying potential outlets for the work in hand.

TABLE I

Title: The official, current name of the publication.

Acronym: A condensed form of the title, it is sometimes erroneously substituted for the official title, or, conversely, the title is mistaken for an acronym. The acronym, when included, appears in parentheses following the title.

Affiliation: An organization, society or group that sponsors one or more publications. One of the prime purposes of the organization in sponsoring a publication is to promote a close association or connection with the membership and support its mutual interests.

Scope & Content: The scope of a publication refers to the range of material it customarily includes. The contents of a periodical refer to the subjects or topics usually covered.

Indexed: This category lists the indexing and abstracting services, either issued as separate publications or as listings within a journal, magazine or electronic source, that partially or fully include the contents of the publication.

Editor: The individual to whom the writer sends a manuscript unless otherwise noted. Since editors change frequently, it is advisable to contact the publisher or scan a current issue of the publication to confirm the name of the editor and the address.

Manuscript Address: The place to which the writer sends a manuscript. In some cases, this may be the work address of the editor.

Student Papers Accepted: Indicates whether material submitted by students in library schools is considered for publication. Generally, editors are more interested in the quality of the manuscript and its appropriateness to the aims of the journal than the educational status of the writer.

Publication Lag Time: The period that lapses between the time an article is accepted and its publication. It is usually expressed as a range of months.

Reprints: A reprint is a copy of the article as it appears in the publication. This category indicates the number of reprints, or the number of copies of the issue in which the article appears, which the writer receives at no cost.

Authorship Restrictions: The policy of the publication that imposes limitations on who is eligible to submit material for publication. Generally, there are few, if any, restrictions.

Abstract Required: Indicates whether the editor requires an abstract to accompany the article submitted, and, if so, the length of the abstract.

Proofs Corrected By: Indicates the individual responsible for checking the printed text for typographical errors.

Payment: States the amount paid in U.S. dollars to the writer as payment for the material. A single figure indicates an average payment.

Number of Copies: Indicates the number of copies of the manuscript the editor requires including the original.

Acknowledgment: States whether it is customary for the editor upon receiving the manuscript to respond to the writer.

Acceptance Lag Time: The period that lapses between the time a manuscript is accepted for publication and the actual publication. It is usually expressed as a range. Within a publication there may be different acceptance lag times dependent, in part, upon the nature of the material submitted.

Format: Describes the appearance of the page, its size, color, type of paper, as well as line spacing and margin width. Information on graphics and illustrations is sometimes included.

Length: Indicates the average length of an article, and is often expressed as a range expressing the length in either words or pages.

Critique Provided: A critique is an evaluation of the submitted manuscript by an editor, an editorial staff, or by a reviewer with subject expertise. This category describes the policy of providing critiques to writers.

Style: Refers to a manual or set of instructions to guide the writer. It is especially useful as a reference source that indicates the punctuation, spelling, capitalization, and practices that are followed by the editor or publisher.

Refereed: A refereed publication is one in which submitted manuscripts are judged by an independent expert or a panel of experts. The referee's role is to assist the editor in evaluating the manuscript. A "blind referee" indicates that the referee has no knowledge as to who authored the manuscript. A "double-blind" review indicates that neither the reviewer nor the writer have any knowledge of the identity of the other.

Reviewed By: Refers to the review procedure used, and describes whether it is done by an editorial board, an editor, an editor with input from staff, or a combination of reviewers.

First Publication: States whether the copyright for the material, when first published, is held by the periodical, the publisher, the writer, or whether an option exists as to who holds the copyright.

Republication: States whether the copyright for material that is reissued is held by the periodical, the publisher, the writer, or whether an option exists as to who holds the copyright.

Subscription Address: The location for requesting information about, or placing an order for, a subscription.

Frequency: The number of times per year the publication is issued.

Circulation: The number of copies of a publication that are distributed by the publisher.

Cost: The current rate, usually expressed in U.S. dollars, of a subscription to the publication. It includes the cost of a single issue of the publication if known.

Telecommunications: The telephone, fax numbers, or electronic mail address of the publisher or editor.

After reviewing the responses to the questionnaires sent to editors of varied library and information science periodicals, several points about preparing a manuscript for publication became apparent. First, before one begins to write, it is important to understand the advantages of identifying either a specific journal or a few journals to which you would consider submitting an article for publication. The contents, scope and style of periodicals, even those publishing in the same subject areas, differ significantly. An awareness of these differences, along with an understanding of the journal's aim and its intended audience are helpful in enabling the writer to preselect an appropriate publication. This is especially true for the novice writer.

The wave of technological advances in communication have advanced the rapid transmittal of information. The widespread acceptance and use of telecommunication in particular have increased the awareness and knowledge of professional issues and concerns world-wide, and created an avenue of easy and rapid access for the writer. Two modes of telecommunication that have gained in popularity, and are useful in communicating with editors are facsimile reproduction and electronic mail.

INSTRUCTIONS FOR AUTHORS

After identifying one or more likely publication sources, contact the editor regarding the availability of an instructional guide for authors. This is frequently a detailed blueprint of specific requirements for formatting the article. It may also specify the journal's general editorial policies, as well as preferred grammatical usage and style. Some journals publish instructions for authors in one issue annually; others neither publish guidelines nor offer instructions to authors. When instructions are available, it is in the writer's interest to follow them. The writer's ability to conform to these instructions may very well increase the likelihood of a favorable review by the editor or others. If you are unfamiliar with the publication, request a sample copy from the publisher or seek a library that subscribes to it.

Unless the writer is instructed otherwise, the following three principal rules should be followed. Manuscripts should be typed double-spaced on clean, white, non-erasable, bond paper 8 1/2″ × 11″. Margins should be at least one-inch on all four sides. The print, whether typed or produced on a printer, should be dark, clear and easily read. Most editors appreciate, and some specifically request, that the abstract, bibliography and footnotes be typed double-spaced also.

Editors and publishers often request the submission of manuscripts that have been prepared in electronic format. Some prescribe a particular software program. WordPerfect 5.1 is commonly requested. Others have the capability and expertise of working with a variety of software programs, systems and languages, and accept diskettes in two sizes. It is the writer's responsibility to determine the editor's or publisher's preferences.

Reading the scope and content section of this *Guide* will assist the writer in selecting a publication suitable for the manuscript, and conversely, in tailoring a manuscript to match the aim of the publication. Whenever possible the *Guide* offers additional information on the preferred length of the abstract and article, the number of manuscript copies required for submission, the reprint policy, the amount of payment for published articles, if any, the format and style requirements, and other editorial policies.

INTERNATIONAL PUBLICATIONS

The responses received to the questionnaire from editors of English-speaking international publications was an encouraging one. Many editors expressed interest in receiving manuscripts from librarians and information specialists throughout the world. This opens avenues for the writer willing to explore the possibility of having an article or the results of research published in an international or foreign journal. The standards and policies of these publications parallel the variety found in library journals published in the United States. Only two terms, both referring to paper size for submitted manuscripts were different. A4 paper, a term frequently used in the United Kingdom, is 210 $\times$ 296 mm or about 8 1/2" $\times$ 11". Foolscap refers to a paper size of 17" $\times$ 13 1/2".

PEER-REVIEW PROCESS

A peer-reviewed article is evaluated for publication by one or more subject specialists within the profession. One of the procedures often used to referee an article is the blind review. To ensure the writer's anonymity in the blind-review process, neither the cover page submitted with the article nor the manuscript pages identify the author by name. A second title page is enclosed with the full name of the author, an abstract, and biographical information for the editor's use.

MAILING THE MANUSCRIPT

Write a brief cover letter to the editor requesting that the enclosed manuscript be considered for publication. Include a short biographical statement and telephone number in the letter, and indicate that a stamped self-addressed envelope is enclosed for the return of your manuscript. In many cases, a rejected manuscript will not be returned to the writer without a self-addressed, stamped envelope. However, if a manuscript has been requested by an editor, further transmittal of it becomes the editor's obligation. When ready for mailing, the pages of the manuscript should be held together with a paper clip, not stapled. If a diskette is included, take precautions to safeguard it to avoid damage in mailing. Diskette wrappers are available in office supply stores and in many stationery stores. This is especially important for 5 1/4" diskettes. Inserting a cardboard backing in the mailing envelope further protects both the manuscript and diskette. The following information should be clearly stated on the label of the diskette: (1) name of the computer or word processor, (2) name of the word processing program or language, (3) file name, and (4) number of diskettes enclosed, e.g., 1 of 2.

The paper copies submitted should be exactly the same as the material on the diskette. Any changes, last minute or otherwise, on the diskette should also be made on the printed pages.

THE REJECTED MANUSCRIPT

A rejected manuscript should not discourage the writer. It can serve as an impetus for an analysis by the writer of the treatment of the subject, and writing skills. Many editors offer brief comments or critiques from subject specialists. These serve as valuable guidelines by focusing attention on areas needing revision. The writer should take the necessary time to reexamine the manuscript in light of the criticism before attempting to resubmit it.

ELECTRONIC JOURNALS AND NEWSLETTERS

The electronic publications included in the *Guide* were selected on the basis of the opportunities they offer to prospective writers. Like their print counterparts, they vary widely in their mission, scope, and contents. Some are brief newsletters that are published irregularly, but frequently. New issues appear whenever the editor has accumulated sufficient material. This has the advantage of rapid dissemination of current news. Other electronic journals, issued on a more regular basis, publish peer-reviewed scholarly articles, or offer their readers general-interest articles on a wide variety of library-related subjects.

Access to these publications is via the Internet, the world's largest computer network. Although the number of computers linked to the Internet has expanded rapidly in recent years, and its use in libraries has increased considerably, the number of electronic journals and newsletters in library and information science is limited.

The aim of these publications is to reach as many potential subscribers as possible which necessitates using communication protocols common to most computers. This limits the publisher's ability to transmit photographs, diagrams or graphics, unless they are ASCII graphics. Since publishers have few options available to create distinctive page layouts or vary the type and size of the printed word, the formats of electronic publications listed in the *Guide* are very similar to each other.

Electronic mail (E-mail) is well established as a medium for rapid communication between writers and editors. A query letter from a writer will generally be delivered almost instantaneously to an editor anywhere in the world. Editors prefer the transmission of all submissions and related correspondence by E-mail as it is a fast and inexpensive means of communication.

Most electronic publications are transmitted to readers as E-mail messages. Users subscribe by sending the following message to the subscription address. In the message section of the E-mail type the following: SUBSCRIBE (name of journal your name). New subscribers generally receive a description of the publication and its affiliation, if any, the editor's address and instructions to writers for submitting articles or news items. Some publications also include instructions for canceling a subscription either temporarily or permanently. Subscribers also receive an explanation on retrieving current and/or back issues of the publication, or individual articles.

Back issues are stored in files available to anyone on the Internet. They may be transferred from the publisher's computer file to the user's computer file through anonymous File Transfer Protocol, known as FTP. Alternatively, back issues may be requested from the list server, which also supports the transfer of files. Both serve as a means of accessing with considerable ease and speed the indexing model for the publication.

There is considerable interest and debate on the future role of electronic journals. At present, they bear only a slight physical resemblance to paper publications. Publishers are developing prototypes with the aim of producing a format that will give readers the look and feel of a paper publication.

Models of distribution have changed dramatically. Some publishers transmit articles as soon as they are ready for distribution, while others give the subscriber the option of requesting available articles from a table of contents. The traditional concept of a journal "issue" has undergone substantial changes in the electronic environment.

At this point in time, electronic journals and newsletters offer limited, but new and exciting publishing opportunities.

Abstracting and Indexing Services Abbreviations

ABI Inform	ABI/INFORM (American Business Information)
Abstr.Engl.Stud.	Abstracts of English Studies
Abstr.Health Care Manage.Stud.	Abstracts of Health Care Management Studies (Ceased)
ACCESS	ACCESS (Australia)
ACM	ACM Guide to Computing Literature
ACM Comp.Rev.	ACM Computing Reviews
AESIS	AESIS Quarterly (Australian Earth Sciences Information System
ALISA	ALISA (Australian Library and Information Science Abstracts
Amer.Hist.&Life	America: History & Life
Anbar	Anbar Publications Ltd.
APAIS	APAIS: Australian Public Affairs Information Service
Art.&Hum.Cit.Ind.	Art & Humanities Citation Index
ASCA	Automatic Subject Citation Alert (Now: Research Alert)
Aus.Educ.Ind.	Australian Education Index
Basic Can.Ind.	Basic Canadian Index
Behav.Abstr.	Behavioural Abstracts
Bibl.Asian.St.	Bibliography of Asian Studies

Bibl.Hist.Med.	Bibliography of the History of Medicine
Bibl.Ind.	Bibliographic Index
Biol.Abstr.	Biological Abstracts
Bk.Rev.Dig.	Book Review Digest
Bk.Rev.Ind.	Book Review Index
B.P.I.	Business Periodicals Index
BPIA	Business Publications Index and Abstracts (Ceased)
Br.Educ.Ind.	British Education Index
Br.Hum.Ind.	British Humanities Index
Bull.Signal.	Bulletin Signaletique 101 (Now: PASCAL)
Bus.Ind.	Business Index
CALL	CALL (Current Awareness–Library Literature)
Cam.Sci.Abstr.	Cambridge Scientific Abstracts
Can.Bus.&Curr.Aff.	Canadian Business and Current Affairs
Can.Educ.Ind.	Canadian Education Index
Can.Mag.Ind.	Canadian Magazine Index
Can.Per.Ind.	Canadian Periodical Index
Cath.Ind.	Catholic Periodical & Literature Index
CBCAD	Current Business & Current Affairs Database
CERDIC	Centre de Recherche et de Documentation des Institutions Cretiennes, Bulletin du CERDIC (Ceased)
Chem.Abstr.	Chemical Abstracts
Child.Lit.Abstr.	Children's Literature Abstracts
Child.Mag.Guide	Children's Magazine Guide

C.I.J.E.	Current Index to Journals in Education
CINAHL	Cumulative Index to Nursing and Allied Health Literature
CISA	CIS Abstracts
Commun.Abstr.	Communication Abstracts
Comp. DTBS	Computer Database
Compumath	Compumath Citation Index
Comput.&Contr.Abstr.	Computer & Control Abstracts
Comput.&Info.Sys.	Computer and Information Systems Abstract Journal
Comput.Cont.	Computer Contents (Ceased)
Comput.Dtbs.	Computer Database
Comput.Lit.Ind.	Computer Literature Index
Comput.Rev.	Computing Reviews
Comput.Sel.	Computer Select
Consum.Ind.	Consumers Index
Cont.Pg.Educ.	Contents Pages In Education
CPI	Christian Periodical Index
Curr.Aw.Abstr.	Current Awareness Abstracts
Curr.Aware.Bio.Sci	Current Awareness in Biological Sciences
Curr.Bk.Rev.Cit.	Current Book Reviews Citations (Ceased)
Curr.Cont.	Current Contents
Curr.Cont/Engin.Tech & Appl.Sci.	Current Contents/Engineering, Technology and Applied Sciences
Curr.Cont./Soc.&Beh.Sci.	Current Contents/Social & Behavioral Sciences
Curr.Work Hist.Med.	Current Work in the History of Medicine
Data Process.Dig.	Data Processing Digest

ECA	Electronics and Communications Abstracts Journal
Econ.Affrs.	Economic Affairs
Econ.St.	Economic Studies
Educ.Admin.Abstr.	Educational Administration Abstracts
Educ.Ind.	Education Index
Educ.Tech.Abstr.	Educational Technology Abstracts
Eng.Ind.	Engineering Index (Now: Engineering Index Monthly)
ERIC	Eric Clearinghouse (See C.I.J.E.)
Excep.Child Educ.Abstr.	Exceptional Child Education Abstracts (Now: Exceptional Child Education Resources)
Excerp.Med.	Excerpta Medica
Fluidex	Fluidex
For.Lib.Inf.Serv.	Foreign Library and Information Service
Geneal.Per.Ind.	Genealogical Periodical Annual Index
Geo.Abstr.	Geographical Abstracts
G.Indian Per.Lit.	Guide to Indian Periodical Literature
G.Perf.Arts	Guide to the Performing Arts
High.Educ.Abstr.	Higher Education Abstracts
Hist.Abstr.	Historical Abstracts
Hosp.Lit.Ind.	Hospital Literature Index
Hum.Ind.	Humanities Index
IBR	IBR (International Bibliography of Book Reviews of Scholarly Literature)
IBZ	Internationale Bibliographie der Zeitschriftenliteratur aus allen Gebietendes Wissens

ILSA	Indian Library Science Abstracts
Ind.Artic.Jew.Stud.	Index of Articles on Jewish Studies
Ind.Den.Lit.	Index to Dental Literature
Indian Bk. Chr.	Indian Book Chronicle
Indian Lib.Sci.Abstr.	Indian Library Science Abstract
Ind.Jew.Per.	Index to Jewish Periodicals
Ind.Med.	Index Medicus
Ind.Per.Art.Relat.Law	Index to Periodical Articles Related to Law
Info.Manage.Ind.	Information Management Index
Inform.Abstr.	Informatics Abstracts
Inform.Bib.	Informationsdienst Bibliothekswesen
Inform.Hot.	Information Hotline
Inform.Sci.Abstr.	Information Science Abstracts
Inform.Tech.Rev.	Information Technology Review
INSPEC	INSPEC (The Institution of Electrical Engineers)
Intl.Bib.Bk.Rev.	International Bibliography of Book Reviews
Intl.Bib.Per.Rev.	International Bibliography of Periodical Literature
Intl.Bib.Zeit.	Internationale Bibliographieder Zeitschriftenliterature
Intl.Civil.Eng.Abstr.	International Civil Engineering Abstracts
Intl.Class.	International Classification
Intl.Nurs.Ind.	International Nursing Index
Intl.Phar.Abstr.	International Pharmaceutical Abstracts
ISMEC	ISMEC Bulletin
LAMP	LAMP (Literature Analysis of Microcomputer Publications)

Leg.Info.Manage.Ind.	Legal Information Management Index
Leg.Per.	Index to Legal Periodicals
LHTN	Library Hi Tech News
Lib.Hi.Tech.Biblio.	Library Hi Tech Bibliography
Lib.Lit.	Library Literature
Lib.Rev.	Library Review
LISA	Library & Information Science Abstracts
Mag.Art.Sum.	Magazine Article Summaries
Mag.Ind.	Magazine Index
Manage.Cont.	Management Contents (Ceased)
Manage.Ind.	Management Index
Media Rev.Dig.	Media Review Digest
Microcomp.Ind.	Microcomputer Index
Mid.East: Abstr.&Ind.	Middle East: Abstracts & Index
M.L.A Int.Bib.	MLA International Bibliography of Books and Articles on the Modern Languages and Literatures
Music Art.Guide	Music Article Guide
Music Ind.	Music Index
Oz.Per.Ind.	Ozark Periodical Index
P.A.I.S.	PAIS Bulletin (Public Affairs Information Service) Now:PAIS International In Print
PASCAL	PASCAL Explore
Pers.Lit.	Personnel Literature
PMR	Popular Magazine Review (Now: Magazine Article Summaries)
Pop.Per.Ind.	Popular Periodical Index
Predi.F&S Ind.U.S.	Predicasts F&S Index United States

PROMT	Predicasts Overview of Markets and Technologies
Psychol.Abstr.	Psychological Abstracts
Ref.Serv.Rev.	Reference Services Review
Ref.Sour.	Reference Sources (Ceased)
Ref.Zh.	Referativnyi Zhurnal
Res.High.Educ.Abstr.	Research into Higher Education Abstracts
Rev. of Revs.	Review of Reviews
RIE	Resources in Education
Sage Pub.Admin.Abstr.	Sage Public Administration Abstracts
SCI	Science Citation Index
Sci.Abstr.	Science Abstracts
Sociol.Educ.Abstr.	Sociology of Education Abstracts
Soc.Sci.Ind.	Social Sciences Index
Soc.Work Res.&Abstr.	Social Work Research & Abstracts
Soft.Abstr.Eng.	Software Abstracts for Engineers
Software Rev.File	Software Reviews on File
SRDS	Standard Rate and Data Services
SSCI	Social Science Citation Index
SSSA	Solid State and Superconductivity Abstracts
Tr.&Ind.Ind.	Trade & Industry Index
UMI	University Microfilms International
Wom.Stud.Abstr.	Women Studies Abstracts
World Text.Abstr.	World Textile Abstracts

Style Manuals
Abbreviations

ALA
: American Library Association. *Guidelines for Writers, Editors and Publishers of Literature in the Library and Information Field.* Adopted by American Library Association Council. 1983. (Five-page pamphlet available from the American Library Association).

AMA
: American Medical Association. Scientific Publications Division. *Style Book and Editorial Manual.* 6th Ed. Chicago: American Medical Association, 1976.

APA
: American Psychological Association. *Publication Manual of the American Psychological Association.* 3rd ed., revisions 1984. Washington, DC: American Psychological Association, [1984], c1983.

Chicago Manual of Style
: University of Chicago Press. *The Chicago Manual of Style: For Authors, Editors, and Copywriters.* 13th ed., revised and expanded. Chicago: University of Chicago Press, 1982.

MLA
: Gibaldi, Joseph, and Walter S. Achtert. *MLA Handbook for Writers of Research Papers.* 3rd ed. New York: Modern Language Association of America, 1988.

New York Times
: *The New York Manual of Style and Usage: A Desk Book of Guidelines for Writers and Editors.* Revised and edited by Lewis Jordan. New York: Quandrangle/New York Times Book Co., 1976.

Turabian
: Turabian, Kate L. *A Manual for Writers of Term Papers, Theses, and Dissertations.* 5th ed. Revised by Bonnie Birtwistle Honigsblum. Chicago: University of Chicago Press, 1987.

Alphabetical Listing
of Periodicals

ACQUISITIONS LIBRARIAN

AFFILIATION: None

SCOPE & CONTENT: Each issue of this unique journal for librarians and information professionals is devoted to a single, broad, well-defined, and practical issue of immediate concern to those working in library/information center acquisitions and collection development. A primary purpose of this journal is to help acquisitions librarians define and extend their roles, responsibilities, and professional status in libraries and information centers and services of all types.

INDEXED: LISA

EDITOR: Bill Katz

MANUSCRIPT ADDRESS: School of Information Science and Policy, Nelson A. Rockefeller College of Public Affairs, State University of New York at Albany, Draper Hall 113, 135 Western Avenue, Albany, NY 12222

EDITORIAL POLICY:
Student Papers Accepted: Yes
Publication Lag Time: 6-12 months
Reprints: 10 plus 1 copy of issue
Authorship Restrictions: None

Abstract Required: 100-150 words
Proofs Corrected By: Editor
Payment: No

THE MANUSCRIPT:
Number of Copies: 2
Acknowledgment: Yes
Acceptance Lag Time:
  2-4 months

Length: 20-30 typed pages
Critique Provided: No
Style: Footnotes and bibliography
  at end of manuscript

Format: Typed, double-spaced, 1″ margins on all sides. Use 8 1/2″ × 11″ bond paper. "Instructions For Authors" available.

REVIEW POLICY:
Refereed: Yes
Reviewed By: Editorial board
  and anonymous specialist referees

Acceptance Rate: 30%

COPYRIGHT HELD BY:
First Publication: Publisher   **Republication:** Publisher

SUBSCRIPTION ADDRESS: The Haworth Press, Production Department,
10 Alice Street, Binghamton, NY 13904

Frequency: Biannual   **Circulation:** 342
Cost: $24 individuals; $75 institutions; $85 libraries

TELECOMMUNICATIONS: Not given

ADVANCES IN LIBRARIANSHIP

AFFILIATION: None

SCOPE & CONTENT: As a scholarly annual, it chronicles essential developments in the field of library and library science. All areas of public, college, university, primary and secondary schools, and special libraries are given up-to-date, critical analysis by experienced practitioners, academicians and other experts engaged in teaching, research and librarianship. Each volume includes a varied assortment of topics written for an international audience. Most manuscripts are solicited.

INDEXED: Curr.Cont./Soc.&Beh.Sci.

EDITOR: Irene P. Godden, Associate Director

MANUSCRIPT ADDRESS: *Advances in Librarianship*, Colorado State University Libraries, Fort Collins, CO 80523

EDITORIAL POLICY:

Student Papers Accepted: No

Publication Lag Time: 6 months
Reprints: 2
Authorship Restrictions: None

Abstract Required: Prefer outline and resume
Proofs Corrected By: Author
Payment: Honoraria paid to contributors

THE MANUSCRIPT:

Number of Copies: 1
Acknowledgment: Yes
Acceptance Lag Time: 2 weeks to 2 months

Length: 5,000-10,000 words
Critique Provided: Not given
Style: House style

Format: Sent with contract when outline accepted by editor.

REVIEW POLICY:

Refereed: Yes
Reviewed By: Editor and editorial board

Acceptance Rate: About 80%

COPYRIGHT HELD BY:

First Publication: Publisher

Republication: Publisher

SUBSCRIPTION ADDRESS: *Advances in Librarianship*, Academic Press, 1250 Sixth Avenue, San Diego, CA 92107

Frequency: Annual
Cost: $57 single volume

Circulation: 1,200

TELECOMMUNICATIONS: Editor: Phone: (303) 491-1836; Fax: (303) 491-1195

ADVANCES IN LIBRARY ADMINISTRATION AND ORGANIZATION

AFFILIATION: None

SCOPE & CONTENT: This annual features essays on major issues for librarians and administrators. Devoted primarily to library research, it provides comprehensive reports of economic, political, social and administrative developments in the field. It includes outstanding historical and conceptual papers covering the theoretical and pragmatic aspects of library management. It is intended for both a national and international audience and includes case studies, bibliographies, and new developments in the field.

INDEXED: Lib.Lit.

EDITOR: Gerald McCabe & Bernard Kreissman

MANUSCRIPT ADDRESS: JAI Press, Inc., 55 Old Post Road, No. 2, P.O. Box 1678, Greenwich, CT 06836

EDITORIAL POLICY:
Student Papers Accepted: Yes   **Abstract Required:** No
Publication Lag Time: 6-9 months   **Proofs Corrected By:** Editor
Reprints: 25   **Payment:** No
Authorship Restrictions: None

THE MANUSCRIPT:
Number of Copies: 3   **Length:** 6,000 words
Acknowledgment: Yes   **Critiques Provided:** Always
Acceptance Lag Time: 2-3 months   **Style:** Standard style sheet

Format: Standard.

REVIEW POLICY:
Refereed: By editors only   **Acceptance Rate:** Most are
Reviewed By: Editor   accepted

COPYRIGHT HELD BY:
First Publication: Publisher   **Republication:** Publisher

SUBSCRIPTION ADDRESS: *Advances in Library Administration and Organization,* JAI Press, Inc., 55 Old Post Road, No. 2, P.O. Box 1678, Greenwich, CT 06836

Frequency: Annual   **Circulation:** Not given
Cost: $38.10 individuals; $63.50 institutions

TELECOMMUNICATION: Not given

ADVANCES IN SERIALS MANAGEMENT

AFFILIATION: None

SCOPE & CONTENT: To provide in-depth studies of all aspects of serials management, including historical studies. Contributors are journal publishers, subscription agents, serials, and acquisition and collection development librarians. Most manuscripts are solicited.

INDEXED: Lib.Lit.

EDITOR: Marcia Tuttle

MANUSCRIPT ADDRESS: *Advances in Serials Management*, University of North Carolina, 215 Flemington Rd., Chapel Hill, NC 27514

EDITORIAL POLICY:
Student Papers Accepted: Yes   **Abstract Required:** Not given
Publication Lag Time: Few months   **Proofs Corrected By:** Author
    to a year   **Payment:** $50
Reprints: 25 to senior author
Authorship Restrictions: Most are
    solicited

THE MANUSCRIPT:
Number of Copies: 2   **Length:** 7,500 to 12,500 words
Acknowledgment: Yes   **Critique Provided:** Always
Acceptance Lag Time: A few weeks   **Style:** *Chicago Manual of Style*

Format: Everything typed double-spaced with no mark-up. Prefer final copy on diskette in ASCII format.

REVIEW POLICY:
Refereed: No   **Acceptance Rate:** 95%
Reviewed By: Editor with input
    from staff

COPYRIGHT HELD BY:
First Publication: Publisher   **Republication:** Publisher
    discourages

SUBSCRIPTION ADDRESS: JAI Press, 55 Old Post Rd., No. 2, P.O. Box 1678, Greenwich, CT 06836

Frequency: Every two years   **Circulation:** Not given
Cost: $38.10 individuals; $63.50 institutions

TELECOMMUNICATIONS: Phone: (919) 962-1067; Fax: (919) 962-0484; E-mail: BITNET:TUTTLE@UNC. Internet: marcia_tuttle@unc.edu.

AFRICAN JOURNAL OF ACADEMIC LIBRARIANSHIP

AFFILIATION: Standing Conference of African University Libraries

SCOPE & CONTENT: The *African Journal of Academic Librarianship* provides a channel for communication, education, and discussion of research methodology and technology for many librarians, especially those in Africa. As a vehicle for the publication of conference papers and proceedings, it frequently covers subjects of general interest including management and technical services, new developments, case studies, and bibliographies. Contributions are welcomed from librarians and information scientists working in academic settings.

INDEXED: LISA

EDITOR: E. Bejide Bankole

MANUSCRIPT ADDRESS: *African Journal of Academic Librarianship*, P.O. Box 46, University of Lagos, Akoka, Lagos, Nigeria

EDITORIAL POLICY:
Student Papers Accepted: No **Abstract Required:** 250 words
Publication Lag Time: 6 months **Proofs Corrected By:** Author
Reprints: 1 **Payment:** No
Authorship Restrictions: None

THE MANUSCRIPT:
Number of Copies: 2 **Length:** 500 words
Acknowledgment: Yes **Critique Provided:** Sometimes
Acceptance Lag Time: 3-4 months **Style:** Standard style sheet

Format: A4 paper.

REVIEW POLICY:
Refereed: Yes **Acceptance Rate:** 70%
Reviewed By: Editor with input from
  staff and blind refereed

COPYRIGHT HELD BY:
First Publication: Journal **Republication:** Journal

SUBSCRIPTION ADDRESS: *African Journal of Academic Librarianship*, P.O. Box 46, University of Lagos, Akoka, Lagos, Nigeria

Frequency: Biannually **Circulation:** 200
Cost: $50 individuals, institutions, and others; $25 single issue

TELECOMMUNICATIONS: Phone: Editor: 524968 (Lagos, Nigeria)

AGAINST THE GRAIN

AFFILIATION: None

SCOPE & CONTENT: This journal serves as a link between scholarly publishers, and librarians of all types: serials, acquisitions, collection development as well as directors in academic, special, medical, and public libraries and vendors of library materials. The intended audience is both national and international in scope. A wide range of subjects, both newsy and pragmatic, relating to library science is covered. Articles on general topics of a practical nature are ranked high on the list of those accepted. State of the art, historical, and case studies are also considered. Book reviews are encouraged. Contributors are librarians, publishers and vendors throughout the United States.

INDEXED: Currently under review

EDITOR: Katina Strauch

MANUSCRIPT ADDRESS: College of Charleston, Citadel Station, Charleston, SC 29409

EDITORIAL POLICY:
Student Papers Accepted: Yes
Publication Lag Time: 1-2 months
Reprints: 2 copies of the issue
Authorship Restrictions: None

Abstract Required: No
Proofs Corrected By: Editor or staff
Payment: No

THE MANUSCRIPT:
Number of Copies: 1
Acknowledgment: Yes
Acceptance Lag Time: 1 month

Length: 1,000-2,000 words
Critique Provided: Sometimes
Style: Standard

Format: None (Prefer machine-readable diskette).

REVIEW POLICY:
Refereed: Yes
Reviewed By: Varies according to material submitted

Acceptance Rate: Good

COPYRIGHT HELD BY:
First Publication: Publisher

Republication: Publisher

SUBSCRIPTION ADDRESS: Katina Strauch, *Against the Grain*, College of Charleston, Citadel Station, Charleston, SC 29409

Frequency: Five times a year
Cost: $25 individuals; $25 institutions; $35 foreign

Circulation: 1,200-1,500

TELECOMMUNICATIONS: Katina Strauch: Phone: (803) 792-8020; Fax: (803) 792-8019; BITNET: STRAUCHK@CITADEL; Internet: strauchk @wando.cofc.edu.

ALCTS NEWSLETTER

AFFILIATION: Association For Library Collections and Technical Services, a Division of the American Library Association

SCOPE & CONTENT: A newsletter that focuses on technical service practices and news items, especially those of interest to members of ALCTS. The intended audience is worldwide. It publishes short articles on topics of current concern, as well as special features including commentaries, new developments, news items, new products, and conference workshop proceedings. New publications are listed, but not reviewed. Most contributors are members of ALCTS.

INDEXED: Lib.Lit.

EDITOR: Ann G. Swartzell

MANUSCRIPT ADDRESS: Conservation Department, 416 Main Library, University of California, Berkeley, CA 94720

EDITORIAL POLICY:

Student Papers Accepted: No
Publication Lag Time: 10 weeks
Reprints: None
Authorship Restrictions: Most manuscripts are solicited

Abstract Required: No
Proofs Corrected By: Editor
Payment: No

THE MANUSCRIPT:

Number of Copies: 1
Acknowledgment: Yes
Acceptance Lag Time: Not given

Length: 500 words maximum
Critique Provided: Not given
Style: Any standard format accepted

Format: Typed double-spaced, or send E-mail.

REVIEW POLICY:

Refereed: No
Reviewed By: Editor

Acceptance Rate: Not given

COPYRIGHT HELD BY:

First Publication: Publisher

Republication: Publisher

SUBSCRIPTION ADDRESS: *ALCTS Newsletter*, Subscriptions, American Library Association, 50 E. Huron St., Chicago, IL 60611

Frequency: 8 issues per year   **Circulation:** 6,150
Cost: $25 individuals; $35 foreign; free to ACLTS members; $5 single issue

TELECOMMUNICATIONS: Editor: E-mail: Internet: aswartze@library.berkeley.edu

ALEXANDRIA: JOURNAL OF NATIONAL & INTERNATIONAL LIBRARY & INFORMATION ISSUES

AFFILIATION: None

SCOPE & CONTENT: This publication discusses and highlights international policy issues relating to national libraries. Subjects covered are of current interest to an international audience. Contributors are librarians worldwide. It includes special "theme" issues, but not reviews.

INDEXED: Not given

EDITOR: Maurice Line

MANUSCRIPT ADDRESS: 10 Blackthorn Lane, Burn Bridge, Harrogate, North Yorkshire HG3 1NZ, U.K.

EDITORIAL POLICY:
Student Papers Accepted: No   **Abstract Required:** No
Publication Lag Time: About 6 months   **Proofs Corrected By:** Editor
Reprints: Not given   **Payment:** Not given
Authorship Restrictions: None

THE MANUSCRIPT:
Number of Copies: 2   **Length:** 5,000-7,000 words
Acknowledgment: Yes   **Critique Provided:** Upon request
Acceptance Lag Time: 1 month   **Style:** House style sheet available

Format: Typed double-spaced on A4 paper.

REVIEW POLICY:
Refereed: Not given   **Acceptance Rate:** About 50%
Reviewed By: Editorial board

COPYRIGHT HELD BY:
First Publication: Not given   **Republication:** Not given

SUBSCRIPTION ADDRESS: Gower Publishing Co, Ltd., Gower House, Croft Rd., Aldershot, Hants GV11 3HR, England

Frequency: Quarterly   **Circulation:** About 200
Cost: $120 individuals and institutions

TELECOMMUNICATIONS: Publishers: Phone: 0252-331551; Editor: Phone and Fax: 0423 87284

AMERICAN ANTIQUARIAN SOCIETY. PROCEEDINGS

AFFILIATION: None

SCOPE & CONTENT: This journal specializes in the publication of tools for scholarship such as bibliographies and primary documents. The focus is scholarship on the cutting edge of the new interdisciplinary field of book history in American culture. The intended audience is national and international.

INDEXED: Not given

EDITOR: John B. Hench

MANUSCRIPT ADDRESS: American Antiquarian Society, 185 Salisbury St., Worcester, MA 01609

EDITORIAL POLICY:

Student Papers Accepted: Not given	**Abstract Required:** Not given
Publication Lag Time: Not given	**Proofs Corrected By:** Not given
Reprints: Not given	**Payment:** Not given
Authorship Restrictions: Not given	

THE MANUSCRIPT:

Number of Copies: Not given	**Length:** Not given
Acknowledgment: Not given	**Critique Provided:** Not given
Acceptance Lag Time: Not given	**Style:** Not given

Format: Not given.

REVIEW POLICY:

Refereed: Not given	**Acceptance Rate:** Not given
Reviewed By: Not given	

COPYRIGHT HELD BY:

First Publication: Not given	**Republication:** Not given

Subscription Address: American Antiquarian Society, 185 Salisbury Street, Worcester, MA 01609

Frequency: Semiannual   **Circulation:** About 1,000
Cost: $45 individuals and institutions; $22.50 single issue

TELECOMMUNICATIONS: Not given

AMERICAN LIBRARIES

AFFILIATION: American Library Association

SCOPE & CONTENT: *American Libraries* is a national magazine published by the American Library Association for its 50,000 members. Not a scholarly journal, it provides independent coverage of news and major developments in and related to the library field at all levels. Among its features are: an open "opinion" column, highlights of life in modern libraries, and concise, current information in all major areas of the field, from intellectual freedom to technology. From one to three articles may be published each month on topics of major importance or special timeliness.

INDEXED: C.I.J.E., Educ.Ind., Inform.Sci.Abstr., LISA, Mag.Ind., Mag.Art.Sum.

EDITOR: Thomas Gaughan

MANUSCRIPT ADDRESS: *American Libraries*, American Library Association, 50 E. Huron St., Chicago, IL 60611

EDITORIAL POLICY:

Student Papers Accepted: Not given	**Abstract Required:** No
Publication Lag Time: 2 or more months	**Proofs Corrected By:** Author
	Payment: $50-200 for most articles
Reprints: Not provided	$30-75 for cartoons
Authorship Restrictions: None	

THE MANUSCRIPT:

Number of Copies: 1	**Length:** 600-2,500 words
Acknowledgment: Upon request	**Critique Provided:** Yes
Acceptance Lag Time: 3-8 weeks	**Style:** Informal, *Chicago Manual of Style* preferred

Format: Double-spaced, letter-or-near-letter quality on plain bond. Prefer line length of about 40 characters, with unjustified (ragged) margins, submit with 5 1/4″ diskette (WordPerfect preferred).

REVIEW POLICY:

Refereed: No	**Acceptance Rate:** Not given
Reviewed By: Editor	

COPYRIGHT HELD BY:

First Publication: Publisher	**Republication:** Publisher

SUBSCRIPTION ADDRESS: *American Libraries*, Subscriptions, American Library Association, 50 E. Huron St., Chicago, IL 60611

Frequency: Monthly, except July/August   **Circulation:** 54,000

Cost: Free to American Library Association members; $60 institutions; $6 single issue

TELECOMMUNICATIONS: American Library Association: Phone: (313) 280-4216; Fax: (312) 440-0901

AMERICAN SOCIETY FOR INFORMATION SCIENCE. BULLETIN

AFFILIATION: American Society for Information Science

SCOPE & CONTENT: The *Bulletin* is a news magazine highlighting topics of interest to the information field. "Cover Stories" appearing in most issues focus on one theme that is explored through one or more articles. Art Information, Accreditation, Government Information Policy, and Managing Information and Technology are examples. It includes news of people and events in ASIS. The general contents, as well as the occasional coverage of world events, are of interest to national and international audiences.

INDEXED: Inform.Sci.Abstr., UMI

Editor: Richard B. Hill

MANUSCRIPT ADDRESS: Bulletin of the American Society for Information Science, ASIS, 8720 Georgia Ave., Ste. 501, Silver Spring, MD 20910-3602

EDITORIAL POLICY:

Student Papers Accepted: Not given   **Abstract Required:** No

Publication Lag Time: 1-2 months usually   **Proofs Corrected By:** Editor

Payment: No

Reprints: Negotiable

Authorship Restrictions: None

THE MANUSCRIPT:

Number of Copies: 1   **Length:** 1,500-2,500 words

Acknowledgment: Yes   **Critique Provided:** No

Acceptance Lag Time: 2 months   **Style:** Not given

Format: Typed, double-spaced; prefer diskette in ASCII format or WordPerfect and paper copy.

REVIEW POLICY:

Refereed: No   **Acceptance Rate:** 90%

Reviewed By: Editor with input from staff

COPYRIGHT HELD BY:

First Publication: Publisher   **Republication:** Publisher

SUBSCRIPTION ADDRESS: Bulletin of the American Society for Information Science, ASIS, 8720 Georgia Ave., Ste. 501, Silver Spring, MD 20910-3602

Frequency: Bimonthly   **Circulation:** 4,000

Cost: $60 U.S., Canada, and Mexico; $70 others; $10 single issue; free to members

TELECOMMUNICATIONS: Richard B. Hill: Phone: (301) 495-0900; Fax: (301) 495-0810

AMERICAN SOCIETY FOR INFORMATION SCIENCE. JOURNAL (JASIS)

AFFILIATION: American Society for Information Science

SCOPE & CONTENT: As a scholarly journal, JASIS is interested in original contributions in the various fields of documentation and information science, and serves as a forum for discussion and implementation. Contributors are mostly academicians in library, information, or computer science. Papers descriptive of an original applied project are as welcome as opinion papers or tutorials. JASIS also publishes Perspectives, Best Student Papers, European Research Letters, Brief Communications, Historical Notes, and Letter to the Editor.

INDEXED: Chem.Abstr., C.I.J.E., Compumath, Curr.Cont./Engin.Tech.&Appl. Sci., Curr.Cont./Soc.Beh.Sci., Eng.Ind., Inform.Sci.Abstr., Lib.Lit., LISA, SSCI

EDITOR: Professor Donald H. Kraft

MANUSCRIPT ADDRESS: Dept. of Computer Science, Louisiana State University, Baton Rouge, LA 70803-4020

EDITORIAL POLICY:
Student Papers Accepted: Yes
Publication Lag Time: About 12 months
Reprints: 1 copy of issue
Authorship Restrictions: No

Abstract Required: Yes, 200 words or less
Proofs Corrected By: Author
Payment: No

THE MANUSCRIPT:
Number of Copies: 3
Acknowledgment: Yes
Acceptance Lag Time: 4-6 months

Length: 4,800 words
Critique Provided: Yes
Style: APA

Format: See "Instructions For Contributors" in January issue.

REVIEW POLICY:
Refereed: Yes
Reviewed By: Blind peer reviewed

Acceptance Rate: 62%

COPYRIGHT HELD BY:
First Publication: Publisher

Republication: Publisher

SUBSCRIPTION ADDRESS: JASIS, Susan Malawski, Fulfillment Manager, Subscription Dept., John Wiley and Sons, Inc., 605 3rd Ave., New York, NY 10158

Frequency: 10 per year
Cost: $375 nonmembers; $500 outside U.S.

Circulation: 4,159 domestic/488 foreign

TELECOMMUNICATIONS: Editor: Phone: (504) 388-1495; Fax: (504) 388-1465; Telenet: kraft@bit.csc.Lsu.edu

APLA BULLETIN

AFFILIATION: Atlantic Provinces Library Association

SCOPE & CONTENT: Focus is to provide a forum for news, information and research by, about, and for the Atlantic Province's library community. The main audience is primarily regional, although a national and international readership is reached through indexing services. Covering a wide range of subjects, it frequently publishes empirical and theoretical research contributed primarily by Atlantic area librarians. Book and computer program reviews are also included.

INDEXED: Can.Bus.&Curr.Aff., Can.Mag.Ind., Can.Per.Ind., LISA

EDITOR: Bradd Burningham

MANUSCRIPT ADDRESS: *APLA Bulletin*, c/o School of Library & Information Studies, Dalhousie University, Halifax, Nova Scotia B3H 4H8, Canada

EDITORIAL POLICY:

Student Papers Accepted: Not given	**Abstract Required:** No
Publication Lag Time: 1-3 months	**Proofs Corrected By:** Editor
Reprints: Varies	**Payment:** No
Authorship Restrictions: None	

THE MANUSCRIPT:

Number of Copies: 1	**Length:** 1,000-2000 words
Acknowledgment: No	**Critique Provided:** Upon request
Acceptance Lag Time: 1-3 months	**Style:** Standard format accepted

Format: WordPerfect diskette appreciated.

REVIEW POLICY:

Refereed: No	**Acceptance Rate:** 75%
Reviewed By: Editor with input from staff	

COPYRIGHT HELD BY:

First Publication: Author	**Republication:** Author

SUBSCRIPTION ADDRESS: *APLA Bulletin*, Atlantic Provinces Library Association, c/o School of Library and Information Studies, Dalhousie University, Halifax, Nova Scotia B3H 4H8, Canada

Frequency: Bimonthly	**Circulation:** 450

Cost: $25 individuals; $25 institutions

TELECOMMUNICATIONS: Not given

ARCHIVUM

AFFILIATION: UNESCO; International Council on Archives (ICA)

SCOPE & CONTENT: *Archivum* is the publication of the International Council on Archives, and has a world-wide circulation. The volumes deal with all the professional aspects of the management of historical and administrative archives, and with the problems relating to the access to archives and historical research. Proceedings have been published with the beginning of the International Congress of Archives in 1950.

INDEXED: Not given

EDITOR: Mr. Andre Vanrie, Editor-in-Chief

MANUSCRIPT ADDRESS: c/o Archives generales du Royaume, Rue de Rysebroek 2-6, B-100 Brussels (Belgium)

EDITORIAL POLICY:
Student Papers Accepted: No
Publication Lag Time: 6 months
Reprints: 10
Authorship Restrictions: No

Abstract Required: 1 page
Proofs Corrected By: Author
Payment: No

THE MANUSCRIPT:
Number of Copies: Not given
Acknowledgment: Yes
Acceptance Lag Time: Not given

Length: 15-30 pages
Critique Provided: Not given
Style: Standard

Format: Typed on A4 paper.

REVIEW POLICY:
Refereed: Yes
Reviewed By: Not given

Acceptance Rate: Not given

COPYRIGHT HELD BY:
First Publication: Author, journal, publisher

Republication: Author, journal, publisher

SUBSCRIPTION ADDRESS: K.G. Saur Verlag Gmbh, Ortlerstrasse 8, Postfach 701620, D-8000 München 70, Federal Republic of Germany

Frequency: Annual
Cost: $75 individuals

Circulation: Not given

TELECOMMUNICATIONS: Fax: 89 76 90 23 50

ART DOCUMENTATION
(Formerly ARLIS Newsletter)

AFFILIATION: Art Libraries Society of North America (ARLIS/NA)

SCOPE & CONTENT: The mission is to encourage the discussion of issues relating to the documenting of art, and to report the activities of the Art Libraries Society of North America. Though the main audience is national, it is read by organizations and individuals in other countries. Contributors are librarians, visual resources curators, and others interested in aspects of art and visual resources, librarianship and management.

INDEXED: Lib.Lit., LISA

EDITOR: Beryl K. Smith

MANUSCRIPT ADDRESS: Rutgers University, Art Library, Voorhees Hall, New Brunswick, NJ 08903

EDITORIAL POLICY:
Student Papers Accepted: No
Publication Lag Time: Generally 6 months
Reprints: Two copies of issue
Authorship Restrictions: None, as long as article complies with editorial policy

Abstract Required: No
Proofs Corrected By: Author
Payment: Not given

THE MANUSCRIPT:
Number of Copies: 1
Acknowledgment: Yes
Acceptance Lag Time: Less than 1 month

Length: 2,500-3,000 words
Critique Provided: Always, if requested
Style: *Chicago Manual of Style*

Format: Typed, double-spaced, one side of sheet only.

REVIEW POLICY:
Refereed: Yes
Reviewed By: Blind refereed

Acceptance Rate: Approximately 50-75%

COPYRIGHT HELD BY:
First Publication: Publisher

Republication: Author/Publisher

SUBSCRIPTION ADDRESS: ARLIS/NA, 3900 E. Timrod Street, Tucson, AZ 85711

Frequency: Quarterly
Cost: $55 individuals; $75 institutions; $35 students; $5 single issue; free with membership

Circulation: 1,350

TELECOMMUNICATIONS: Not given

ART REFERENCE SERVICES QUARTERLY

AFFILIATION: None

SCOPE & CONTENT: The new *Art Reference Services Quarterly* will be a forum for those professionals who provide architectural and visual arts reference and information services in academic, museum, and public library settings. This important journal will provide practical and theoretical articles about a wide range of reference issues, with the focus on the service needs associated with architecture and the visual arts broadly defined to include architecture, interior design, landscape architecture, urban planning, art history, archaeology, photography, and studio arts.

INDEXED: Not given

Editor: Edward H. Teague

MANUSCRIPT ADDRESS: Architecture and Fine Arts Library, 201 Fine Arts, Building "A", Gainesville, FL 32611

EDITORIAL POLICY:
Student Papers Accepted: Yes **Abstract Required:** About 100 words
Publication Lag Time: 6-12 months
Reprints: 10 plus 1 copy of issue **Proofs Corrected By:** Editor
Authorship Restrictions: No **Payment:** No

THE MANUSCRIPT:
Number of Copies: 3 **Length:** 5-50 pages
Acknowledgment: Yes **Critique Provided:** Yes
Acceptance Lag Time: 3-6 months **Style:** *Chicago Manual of Style*

Format: Typed, double-spaced on 8 1/2″ bond paper with 1″ margins on four sides.

REVIEW POLICY:
Refereed: Yes **Acceptance Rate:** 30%
Reviewed By: Editorial board and anonymous specialist referees

COPYRIGHT HELD BY:
First Publication: Publisher **Republication:** Publisher

Subscription Address: The Haworth Press, 10 Alice Street, Binghamton, NY 13904-1580

Frequency: Quarterly **Circulation:** Not given
Cost: $18 individuals; $24 institutions; $24 libraries

TELECOMMUNICATIONS: Not given

ASIAN LIBRARIES

AFFILIATION: None

SCOPE & CONTENT: *Asian Libraries* publishes original articles of interest to library and information service professionals around the world with particular reference to Asia and the Pacific. Contributors are library school faculty, administrators, and information professionals from Asia and occasionally United States, Canada, and Europe.

INDEXED: No

EDITOR: James Pruess

MANUSCRIPT ADDRESS: Library Marketing Services Ltd., G.P.O. Box 701, Bangkok 10501, Thailand

EDITORIAL POLICY:
Student Papers Accepted: No
Publication Lag Time: 2-5 months
Reprints: None
Authorship Restrictions: None

Abstract Required: Yes, 200 words
Proofs Corrected By: Editor
Payment: Only for articles commissioned by editor

THE MANUSCRIPT:
Number of Copies: 1 hard copy
Acknowledgment: Yes
Acceptance Lag Time: 2 weeks-3 months

Length: 2000-3500 words
Critique Provided: Yes
Style: House style

Format: Written in English, double-spaced on A4 white paper with abstract, references, and citations in text. Computer diskette required.

REVIEW POLICY:
Refereed: Yes
Reviewed By: Editor and editorial board

Acceptance Rate: 80%

COPYRIGHT HELD BY:
First Publication: Publisher

Republication: Publisher

SUBSCRIPTION ADDRESS: Library Marketing Services Ltd., G.P.O. Box 701 Bangkok 10501, Thailand

Frequency: Quarterly
Cost: $48 individuals, $72 institutions, $24 single issue

Circulation: 1,000

TELECOMMUNICATIONS: Editor: Phone: (66-2) 247-1032; Fax: (66-2) 247-1033

ASLIB INFORMATION

AFFILIATION: The Association for Information Management (ASLIB)

SCOPE & CONTENT: This journal provides a forum for Association for Information Management members in order to provide up-to-date information on world issues. Each issue covers a particular topic in depth, as well as providing news and reviews. Information technology, online, CD-ROM, information sources, and management of information services are some of the topics most often covered.

INDEXED: LISA

EDITOR: Moira Duncan

MANUSCRIPT ADDRESS: ASLIB, Information House, 20-24 Old Street, London, ECIV 9AP, England

EDITORIAL POLICY:
Student Papers Accepted: Yes   **Abstract Required:** No
Publication Lag Time: 2 months   **Proofs Corrected By:** Editor
Reprints: 5 issues of journal   **Payment:** No
Authorship Restrictions: No

THE MANUSCRIPT:
Number of Copies: 1   **Length:** 2,000 words
Acknowledgment: Yes   **Critique Provided:** Not usually
Acceptance Lag Time: 2-3 weeks   **Style:** House style sheet available

Format: Use A4 paper with 1″ margins on other side of text. Submit with 3 1/4″ diskette in ASCII format.

REVIEW POLICY:
Refereed: Yes   **Acceptance Rate:** 70%
Reviewed By: Editor, input from staff

COPYRIGHT HELD BY:
First Publication: Publisher   **Republication:** Publisher

SUBSCRIPTION ADDRESS: Moira Duncan, ASLIB, 20-24 Old Street, London, ECIV 9AP, England

Frequency: 10 per year   **Circulation:** 3,000
Cost: Not given

TELECOMMUNICATIONS: Phone: +44 (0) 71 253 4488; +44 (0) 71 430 0514

ASLIB PROCEEDINGS

AFFILIATION: The Association for Information Management (ASLIB)

SCOPE & CONTENT: The main thrust of this journal is to publish proceedings of seminars and conferences in the broad area of information management. Information technology, sources, and management are the subjects most frequently covered. Contributors are specialists in the field of information management. It includes case studies, commentaries and letters.

INDEXED: Curr.Aw.Abstr., Lib.Lit., LISA

EDITOR: Moira Duncan

MANUSCRIPT ADDRESS: ASLIB, Information House, 20-24 Old Street, London, ECIV 9AP, England

EDITORIAL POLICY:
Student Papers Accepted: No
Publication Lag Time: 3 months maximum
Reprints: 10
Authorship Restrictions: Not given

Abstract Required: About 100 words
Proofs Corrected By: Author
Payment: No

THE MANUSCRIPT:
Number of Copies: 2
Acknowledgment: Yes
Acceptance Lag Time: 1-2 months

Length: 3,000 words
Critique Provided: Not usually
Style: House style sheet available

Format: Use A4 paper, double-spaced, single side only and provide diskette.

REVIEW POLICY:
Refereed: Yes
Reviewed By: Editor with input from staff

Acceptance Rate: 70-80%

COPYRIGHT HELD BY:
First Publication: Author/Publisher

Republication: Author/Publisher

SUBSCRIPTION ADDRESS: Moira Duncan, ASLIB, 20-24 Old Street, London, ECIV 9AP, England

Frequency: 10 per year
Cost: Not given

Circulation: 3,000

TELECOMMUNICATIONS: Phone: +44 (0) 71 253 4488; Fax: +44 (0) 71 430 0514

ASSISTANT LIBRARIAN

AFFILIATION: Association of Assistant Librarians, Group of The Library Association

SCOPE & CONTENT: The aim is to provide a forum for debating issues; developing awareness, news, views and opinions on issues in the library and information world. Focusing on generalists issues, it encourages perspectives from younger and newer entrants in the profession. Support for professional development is ranked high among the types of articles accepted for publication. It includes book and video reviews.

INDEXED: LISA

EDITOR: Nigel Ward

MANUSCRIPT ADDRESS: Sherwood Library, Spondon Street, Mansfield Road, Nottingham, NG5 4AB, U.K.

EDITORIAL POLICY:
Student Papers Accepted: Yes   **Abstract Required:** No
Publication Lag Time: Varies   **Proofs Corrected By:** Editor
Reprints: 2   **Payment:** No
Authorship Restrictions: None

THE MANUSCRIPT:
Number of Copies: 1   **Length:** 1,500-2,500 words
Acknowledgment: Yes   **Critique Provided:** Sometimes
Acceptance Lag Time: Not given   **Style:** No specific one

Format: No specific format.

REVIEW POLICY:
Refereed: No   **Acceptance Rate:** 80%
Reviewed By: Editor

COPYRIGHT HELD BY:
First Publication: Publisher   **Republication:** Publisher

SUBSCRIPTION ADDRESS: Nigel Ward, Sherwood Library, Spondon Street, Mansfield Road, Nottingham, NG5 4AB, U.K.

Frequency: Monthly   **Circulation:** 10,000
Cost: $43 individuals; $5 single issue

TELECOMMUNICATIONS: Editors: Phone: (0) 602 606680

AUDIOVISUAL LIBRARIAN

AFFILIATION: Library Association Audiovisual Group, U.K., ASLIB Audiovisual Group, U.K.

SCOPE & CONTENT: This international journal covers multimedia developments of interest to librarians, information specialists, archivists and educators. Subjects covered are all related to audiovisual/multimedia relevant to a target audience. Contributors are predominantly international librarians and others from associated fields. Reviews, state-of-the-art equipment and news are regular features. Includes reviews of books, videos, audio, and computer programs.

INDEXED: Lib.Lit., LISA

EDITOR: Dr. Anthony Hugh Thompson

MANUSCRIPT ADDRESS: The Coach House Frongog, Llanbadarn Fawr, Aberystwyth, Wales SY23 3HN U.K.

EDITORIAL POLICY:

Student Papers Accepted: Only appropriate ones
Publication Lag Time: 1 month minimum
Reprints: 1 copy of issue
Authorship Restrictions: No

Abstract Required: No
Proofs Corrected By: Editor
Payment: No

THE MANUSCRIPT:

Number of Copies: 1
Acknowledgment: Yes
Acceptance Lag Time: Varies

Length: 3,000 words
Critique Provided: Always
Style: Journal style

Format: Typed on ASCII or any other popular word processor, include diskette.

REVIEW POLICY:

Refereed: No
Reviewed By: Editor

Acceptance Rate: High

COPYRIGHT HELD BY:

First Publication: Journal

Republication: Journal

SUBSCRIPTION ADDRESS: Audiovisual Librarian. Bailey Management Services. 127 Sandgate Road, Folkstone, Kent CT202BL, U.K.

Frequency: Quarterly
Cost: £33 in U.K.; £39 overseas and U.S.

Circulation: 3,000 internationally

TELECOMMUNICATIONS: Phone: (0) 970 617322; Fax: (0) 974 298513

AUSTRALIAN LIBRARY REVIEW
(Formerly Riverina Library Review)

AFFILIATION: Centre for Information Studies

SCOPE & CONTENT: *Australian Library Review* covers all aspects of library and information science. Articles most frequently published are practical, followed by descriptions of the state of the art articles and case studies. It includes book reviews, bibliographies, and special-theme issues. Contributors are academicians and practitioners from all parts of the world, but especially from Australia and the Pacific.

INDEXED: ALISA, LISA

EDITOR: Dr. G.E. Gorman

MANUSCRIPT ADDRESS: Australian Library Review, Centre for Information Studies, Charles Stuart University, P.O. Box 588, Wagga Wagga, N.S.W. 2650 Australia

EDITORIAL POLICY:

Student Papers Accepted: No

Publication Lag Time: 3-6 months

Reprints: 6

Authorship Restrictions: None

Abstract Required: Yes, 50-100 words

Proofs Corrected By: Author

Payment: No

THE MANUSCRIPT:

Number of Copies: 2

Acknowledgment: Yes

Acceptance Lag Time: 1-3 months

Length: 4,000-6,000 words

Critique Provided: Sometimes

Style: House style sheet available

Format: Manuscript should be typed or word processed, double-spaced on one side only, on white A4 paper with four centimeter margins on all sides or submit diskette (Microsoft Word or Apple MacIntosh).

REVIEW POLICY:

Refereed: Yes

Reviewed By: Editor with input from staff

Acceptance Rate: Not given

COPYRIGHT HELD BY:

First Publication: Not given

Republication: Author

SUBSCRIPTION ADDRESS: Australian Library Review, Centre for Information Studies, Charles Stuart University, P.O. Box 588, Wagga Wagga, N.S.W., Australia 2650

Frequency: Quarterly

Circulation: 1,000

Cost: (Australian dollars) $30 individuals and institutions; $7.50 single issue.

TELECOMMUNICATIONS: Not given

BEHAVIORAL & SOCIAL SCIENCES LIBRARIAN

AFFILIATION: None

SCOPE & CONTENT: From its inception in 1979, *Behavioral & Social Sciences Librarian* has focused on the production, collection, organization, dissemination, retrieval, and use of information in the social and behavioral sciences. The ongoing purpose of this unique journal is to publish articles on all aspects of behavioral and social science information, with emphasis on librarians, libraries, and the users of social science information in libraries and information centers.

INDEXED: ALISA, C.I.J.E., CINAHL, Comput.&Info.Sys., Curr.Cont., Excerp.Med., Inform.Sci.Abstr., Lib.Lit., LISA, P.A.I.S., Psychol.Abstr., Ref.Zh., Sci.Abstr., Soc.WorkRes.&Abstr., SSCI, Wom.Stud.Abstr.

EDITOR: Michael F. Winter

MANUSCRIPT ADDRESS: Behavioral Sciences Librarian, Shields Library, University of California, Davis, Davis, CA 95616-5292

EDITORIAL POLICY:
Student Papers Accepted: Yes
Publication Lag Time: Not given
Reprints: 10 plus 1 copy of issue
Authorship Restrictions: None
Abstract Required: About 100 words
Proofs Corrected By: Editor
Payment: No

THE MANUSCRIPT:
Number of Copies: 3
Acknowledgment: Yes
Acceptance Lag Time: Not given
Length: Approx. 15-20 pages
Critique Provided: Not given
Style: *Chicago Manual of Style* or APA

Format: Typed, double-spaced on 8 1/2″ bond paper with 1″ margins on all four sides. Guidelines of the American Sociological Association are also acceptable.

REVIEW POLICY:
Refereed: Yes
Acceptance Rate: Not given
Reviewed By: Editorial board and anonymous specialist referees

COPYRIGHT HELD BY:
First Publication: Publisher
Republication: Publisher

SUBSCRIPTION ADDRESS: The Haworth Press, Production Department, 10 Alice Street, Binghamton, NY 13904-1580

Frequency: 2 per year
Circulation: 437
Cost: $35 individuals; $75 institutions; $75 libraries

TELECOMMUNICATIONS: Phone: (916) 752-3058

THE BOOKMARK

AFFILIATION: A publication of the New York State Library

SCOPE & CONTENT: Each issue is devoted exclusively to a theme edited by a practitioner in the field, and has approximately 17 to 25 articles on a well-defined topic written by educators and librarians. The Spring 1992 issue examines "Libraries, Users and Copyright: Proprietary Rights and Wrongs." Other past issues have covered, "Youth Services," "Family History Resources," and "Clarifying and Defining Library Services." The broad scope and treatment have particular appeal to New York librarians. Most contributors are invited to submit manuscripts based on the theme of the issue.

INDEXED: CALL, Lib.Lit., P.A.I.S.

EDITOR: Joseph F. Shubert

MANUSCRIPT ADDRESS: *The Bookmark*, New York State Library, Albany, NY 12230

EDITORIAL POLICY:
Student Papers Accepted: No   **Abstract Required:** No
Publication Lag Time: Up to 6 months   **Proofs Corrected By:** Editor
Reprints: Not given   **Payment:** No
Authorship Restrictions: None

THE MANUSCRIPT:
Number of Copies: 2   **Length:** Not specified
Acknowledgment: 1 month to 1 year   **Critique Provided:** No
Acceptance Lag Time: Not given   **Style:** "Guidelines for Authors"
                available.

Format: One paper copy and one copy on either diskette (an IBM PC with MS-DOS is greatly preferred) or send via E-mail. (See Telecommunications).

REVIEW POLICY:
Refereed: No   **Acceptance Rate:** Not given
Reviewed By: Not given

COPYRIGHT HELD BY:
First Publication: Not given   **Republication:** Not given

SUBSCRIPTION ADDRESS: *The Bookmark*, Subscriptions, New York State Library, Albany, NY 12230

Frequency: Quarterly   **Circulation:** 4,000
Cost: $15.00 individuals and institutions; $20.00 outside of the U.S., Canada and Mexico; $4.00 single issue, mailed 4th class; ($6.00 mailed first class)

TELECOMMUNICATIONS: Andy Mace: (518) 474-8541; BITNET: USERGLN9@RPITSMTS, E-mail: AMACE%SEDOFIS@VM1.NYSED.GOV

THE BOTTOM LINE

AFFILIATION: None

SCOPE & CONTENT: This journal strives to keep librarians up-to-date about financial management tools, theories, trends, and business techniques. Articles cover such topics as budgeting, cash management, economic trends, endowments, investments, leasing, insurance, grants, resource allocation, cost analysis, accounting systems, financial technology, fiscal planning and alternate funding. Its aim is to assist librarians in operating libraries on a more fiscally sound basis.

INDEXED: Not given

EDITOR: Frances B. Bradburn

MANUSCRIPT ADDRESS: *The Bottom Line*, J. Y. Joyner Library, East Carolina University, Greenville, NC 27858-4353

EDITORIAL POLICY:

Student Papers Accepted: No	**Abstract Required:** No
Publication Lag Time: 3 months	**Proofs Corrected By:** Editor
Reprints: Not given	**Payment:** No
Authorship Restrictions: None	

THE MANUSCRIPT:

Number of Copies: 2	**Length:** 5,000 words
Acknowledgment: Yes	**Critique Provided:** Upon request
Acceptance Lag Time: 8 weeks	**Style:** *Chicago Manual of Style*

Format: Typed, double-spaced on one side of 8 1/2″ × 11″ nonerasable white paper with a 1″ margin on all sides. Footnotes should follow the body of manuscript. Include a short biographical sketch of author.

REVIEW POLICY:

Refereed: No	**Acceptance Rate:** Not given
Reviewed By: Editor and editorial board	

COPYRIGHT HELD BY:

First Publication: Publisher	**Republication:** Publisher

SUBSCRIPTION ADDRESS: *The Bottom Line*, Neal-Schuman Publishers, 100 Varick St., New York, NY 10013

Frequency: Quarterly	**Circulation:** Not given

Cost: $49.94 in U.S.; $60 in Canada; $65 other foreign countries

TELECOMMUNICATIONS: Editor: Phone: (919) 757-6076; Fax: (919) 757-6618

BRIO

AFFILIATION: *BRIO* is the journal of the British branch of the International Association of Music Libraries (IAML (U.K.)), Archives and Documentation Centres

SCOPE & CONTENT: The aim is to publish news of the United Kingdom branch's activities; to review music library/bibliographical publications; to publish articles on bibliographical and/or musicological topics; and to report on current topics and trends in music librarianship. Editor encourages communication from anyone who has enlightening manuscripts about music librarianship or music bibliography. It includes reviews of books and musical scores.

INDEXED: LISA, Music Ind.

EDITOR: John Wagstaff

MANUSCRIPT ADDRESS: Music Faculty Library, University of Oxford, St. Aldate's, Oxford OXI 1PB, U.K.

EDITORIAL POLICY:
Student Papers Accepted: No
Publication Lag Time: 1 year maximum
Reprints: 1 copy of the issue
Authorship Restrictions: None

Abstract Required: No
Proofs Corrected By: Author
Payment: No

THE MANUSCRIPT:
Number of Copies: 2
Acknowledgment: Yes
Acceptance Lag Time: A few weeks

Length: 2,500-3,500 words
Critique Provided: Upon request
Style: Not given

Format: Typed neatly, double-spaced.

REVIEW POLICY:
Refereed: No
Reviewed By: Editor, with input from staff

Acceptance Rate: 80%

COPYRIGHT HELD BY:
First Publication: Journal

Republication: Journal

SUBSCRIPTION ADDRESS: Tony Reed, Publications Officer, Music Section, British Library Document Supply Centre, Boston, SPA, Wetherby, West Yorkshire LS23 7BQ, U.K.

Frequency: 2 per year
Cost: $42.50 individuals and institutions

Circulation: About 550

TELECOMMUNICATIONS: Phone: (0) 865 276146; E-mail: LIBMUS@UK.AC.OX.VAX

BRITISH JOURNAL OF ACADEMIC LIBRARIANSHIP

AFFILIATION: None

SCOPE & CONTENT: An international journal designed to explore the range of issues of current concern to academic librarians; it focuses on information technology; major cooperative or commercial library systems; the development of in-house systems, particularly those involving microcomputer applications; developments in academic library management; Management Information Systems; marketing (including user studies and user education); collection management; the academic role of the librarian; the influence of national library policy and national educational policy on the academic library; the physical library environment; conservation and preservation; education, training and staff development; research in academic librarianship; and the future of the academic library.

INDEXED: Lib.Lit.

EDITOR: Dr. Colin Harris

MANUSCRIPT ADDRESS: Head of Academic Information Services, University of Salford, Salford, MS 4WT, U.K.

EDITORIAL POLICY:

Student Papers Accepted: No	**Abstract Required:** Yes
Publication Lag Time: Not given	**Proofs Corrected By:** Editor
Reprints: 20	**Payment:** No
Authorship Restrictions: None	

THE MANUSCRIPT:

Number of Copies: 2	**Length:** 5,000-7,000 words
Acknowledgment: Yes	**Critique Provided:** Not given
Acceptance Lag Time: Not given	**Style:** Not given

Format: Any format, manuscript or diskette in ASCII format.

REVIEW POLICY:

Refereed: Yes	**Acceptance Rate:** Not given
Reviewed By: Blind refereed, editor and editorial board	

COPYRIGHT HELD BY:

First Publication: Author, publisher	**Republication:** Author, publisher

SUBSCRIPTION ADDRESS: Taylor Graham Publishing, 500 Chesham House, 150 Regent Street, London, WIR 5FA, U.K.

Frequency: 3 per year	**Circulation:** Not given
Cost: $103 institutions; $35 single issue	

TELECOMMUNICATIONS: Not given

BRITISH LIBRARY JOURNAL

AFFILIATION: None

SCOPE & CONTENT: This journal promotes and publishes research on the contents and history of the British library collections. The subjects covered are history, literature and archives, but it does not cover information science. Contributors are members of the international scholarly community. Special "theme" issues are one of the special features published.

INDEXED: Hist.Abstr.

EDITOR: Dr. C. J. Wright

MANUSCRIPT ADDRESS: *British Library Journal,* British Library, Great Russell Street, London, WC1B 3D9, U.K.

EDITORIAL POLICY:
Student Papers Accepted: No
Publication Lag Time: 2 years
Reprints: 25
Authorship Restrictions: None

Abstract Required: No
Proofs Corrected By: Author
Payment: No

THE MANUSCRIPT:
Number of Copies: 2
Acknowledgment: Yes
Acceptance Lag Time: 6 months

Length: About 5,000-10,000 words
Critique Provided: Not usually
Style: House style sheet available

Format: Typed, double-spaced on one side only of A4 paper.

REVIEW POLICY:
Refereed: Yes
Reviewed By: Editor and external referees

Acceptance Rate: Not given

COPYRIGHT HELD BY:
First Publication: Publisher

Republication: Publisher

SUBSCRIPTION ADDRESS: Publications Sales Unit, The British Library, Boston SPA, Wetherby, West Yorkshire, LS23 7BQ, U.K.

Frequency: Biannually
Cost: $60 individuals, institutions, others; $30 single issue

Circulation: About 1,000

TELECOMMUNICATIONS: Phone: (0) 71 323-7516; Fax: (0) 71 323-7745

BULLETIN OF THE CONGREGATIONAL LIBRARY

AFFILIATION: The American Congregational Association

SCOPE & CONTENT: To inform interested parties of the contents of new books added to the Congregational Library's collection in the preceding four months, and to publish brief articles relating to the Congregational and United Church of Christ denominations of churches. Articles are historical or biographical in nature.

INDEXED: No

EDITOR: Dr. Harold F. Worthley

MANUSCRIPT ADDRESS: The Congregational Library, 14 Beacon St. Boston, MA 02108

EDITORIAL POLICY:

Student Papers Accepted: Not given   **Abstract Required:** Not given

Publication Lag Time: 2 years   **Proofs Corrected By:** Author, but

Reprints: Usually 10   not usually

Authorship Restrictions: None   **Payment:** No

THE MANUSCRIPT:

Number of Copies: Not given   **Length:** Not given

Acknowledgment: Not given   **Critique Provided:** Sometimes

Acceptance Lag Time: 2 months   **Style:** Not given

Format: Not given.

REVIEW POLICY:

Refereed: No   **Acceptance Rate:** Not given

Reviewed By: Editor

COPYRIGHT HELD BY:

First Publication: Author   **Republication:** Journal

SUBSCRIPTION ADDRESS: *Bulletin of the Congregational Library,* The Congregational Library, 14 Beacon St., Boston, MA 02108

Frequency: 3 issues per year   **Circulation:** 1,000
Cost: $5 individuals; $5 institutions; $2 single issue

TELECOMMUNICATIONS: Phone: (617) 523-0470; Fax: (617) 523-0491

CANADIAN LIBRARY JOURNAL (CLJ)

AFFILIATION: Canadian Library Association

SCOPE & CONTENT: This refereed bimonthly publication provides a forum for the discussion, analysis and evaluation of issues in librarianship. Contributors are from a cross section of public, academic, special, and school librarians, as well as library administrators and trustees. Special features include case studies, commentaries, new developments, special "theme" issues, bibliographies, and conferences or workshops. Theoretical research is ranked high among the types of articles published.

INDEXED: CALL, Can.Bus.&Curr.Aff., Can.Per.Ind., C.I.J.E., International Index to Multi-Media Information, Leg.Info.Manage.Ind., Lib.Lit., LISA

EDITOR: Jacqueline Easby

MANUSCRIPT ADDRESS: *Canadian Library Journal,* c/o Canadian Library Association, 602-200 Elgin Street, Ottawa, Ontario K1Z 5E3, Canada

EDITORIAL POLICY:

Student Papers Accepted: Yes   **Abstract Required:** 50-100 words
Publication Lag Time: 6 months   **Proofs Corrected By:** Editor
Reprints: 2 copies of issue   **Payment:** Not given
Authorship Restrictions: None

THE MANUSCRIPT:

Number of Copies: 2   **Length:** 4,000-8,000 words per
Acknowledgment: Yes   page
Acceptance Lag Time: 2- months   **Critique Provided:** Upon request
   Style: *Chicago Manual of Style*

Format: Type manuscript, double-spaced and submit on unfolded paper. If manuscript is composed on a word processor, indicate diskette size and software used.

REVIEW POLICY:

Refereed: Yes   **Acceptance Rate:** Varies, about
Reviewed By: Blind refereed   20-40%

COPYRIGHT HELD BY:

First Publication: Journal   **Republication:** Author/Journal/
   Publisher

SUBSCRIPTION ADDRESS: *Canadian Library Journal,* c/o Canadian Library Association, 602-200 Elgin Street, Ottawa, Ontario K1Z 5E3, Canada

Frequency: Bimonthly   **Circulation:** 4,600
Cost: $45 (in Canadian dollars) members; $50 U.S.; $55 foreign; $8 single issue

TELECOMMUNICATIONS: Phone: (613) 232-9625; Fax: (613) 563-9895; Envoy 100: CLA.PUBS

CATALOGING & CLASSIFICATION QUARTERLY

AFFILIATION: None

SCOPE & CONTENT: Designed to provide an international forum, this journal is devoted to all aspects of bibliographic access and control for all forms of library materials in all types of libraries. It publishes full-length research and review articles, management-oriented articles, and descriptions of new programs and technology. Subjects include descriptive cataloging, subject analysis, classification, and the full spectrum of the creation, management, content, and use of bibliographic records. This journal includes contemporary and historical perspectives, theory and scholarly research and practical applications.

INDEXED: Bull.Signal., Cam.Sci.Abstr., C.I.J.E., Comput.&Contr.Abstr., Curr. Aw.Bull., Ind.Per.Art.Relat.Law., Inform.Sci.Abstr., INSPEC, Lib.Lit., LISA, Ref.Zh.

EDITOR: Ruth C. Carter

MANUSCRIPT ADDRESS: 121 Pikemont Drive, Wexford, PA 15260

EDITORIAL POLICY:

Student Papers Accepted: No
Publication Lag Time: About 7-9 months
Reprints: 10
Authorship Restrictions: None

Abstract Required: About 100 words
Proofs Corrected By: Editor
Payment: No

THE MANUSCRIPT:

Number of Copies: 3
Acknowledgment: Yes
Acceptance Lag Time: 3-4 months

Length: Prefer 15-20 pages
Critique Provided: Always
Style: *Chicago Manual of Style*

Format: Typed, double-spaced on white 8 1/2″ × 11″ bond paper with at least a 1″ margin on all sides. Final copy submitted in print and on diskette.

REVIEW POLICY:

Refereed: Yes
Reviewed By: Editorial board and blind refereed

Acceptance Rate: 75%

COPYRIGHT HELD BY:

First Publication: Publisher

Republication: Author/Publisher

SUBSCRIPTION ADDRESS: *Cataloging & Classification Quarterly*, The Haworth Press, 10 Alice Street, Binghamton N.Y., 13904-1580

Frequency: Quarterly
Cost: $40 individuals; $115 institutions

Circulation: About 1,100

TELECOMMUNICATIONS: Editor: Phone: (412)648-7710; Fax: (412)648-7887; Home phone: (412)935-1752; BITNET: RCC13@PITTVMS; Internet: rcc13@vms.cis.pitt.edu

CATHOLIC LIBRARY WORLD

AFFILIATION: Catholic Library Association

SCOPE & CONTENT: *Catholic Library World* is the official journal of the Catholic Library Association. It was recently redesigned to reflect both news items of interest to its members as well as the professional needs and concerns of librarians. The "News and Notes" section provides short current awareness information on people, places, products and publications. Articles are scholarly, covering a wide range of subjects aimed at those involved in education at the high school and post secondary levels, as well as the needs of children. It also serves library educators and students, and covers parish and community concerns. Book and video reviews are included. Contributors are from the general library community.

INDEXED: Bk.Rev.Ind., Cath.Ind., CERDIC, C.I.J.E., Lib.Lit., LISA

EDITOR: Anthony Prete

MANUSCRIPT ADDRESS: *Catholic Library World*, 461 W. Lancaster Ave., Haverford, PA 19041

EDITORIAL POLICY:

Student Papers Accepted: Yes	**Abstract Required:** No
Publication Lag Time: Not given	**Proofs Corrected By:** Author
Reprints: Not given	**Payment:** Not given
Authorship Restrictions: None	

THE MANUSCRIPT:

Number of Copies: 2	**Length:** 5,000-6,000 words
Acknowledgment: Yes	**Critique Provided:** Upon request
Acceptance Lag Time: Not given	**Style:** Not given

Format: Submit one copy on diskette, IBM, or compatible, WordPerfect or WordStar preferred. Other formats will be accepted, if inquiry made first.

REVIEW POLICY:

Refereed: No	**Acceptance Rate:** Not given
Reviewed By: Editor	

COPYRIGHT HELD BY:

First Publication: Publisher	**Republication:** Publisher

SUBSCRIPTION ADDRESS: *Catholic Library World*, Catholic Library Association, 461 W. Lancaster Ave. Haverford, PA 19041

Frequency: Quarterly   **Circulation:** Not given
Cost: $60 individuals; $70 Canada and foreign; $8.50 single issue

TELECOMMUNICATIONS: Editor: Phone: (215) 649-5250; Fax: (215) 896-1991

CD-ROM LIBRARIAN

AFFILIATION: None

SCOPE & CONTENT: The focus of this publication is to inform and keep readers up-to-date with trends and developments in the area of CD-ROM and compact optical media. Contributors are librarians, end-users and industry representatives. Articles cover a wide range of subjects that include networking, standards, reviews of computer hardware and programs, and system performance functioning.

INDEXED: Comput.Rev., Lib.Lit., LISA

EDITOR: Norman Desmarais

MANUSCRIPT ADDRESS: *CD-ROM Librarian*, 467 River Road, Lincoln, RI 02865

EDITORIAL POLICY:

Student Papers Accepted: Yes
Publication Lag Time: 3-4 months
Reprints: 1-2
Authorship Restrictions: None

Abstract Required: No
Proofs Corrected By: Editor
Payment: $50 reviews; $100 articles

THE MANUSCRIPT:

Number of Copies: 1
Acknowledgment: Yes
Acceptance Lag Time: Within 3 weeks

Length: 1,500-3,000 words
Critique Provided: Sometimes, upon request
Style: *Chicago Manual of Style*

Format: Paper copy and diskette, (WordPerfect, ASCII or compatible).

REVIEW POLICY:

Refereed: Yes
Reviewed By: Editor

Acceptance Rate: 80%

COPYRIGHT HELD BY:

First Publication: Publisher

Republication: Publisher

SUBSCRIPTION ADDRESS: *CD-ROM Librarian*, Meckler Corp., 11 Ferry Lane W., Westport, CT 06880

Frequency: Monthly

Circulation: Not given

Cost: $33 individuals; $79.50 institutions; $15 additional outside the U.S.; $10 single issue

TELECOMMUNICATIONS: Phone: (401) 865-2241; Fax: (401) 865-2057; BITNET: NP180003@BROWNVM

CD-ROM PROFESSIONAL

AFFILIATION: None

SCOPE & CONTENT: *CD-ROM Professional* focuses exclusively on the CD-ROM. Articles cover the selection, evaluation, purchase and operation of CD-ROM titles, work stations, networks and related equipment. It provides practical information on all aspects of CD-ROM publishing. Columns are headed News, New Titles, DataBasics, Discware, Multimedia, Hardware, Standards, Conference Calendar, Q&A and Book Reviews.

INDEXED: ABI/Inform, Curr.Aw.Abstr., ERIC, LHTN, LISA

EDITOR: Nancy K. Herther

MANUSCRIPT ADDRESS: 407 Kingston Ave., St. Paul, MN 55117

EDITORIAL POLICY:
Student Papers Accepted: No
Publication Lag Time: 10 weeks
Reprints: 5-10 tearsheets;
   5-6 copies issue
Authorship Restrictions: Not given

Abstract Required: No
Proofs Corrected By: Author
Payment: $50 brief reviews;
   $200-500 articles

THE MANUSCRIPT:
Number of Copies: 2
Acknowledgment: Yes
Acceptance Lag Time: 1-3 months

Length: 2,000
Critique Provided: Always
Style: House style upon request;
   not published

Format: One paper copy and one copy on diskette.

REVIEW POLICY:
Refereed: Yes   **Acceptance Rate:** 33%
Reviewed By: Editorial board, editorial staff, and other subject specialists as
   needed

COPYRIGHT HELD BY:
First Publication: Publisher   **Republication:** Publisher

SUBSCRIPTION ADDRESS: *CD-ROM Professional*, Subscription Department, 462 Danbury Road, Wilton, CT 06897

Frequency: Bimonthly   **Circulation:** 5,000
Cost: $86 U.S. & Canada individuals and institutions; $10 single issue; $121
   foreign countries

TELECOMMUNICATIONS: Editor: Phone: (612) 771-9939

THE CHRISTIAN LIBRARIAN

AFFILIATION: Association of Christian Librarians

SCOPE & CONTENT: The focus is on communication of Christian interpretations on the theory and practice of library science. Contributors are Christian librarians in institutions of higher learning as well as evangelical scholars. Special features include bibliographic articles and book reviews.

INDEXED: CPI, Inform.Sci.Abstr., Lib.Lit.

EDITOR: Ron Jordahl

MANUSCRIPT ADDRESS: *The Christian Librarian*, Prairie Theological Library, P.O. Box 4000, Three Hills, Alberta TOM 2AO Canada

EDITORIAL POLICY:
Student Papers Accepted: Yes
Publication Lag Time: 6 months
Reprints: 2
Authorship Restrictions: None
Abstract Required: Yes, 100 to 150 words
Proofs Corrected By: Editor
Payment: No

THE MANUSCRIPT:
Number of Copies: 1
Acknowledgment: Yes
Acceptance Lag Time: 4 weeks
Length: 3,500 words
Critique Provided: Always
Style: Style sheet available

Format: 8 1/2" × 11" white bond, double-spaced, 1" margins.

REVIEW POLICY:
Refereed: No
Acceptance Rate: 80%
Reviewed By: Editor with input from staff

COPYRIGHT HELD BY:
First Publication: Journal
Republication: Author

SUBSCRIPTION ADDRESS: Stephen P. Brown, *The Christian Librarian*, P.O. Box 4, Cedarville, OH 45314

Frequency: Quarterly
Circulation: 465
Cost: $20 individuals; $20 institutions; $5 single issue

TELECOMMUNICATIONS: Editor: Phone: (403) 443-5511; Fax: (403) 443-5540

CHURCH AND SYNAGOGUE LIBRARIES (CSLA)

AFFILIATION: Church and Synagogue Library Association

SCOPE & CONTENT: CSLA provides inspirational and educational guidance for persons establishing and maintaining libraries and media centers for religious congregations. Contributors are members and nonmembers of the association, publishers, and suppliers who write about everything that applies to the small religious library: organizing, selecting materials, cataloging and promotion. Book and video reviews are included.

INDEXED: Not given

EDITOR: Lorraine Burson

MANUSCRIPT ADDRESS: P.O. Box 19357, Portland, OR 97280-0357

EDITORIAL POLICY:
Student Papers Accepted: No
Publication Lag Time: 1-12 months
  or longer
Reprints: 2-3
Authorship Restrictions: None

Abstract Required: No
Proofs Corrected By: Editor
Payment: No

THE MANUSCRIPT:
Number of Copies: 1
Acknowledgment: Yes
Acceptance Lag Time: 2 weeks

Length: 750-900 words
Critique Provided: Not usually
Style: "Author's Guidelines"
  available

Format: Typed, double-spaced on one side of white paper.

REVIEW POLICY:
Refereed: Yes
Reviewed By: Editor

Acceptance Rate: 100% if
  recruited, less
  author is unknown

COPYRIGHT HELD BY:
First Publication: Publisher

Republication: Author

SUBSCRIPTION ADDRESS: *Church and Synagogue Libraries*, Church and Synagogue Library Association, P.O. Box 19357, Portland, OR 97280-0357

Frequency: Bimonthly
Cost: $18 individuals; $3 single issue

Circulation: 3,100

TELECOMMUNICATIONS: Editor: Phone: (503) 244-6919

COLLECTION BUILDING

AFFILIATION: None

SCOPE & CONTENT: *Collection Building* seeks to address the issues and problems encountered by librarians working in the field of collection development. It publishes both the broad, wide-ranging essay on the field as a whole as well as the specific-issue article, and includes practical, how-to articles along with research-oriented articles and subject bibliographies. It is designed for the multidisciplinary academic and professional librarian.

INDEXED: Inform.Sci.Abstr., Lib.Lit.

EDITOR: Arthur Curley, Director

MANUSCRIPT ADDRESS: Boston Public Library, Copley Square, Boston, MA 02117

EDITORIAL POLICY:
Student Papers Accepted: Yes   **Abstract Required:** No
Publication Lag Time: 3 months   **Proofs Corrected By:** Publisher
Reprints: 1 copy of issue   **Payment:** $50
Authorship Restrictions: No

THE MANUSCRIPT:
Number of Copies: 2   **Length:** 15-25 pages
Acknowledgment: Yes   **Critique Provided:** Yes
Acceptance Lag Time: 3 months   **Style:** *Chicago Manual of Style*

Format: "Guidelines For Authors" available. Type manuscript on 8 1/2" × 11" white bond paper with at least 1" margins on all sides with self-addressed, stamped envelope included.

REVIEW POLICY:
Refereed: Yes   **Acceptance Rate:** Not given
Reviewed By: Peer reviewed

COPYRIGHT HELD BY:
First Publication: Publisher   **Republication:** Publisher

SUBSCRIPTION ADDRESS: *Collection Building*, Neal-Schuman Publishers, 100 Varick St., New York, NY 10013

Frequency: Quarterly   **Circulation:** Not given
Cost: $55 annually

TELECOMMUNICATIONS: Susan Benson Holt, Editor: Phone: (212) 925-8650; Fax: (212) 219-8916. Coeditor: Kay Cassell, Assistant Director, Branch Programs and Services, New York Public Library, 6 East 40th St., New York, NY 10016

COLLECTION MANAGEMENT

AFFILIATION: None

SCOPE & CONTENT: *Collection Management* focuses on the important tasks of collection management and development. An essential resource for all librarians involved in this dynamic field, it examines the latest developments in the field and their implications for college, university, and research libraries of all types. It presents many different kinds of articles on an extensive range of topics–some pragmatic and topical, others theoretical, and still others state-of-the-art.

INDEXED: Behav.Abstr., Bull.Signal., CALL, Leg.Info.Manage.Ind., Lib.Lit., LISA

EDITOR: Peter Gellatly

MANUSCRIPT ADDRESS: The Haworth Press, 10 Alice Street, Binghamton, NY 13904-1580

EDITORIAL POLICY:
Student Papers Accepted: Occasionally
Publication Lag Time: 3-6 months
Reprints: 10 reprints and 1 copy of issue
Authorship Restrictions: None
Abstract Required: About 100 words
Proofs Corrected By: Editor
Payment: No

THE MANUSCRIPT:
Number of Copies: 3
Acknowledgment: Yes
Acceptance Lag Time: 1-2 months
Length: 3,000-4,000 words
Critique Provided: Sometimes
Style: *Chicago Manual of Style*

Format: Typed, double-spaced on white 8 1/2″ × 11″ bond paper with 1″ margins on all sides. "Instruction For Authors" available.

REVIEW POLICY:
Refereed: Yes
Acceptance Rate: About 65-70%
Reviewed By: Editor with input from staff, editorial board and blind refereed

COPYRIGHT HELD BY:
First Publication: Publisher
Republication: Publisher

SUBSCRIPTION ADDRESS: The Haworth Press, 10 Alice Street, Binghamton, NY 13904-1580

Frequency: Quarterly
Circulation: 900
Cost: $45 individuals; $120 institutions; $120 libraries

TELECOMMUNICATIONS: Not given

COLLEGE AND RESEARCH LIBRARIES (C&RL)

AFFILIATION: American Library Association

SCOPE & CONTENT: As the official journal of the Association of College & Research Libraries (ACRL), a division of the American Library Association, this publication is devoted almost exclusively to research articles covering a wide variety of current topics of academic interest. Articles are written by professors of library science and practitioners with substantial experience in their subject areas. Topics in a recent issue ranged from an empirical study of the merits of direct observation of periodical usage to a solution for journal price escalation. Selected book reviews, letters to the editor and research notes are included in this scholarly journal.

INDEXED: C.I.J.E., Inform.Sci.Abstr., LISA, SSCI

EDITOR: Gloriana St.Clair

MANUSCRIPT ADDRESS: c/o E506 Pattee Library, Pennsylvania State University Library, University Park, PA 16802

EDITORIAL POLICY:

Student Papers Accepted: Yes	**Abstract Required:** Yes
Publication Lag Time: 8-10 months	**Proofs Corrected By:** Author/
Reprints: Yes	Editor
Authorship Restrictions: None	**Payment:** No

THE MANUSCRIPT:

Number of Copies: 3	**Length:** 20 pages
Acknowledgment: Yes	**Critique Provided:** Yes
Acceptance Lag Time: 8-10 weeks	**Style:** *Chicago Manual Of Style* (modified by ALA standards)

Format: See "Instructions to Authors" in January issue.

REVIEW POLICY:

Refereed: Yes (Double blind)	**Acceptance Rate:** 40%

Reviewed By: Editorial board and selected reviewers

COPYRIGHT HELD BY:

First Publication: Journal	**Republication:** Journal

SUBSCRIPTION ADDRESS: American Library Association, 50 E. Huron Street, Chicago, IL 60611

Frequency: Bimonthly	**Circulation:** 13,000

Cost: $22.50 to ACRL members, included in membership dues; $45 nonmembers, U.S.; $50 Canada and Mexico; $55 other countries; $12 single issue. Retrospective subscriptions not accepted.

TELECOMMUNICATIONS: None

COLLEGE & RESEARCH LIBRARIES NEWS (C&RL News)

AFFILIATION: Association of College & Research Libraries; A Division of the American Library Association

SCOPE & CONTENT: As the official news magazine of the Association of College and Research Libraries, a division of the American Library Association, it serves as a vehicle for information among college and research libraries. *C&RL News* reports on items pertinent to academic and research librarianship, including information on bibliographic instruction, continuing education, appointments, acquisition of special collections, grants to libraries, new technology, and publications (brief notices). The contents are timely and of practical value to the people in the field.

INDEXED: C.I.J.E., Curr.Cont./Soc.&Beh.Sci., Inform.Sci.Abstr., Lib.Lit., LISA, SSCI

EDITOR: Mary Ellen K. Davis

MANUSCRIPT ADDRESS: ACRL/ALA, 50 E. Huron St., Chicago, IL 60611-2795

EDITORIAL POLICY:

Student Papers Accepted: Yes   **Abstract Required:** No
Publication Lag Time: 1-12 months   **Proofs Corrected By:** Editor
Reprints: 2 copies of issue   **Payment:** No
Authorship Restrictions: No

THE MANUSCRIPT:

Number of Copies: 2   **Length:** 500-3,000 words
Acknowledgment: Yes   **Critique Provided:** On request
Acceptance Lag Time: 8-12 weeks   **Style:** *Chicago Manual of Style* or Turabian

Format: If manuscript is prepared on word processor, please supply electronic version. Preferably WordPerfect 5.1 or ASCII on 5 1/4" or 3 1/2" diskettes.

REVIEW POLICY:

Refereed: No   **Acceptance Rate:** About 50%
Reviewed By: Editor

COPYRIGHT HELD BY:

First Publication: Publisher   **Republication:** Not given

SUBSCRIPTION ADDRESS: ALA Subscriptions, 50 E. Huron St., Chicago, IL 60611-2795

Frequency: 11 issues   **Circulation:** Not given
Cost: $7.50 for members of ACRL; $20 for nonmembers; $4.50 single issue

TELECOMMUNICATIONS: BITNET: U38398@UICVM.

COMMITTEE ON EAST ASIAN LIBRARIES. BULLETIN
(CEAL Bulletin)

AFFILIATION: Association For Asian Studies, Committee On East Asian Libraries

SCOPE & CONTENT: The CEAL Bulletin serves as a medium for East Asian Library problems of concern, and as an aid in the formulation of programs for the development of East Asian library resources, bibliographic controls, and access. The improvement of interlibrary and international cooperation in East Asian library development and services is a continual focus. The main contributors are librarians working with East Asian collections, East Asian studies scholars, and rare book/special collections curators.

INDEXED: Bibl.Asian.St., Lib.Lit.

EDITOR: Edward Martinique

MANUSCRIPT ADDRESS: Collection Development Department, CB #3918 Davis Library, University Of North Carolina, Chapel Hill, NC 27599-3918

EDITORIAL POLICY:

Student Papers Accepted: No	**Abstract Required:** No
Publication Lag Time: Within 4 months	**Proofs Corrected By:** Author
Reprints: None	**Payment:** No
Authorship Restrictions: None	

THE MANUSCRIPT:

Number of Copies: 1	**Length:** 3,000-5,000 words
Acknowledgment: No	**Critique Provided:** Always
Acceptance Lag Time: Varies	**Style:** Not given

Format: Typed, double-spaced, no paragraph indentation, name and affiliation of contributor.

REVIEW POLICY:

Refereed: No	**Acceptance Rate:** Not given
Reviewed By: Not given	

COPYRIGHT HELD BY:

First Publication: Author	**Republication:** Author

SUBSCRIPTION ADDRESS: *Committee On East Asian Libraries*, c/o Japanese Studies, 310 Main Library, 1858 Neil Avenue Mall, Columbus, OH 43210-1286

Frequency: 3 times a year	**Circulation:** 309

Cost: $15 individuals; $25 institutions; $10 single issue

TELECOMMUNICATIONS: Phone: (614) 292-3502; Fax: (614) 292-7859; E-mail: DONOVAN.1@OSU.EDU

COMPUTERS IN LIBRARIES

AFFILIATION: None

SCOPE & CONTENT: Articles are published on a wide variety of topics, all relating to computers in libraries. Most articles cover the practical applications of computer technology in libraries. *Computers in Libraries,* formerly called *Small Computers in Libraries,* appeals to a national and international audience. Contributors are generally from institutions of higher learning. Review of books, computer hardware, products, and programs are included.

INDEXED: ACM, Comp.Dtbs., Comput.Rev., Inform.Sci.Abstr., LHTN, Lib.Lit., Microcomp.Ind.

EDITOR: Nancy Nelson, Editor-In-Chief

MANUSCRIPT ADDRESS: Meckler Corp., 11 Ferry Lane West, Westport, CT 06880-9760

EDITORIAL POLICY:
Student Papers Accepted: No
Publication Lag Time: 2-4 months
Reprints: 2 copies of issue
Authorship Restrictions: None

Abstract Required: No
Proofs Corrected By: Editor
Payment: Negotiated article by article

THE MANUSCRIPT:
Number of Copies: 1
Acknowledgment: Yes
Acceptance Lag Time: 2-4 weeks

Length: 2,500 words
Critique Provided: Sometimes
Style: Not given

Format: No specific format.

REVIEW POLICY:
Refereed: No
Reviewed By: Editorial board and editor

Acceptance Rate: 50%

COPYRIGHT HELD BY:
First Publication: Publisher

Republication: Publisher

SUBSCRIPTION ADDRESS: *Computers in Libraries,* Meckler Corp., 11 Ferry Lane W., Westport, CT 06880-9760

Frequency: Monthly, except July/August   **Circulation:** 4,000
Cost: $35 individuals; $77 institutions; $18 additional for foreign rates

TELECOMMUNICATIONS: Editor: Phone: (203) 226-6967; Fax: (203) 454-5840; Internet: nancy@meckler.jvnc.net

COMPUTERS IN THE SCHOOLS

AFFILIATION: None

SCOPE & CONTENT: *Computers in the Schools* is supported by an editorial review board of prominent specialists in the school and educational setting. Material presented in this journal goes beyond the "how we did it" magazine article or handbook by offering serious discussions for educators, administrators, computer center directors, and special service providers in the school setting. Articles emphasize the practical aspect of any application but also tie theory to practice, relate present accomplishments to past efforts and future trends, identify conclusions and their implications, and discuss the theoretical and philosophical basis for the application.

INDEXED: Child.Educ.Abstr., C.I.J.E., Comput.Cont., Comput.Rev., Cont.Pg. Educ., Educ.Tech.Abstr., Excep.Child.Educ.Abstr., LAMP, Social.Educ.Abstr., Ref.Zh.

EDITOR: D. LaMont Johnson, PhD

MANUSCRIPT ADDRESS: College of Education, University of Nevada-Reno, Reno, NV 89557-0029

EDITORIAL POLICY:

Student Papers Accepted: Yes	**Abstract Required:** 100 words
Publication Lag Time: Not given	**Proofs Corrected By:** Editor
Reprints: Not given	**Payment:** No
Authorship Restrictions: None	

THE MANUSCRIPT:

Number of Copies: 4	**Length:** 10-20 pages
Acknowledgment: Yes	**Critique Provided:** Not given
Acceptance Lag Time: Not given	**Style:** APA

Format: Typed, double-spaced, 1″ margins on all four sides on 8 1/2″ × 11″ bond paper, plus diskette.

REVIEW POLICY:

Refereed: Yes	**Acceptance Rate:** Not given
Reviewed By: Editorial board and subject specialists	

COPYRIGHT HELD BY:

First Publication: Publisher	**Republication:** Publisher

SUBSCRIPTION ADDRESS: The Haworth Press, Inc., 10 Alice Street, Binghamton, NY 13904-1580

Frequency: Quarterly	**Circulation:** 452

Cost: $32 individuals; $60 institutions; $105 libraries

TELECOMMUNICATIONS: Editor: Phone: (702) 784-4961

CONCEPTS IN COMMUNICATION INFORMATICS AND LIBRARIANSHIP (CICIL)

AFFILIATION: None

SCOPE & CONTENT: This journal includes the interrelated fields of communication, informatics and librarianship. It provides a forum for professionals to disseminate their research. Contributors are scholars and academicians. Librarians with an interest or expertise in special areas are often contributors to the special theme volumes. Other volumes include theoretical research, historical and biographical documentation, case studies and state-of-the-art articles. There are no reviews. CICIL is an irregular serial published several times per year. All contributors whose work falls within the scope of the serials are welcomed.

INDEXED: Curr.Aw.Abstr., Econ.Affrs., Econ.St., Indian Lib.Sci.Abstr., Indian Bk.Chr., Intl.Class., Lib.Rev.

EDITOR: Dr. S.P. Argawal

MANUSCRIPT ADDRESS: B5/73, Azad Apartments, Sri Aurobindo Marg, New Delhi 110016 India

EDITORIAL POLICY:
Student Papers Accepted: Yes   **Abstract Required:** Yes
Publication Lag Time: Varies   **Proofs Corrected By:** Author
Reprints: No   **Payment:** Varies
Authorship Restrictions: None

THE MANUSCRIPT:
Number of Copies: 1   **Length:** 150-1,000 words
Acknowledgment: Yes   **Critique Provided:** Not usually
Acceptance Lag Time: 3 months   **Style:** Standard style sheet

Format: Standard style information available upon request

REVIEW POLICY:
Refereed: Yes   **Acceptance Rate:** 40%
Reviewed By: Editor and specialists

COPYRIGHT HELD BY:
First Publication: Varies   **Republication:** Varies

SUBSCRIPTION ADDRESS: Concept Publishing Company, A/15-16, Commercial Block, Mohan Garden, New Delhi 110059

Frequency: Irregular   **Circulation:** 500-1,000
Cost: Price list available on request

TELECOMMUNICATIONS: Editor: Phone: 666451 or 6864638; Publishers: Phone: 5554042 or 5504042; Telex: 31-76106 DK IN; Fax: (011) 559 8898

CONSERVATION ADMINISTRATION NEWS

AFFILIATION: None

SCOPE & CONTENT: Devoted to library and archival preservation and conservation, *Conservation Administration News* covers many phases of disaster planning and recovery, in addition to security measures. The main contributors are librarians, conservators, preservationists, archivists, museum curators, and record managers. Book, film, video, and audio reviews are also included.

INDEXED: Lib.Lit.

EDITOR: Toby Murray

MANUSCRIPT ADDRESS: McFarlin Library, University of Tulsa, 600 S. College Ave., Tulsa, OK 74104

EDITORIAL POLICY:

Student Papers Accepted: No	**Abstract Required:** No
Publication Lag Time: 1-6 months	**Proofs Corrected By:** Editor
Reprints: 1 issue	**Payment:** No
Authorship Restrictions: None	

THE MANUSCRIPT:

Number of Copies: 1	**Length:** 1,200 words
Acknowledgment: Yes	**Critique Provided:** Sometimes
Acceptance Lag Time: Immediate	**Style:** *Chicago Manual of Style*

Format: Double-spaced, typed manuscripts or computer disks.

REVIEW POLICY:

Refereed: No	**Acceptance Rate:** 99%
Reviewed By: Managing editor	

COPYRIGHT HELD BY:

First Publication: Material not copyrighted	**Republication:** Journal

SUBSCRIPTION ADDRESS: Toby Murray, McFarlin Library, University of Tulsa, 600 S. College Ave., Tulsa, OK 74104

Frequency: Quarterly   **Circulation:** About 700
Cost: $24 individuals; $24 institutions; $24 others; $6 single issue

TELECOMMUNICATIONS: Not given

CORPORATE LIBRARY UPDATE

AFFILIATION: None

SCOPE & CONTENT: *Corporate Library Update* is a bimonthly newsletter aimed at bringing news of interest to information managers and special librarians. It covers reviews of new books, events occurring in corporate and special libraries, and announcements of conferences and programs. It accepts press releases, brief news items and opinion pieces. It does not publish feature-length articles.

INDEXED: Not given

EDITOR: Susan S. DiMattia, Editor

MANUSCRIPT ADDRESS: Cahners Publishing Company, 249 W. 17th Street, 6th Floor, New York, NY 10011

EDITORIAL POLICY:
Student Papers Accepted: Not given   **Abstract Required:** Not given
Publication Lag Time: Not given   **Proofs Corrected By:** Not given
Reprints: Not given   **Payment:** Not given
Authorship Restrictions: Not given

THE MANUSCRIPT:
Number of Copies: Not given   **Length:** Not given
Acknowledgment: Not given   **Critique Provided:** Not given
Acceptance Lag Time: Not given   **Style:** Not given

Format: Not given.

REVIEW POLICY:
Refereed: Not given   **Acceptance Rate:** Not given
Reviewed By: Not given

COPYRIGHT HELD BY:
First Publication: Not given   **Republication:** Not given

SUBSCRIPTION ADDRESS: Not given

Frequency: Bimonthly   **Circulation:** Not given
Cost: Not given

TELECOMMUNICATIONS: Not given

CURRENT STUDIES IN LIBRARIANSHIP

AFFILIATION: None

SCOPE & CONTENT: Primarily a journal devoted to student research in librarianship, it includes a wide range of studies that address state-of-the-art issues, or current topics that also cover experimental data and conclusions. Contributors are students enrolled in MLS and PhD programs, as well as practitioners and professors.

INDEXED: LISA

EDITOR: Rashelle Karp

MANUSCRIPT ADDRESS: College of Library Science, Clarion University of Pennsylvania, Clarion, PA 16214

EDITORIAL POLICY:
Student Papers Accepted: Yes
Publication Lag Time: About 6 months
Reprints: 2 copies of issue
Authorship Restrictions: None

Abstract Required: Yes, about 100 words
Proofs Corrected By: Editor
Payment: No

THE MANUSCRIPT:
Number of Copies: 2
Acknowledgment: Yes
Acceptance Lag Time: About 2 months

Length: 1,000-2,000 words
Critique Provided: Sometimes
Style: APA

Format: Refer to previous issue as a guide.

REVIEW POLICY:
Refereed: No   **Acceptance Rate:** 80%
Reviewed By: Editor with input from staff

COPYRIGHT HELD BY:
First Publication: Not copyrighted   **Republication:** Not applicable

SUBSCRIPTION ADDRESS: Rashelle Karp, Current Studies in Librarianship, College of Library Science, Clarion University of Pennsylvania, Clarion, PA 16214

Frequency: Annual   **Circulation:** About 100
Cost: $10 individuals; $10 institutions; $10 single issue

TELECOMMUNICATIONS: Editor: Phone: (814) 226-5157

DIKTA

AFFILIATION: Southern Conference of Librarians for the Blind and Physically Handicapped

SCOPE & CONTENT: To provide a forum for the discussion of issues of interest to librarians serving patrons with print disabilities. Major audience is Southern librarians, but subscribers include national and international librarians. Reviews of books, videos, computer hardware, and accessible equipment, e.g., reading machines, Braille embossers, speech synthesizers are also added features. Contributors are generally librarians and rehabilitation professionals.

INDEXED: Not given

EDITOR: Michael G. Gunde

MANUSCRIPT ADDRESS: 420 Platt Street, Daytona Beach, FL 32114

EDITORIAL POLICY:

Student Papers Accepted: Yes	**Abstract Required:** No
Publication Lag Time: 3-6 months	**Proofs Corrected By:** Author
Reprints: 2	**Payment:** No
Authorship Restrictions: None	

THE MANUSCRIPT:

Number of Copies: 1	**Length:** About 2,000 words
Acknowledgment: Yes	**Critique Provided:** Always
Acceptance Lag Time: Usually 30 days	**Style:** *Chicago Manual of Style*

Format: Typed, double spaced, on diskette in WordPerfect also acceptable.

REVIEW POLICY:

Refereed: No	**Acceptance Rate:** 75%
Reviewed By: Editor	

COPYRIGHT HELD BY:

First Publication: Author	**Republication:** Author

SUBSCRIPTION ADDRESS: Joyce L. Smith, Huntsville Subregional Library for the Blind and Physically Handicapped, P.O. Box 443, Huntsville, AL 35801

Frequency: Biannually	**Circulation:** 120
Cost: $10 individuals; $20 institutions	

TELECOMMUNICATIONS: Not given

DOCUMENTS TO THE PEOPLE (DTTP)

AFFILIATION: ALA/GODORT, American Library Association Government Documents Round Table

SCOPE & CONTENT: As the official publication of the Government Documents Round Table, a unit of the American Library Association, it provides current information on government publications, technical reports, and maps at local, state, national, and international levels. It alerts the membership to current news with reports, announcements and information of interest to government document librarians. The intended audience is primarily national, but includes some international readers.

INDEXED: Lib.Lit.

EDITOR: Mary Redmond

MANUSCRIPT ADDRESS: New York State Library, Legislative/Governmental Services, Cultural Education Center, Albany, NY 12230

EDITORIAL POLICY:

Student Papers Accepted: Yes

Abstract Required: No

Publication Lag Time: 2-5 months

Proofs Corrected By: Editor

Reprints: One copy of issue

Payment: No

Authorship Restrictions: No

THE MANUSCRIPT:

Number of Copies: 2 (diskette and printout)

Length: About 2-3 pages long

Acknowledgment: Yes

Critique Provided: Only if not accepted

Acceptance Lag Time: 1 month or less

Style: Not given

Format: Not given.

REVIEW POLICY:

Refereed: No

Acceptance Rate: Almost all accepted

Reviewed By: Editor, with input from subject specialists

COPYRIGHT HELD BY:

First Publication: Optional

Republication: Optional

SUBSCRIPTION ADDRESS: Sinai Rocha, Distribution Manager, Reference, Moody Library, Baylor University, BU Box 7148, Waco, TX 76798-7148

Frequency: Quarterly

Circulation: About 1,800

Cost: Annual subscription for all is $20 in North America and $25 elsewhere. Inquire about price of single issues from UMI, 300 N. Zeeb Road, Ann Arbor, MI 48106

TELECOMMUNICATIONS: Editor: Phone: (518) 474-3940 Fax: (518) 474-5163; BITNET: USERGLN9@RPITSMTS

EDUCATION FOR INFORMATION

AFFILIATION: None

SCOPE & CONTENT: As an international journal, it covers all aspects of education and training for the information profession. It includes full-length articles, a section on computer software applications for education and training, and short communications on matters of current concern. The news section reports on significant activities and events worldwide and in-depth book reviews complete each issue. There is also an extensive bibliography of publications on education and training in the third issue of each volume. Members of the editorial staff are library and information science educators worldwide.

INDEXED: Br.Educ.Ind., Comput.Lit.Ind., Curr.Cont., Educ.Tech.Abstr., Eng.Ind., ERIC, INSPEC, LISA

EDITOR: J.A. Large

MANUSCRIPT ADDRESS: McGill University, Graduate School of Library and Information Studies, McLennon Library Building, 3459 McTavish Street, Montreal, Quebec H3A 1Y1, Canada

EDITORIAL POLICY:

Student Papers Accepted: No

Abstract Required: 200 words

Publication Lag Time: 3-12 months

Proofs Corrected By: Author

Reprints: 20

Payment: No

Authorship Restrictions: None

THE MANUSCRIPT:

Number of Copies: 2

Length: Varies

Acknowledgment: Yes

Critique Provided: Always

Acceptance Lag Time: About 4 weeks

Style: House style sheet available to prospective authors

Format: Typed on one side, double-spaced (including footnotes, references and abstracts) with wide margins. Authors are encouraged to submit manuscripts in machine-readable form on 3 1/2" or 5 1/4" diskette in English. "Information to Authors" available.

REVIEW POLICY:

Refereed: Yes

Acceptance Rate: 70%

Reviewed By: Blind refereed

COPYRIGHT HELD BY:

First Publication: Publisher

Republication: Publisher

SUBSCRIPTION ADDRESS: *Education for Information*, IOS Press, Van Diemenstraat 94, 1013 CN Amsterdam, Netherlands

Frequency: Quarterly

Circulation: 1,000-1,500

Cost: $193 (Dfl. 335.00) individuals and institutions

TELECOMMUNICATIONS: Phone: (415) 398-4204; Fax: (514) 398-7193; E-mail: INAW@MUSICB.MCGILL.CA

EDUCATION FOR LIBRARY AND INFORMATION SERVICES: Australia (ELISA)

AFFILIATION: Australian Library and Information Association

SCOPE & CONTENT: This publication is a forum for the concerns and interests of library educators, both national and international. All aspects of library education are covered. Special feature issues include commentaries, new developments, special "theme" issues, news items, and conference and workshop proceedings.

INDEXED: Aus.Educ.Inc., ERIC, LISA

EDITOR: Kate Beattie

MANUSCRIPT ADDRESS: 1 Elgin Place, Carlton, Victoria, Australia 3053

EDITORIAL POLICY:

Student Papers Accepted: No	**Abstract Required:** No
Publication Lag Time: 3-6 months	**Proofs Corrected By:** Editor
Reprints: No	**Payment:** No
Authorship Restrictions: No	

THE MANUSCRIPT:

Number of Copies: 2	**Length:** About 2,500 words
Acknowledgment: Yes	**Critique Provided:** Sometimes,
Acceptance Lag Time: 2 months	upon request
	Style: APA

Format: Paper copy.

REVIEW POLICY:

Refereed: Yes	**Acceptance Rate:** 90%
Reviewed By: Editor	

COPYRIGHT HELD BY:

First Publication: Author	**Republication:** Author

SUBSCRIPTION ADDRESS: Australian Library and Information Association, P.O. Box E441, Queen Victoria Terrace, A.C.T., Australia 2600

Frequency: 3 issues a year   **Circulation:** 300
Cost: $19.50 individuals; $23.50 institutions; $36 air mail; $6.50 single issue

TELECOMMUNICATIONS: Phone: (3) 347 9194

EDUCATION LIBRARIES JOURNAL

AFFILIATION: None

SCOPE & CONTENT: *Education Libraries Journal* publishes articles on all aspects of education and libraries, including the role of libraries and educators. Educational bibliographies and book reviews are also covered.

INDEXED: Br.Educ.Ind., IBR, IBZ, LISA

EDITOR: Claire Drinkwater

MANUSCRIPT ADDRESS: Institute of Education Library, 20 Bedford Way, London, WCIH OAL, England

EDITORIAL POLICY:

Student Papers Accepted: No

Publication Lag Time: 3-12 months

Reprints: 6 copies of issue

Authorship Restrictions: None

Abstract Required: About 100 words

Proofs Corrected By: Editor

Payment: No

THE MANUSCRIPT:

Number of Copies: 1

Acknowledgment: Yes

Acceptance Lag Time: 1 month

Length: 2,000-6,000 words

Critique Provided: Brief reason for rejection given

Style: Not given

Format: Typed, double-spaced, notes and references numbered at end of article.

REVIEW POLICY:

Refereed: No

Acceptance Rate: 75%

Reviewed By: Editor with input from staff

COPYRIGHT HELD BY:

First Publication: Journal

Republication: Journal

SUBSCRIPTION ADDRESS: Rey Augustin, Business Manager ELJ, Institute of Education Library, 20 Bedford Way, London WCIH OAL, England

Frequency: 3 issues a year

Circulation: About 400

Cost: $20 individuals; $20 institutions; $8 single issue

TELECOMMUNICATIONS: Phone: (071) 612-6060; Fax: (071) 612-0126

EMERGENCY LIBRARIAN

AFFILIATION: None

SCOPE & CONTENT: Promotes excellence in library services for children and young adults through thought-provoking and challenging articles, regular review columns, and critical analysis of management and programming issues. Teachers, librarians, professors, teacher-librarians, and administrators contribute case studies, commentaries, and bibliographies. Reviews of: books, video, audio, and computer programs are also included.

INDEXED: Basic Can.Ind., Bk.Rev.Ind., Can.Educ.Ind., Can.Mag.Ind., Can. Per.Ind., Child.Mag.Guide, C.I.J.E., Inform.Sci.Abstr., Lib.Lit., LISA

EDITOR: Ken Haycock

MANUSCRIPT ADDRESS: Dyad Services, P.O. Box 46258, Station G, Vancouver, B.C. V6R 4G6, Canada

EDITORIAL POLICY:
Student Papers Accepted: No
Publication Lag Time: Varies, within 1 year
Reprints: 2
Authorship Restrictions: None

Abstract Required: No
Proofs Corrected By: Editor
Payment: $50

THE MANUSCRIPT:
Number of Copies: 1
Acknowledgment: Yes
Acceptance Lag Time: About 8 weeks

Length: 5-12 pages double-spaced
Critique Provided: Upon request
Style: Author's guidelines available

Format: Typewritten, double-spaced.

REVIEW POLICY:
Refereed: Yes
Reviewed By: Blind refereed

Acceptance Rate: Not given

COPYRIGHT HELD BY:
First Publication: Publisher

Republication: Publisher

SUBSCRIPTION ADDRESS: *Emergency Librarian*, Dept. 284, P.O. Box C34069, Seattle, WA 98124-1069

Frequency: Five times per year   **Circulation:** 7,500
Cost: $47 individuals, $47 institutions, $10 single issue

TELECOMMUNICATIONS: Phone: (604) 734-0255; Fax: (604) 734-0221

FID NEWS BULLETIN

AFFILIATION: None

SCOPE & CONTENT: This journal reflects developments in FID (International Federation for Information and Documentation) for the benefit of its members; to provide members with up-to-date information on recent publications and developments in the information field. Information services, training for information management, and technological developments in the information world are some of the subjects covered. A calendar of meetings and conferences in the field of information services, as well as book reviews are included.

INDEXED: None

EDITOR: Theresa M. Stanton

MANUSCRIPT ADDRESS: FID Secretariat, P.O. Box 90402, 2509 LK The Hague, The Netherlands

EDITORIAL POLICY:
Student Papers Accepted: No
Publication Lag Time: Approx. 2 months
Reprints: 5
Authorship Restrictions: No

Abstract Required: No
Proofs Corrected By: Editor, unless author requests
Payment: No

THE MANUSCRIPT:
Number of Copies: 1
Acknowledgment: Yes
Acceptance Lag Time: 2 weeks

Length: 2,500-3,000 words
Critique Provided: Sometimes
Style: Not given

Format: Manuscript should be delivered as word copy and in WordPerfect diskette. Alternatively, it could be sent via E-mail.

REVIEW POLICY:
Refereed: Yes
Reviewed By: Editorial board and editor

Acceptance Rate: 80%

COPYRIGHT HELD BY:
First Publication: Publisher

Republication: Publisher

SUBSCRIPTION ADDRESS: FID Secretariat, P.O. Box 90402, 2509 LK The Hague, The Netherlands

Frequency: Monthly; double issue for July/August

Circulation: 1,800

Cost: $80 individuals; $80 institutions; free to members.

TELECOMMUNICATIONS: Phone: +31-(0)70-3140671; Fax: +31-(0)70-3140667; Telex: 34402KBGVNL; E-mail: GEOMAIL: GEO2:FID; Internet: fid@geo2.geomail.org; Dasnet: (DCFGN2)FID

FOCUS ON INDIANA LIBRARIES

AFFILIATION: Indiana Library Federation and Indiana State Library

SCOPE & CONTENT: This is a joint publication of the Indiana Library Federation and the Indiana State Library. It disseminates news and information of interest to librarians and others working in or with Indiana libraries, specifically legislative updates and program highlights, federation business, continuing education and general news. Contributors are members of the Indiana Library Community.

INDEXED: None

EDITOR: Raquel Ravinet

MANUSCRIPT ADDRESS: 1500 N. Delaware Street, Indianapolis, IN 46202

EDITORIAL POLICY:
Student Papers Accepted: No   **Abstract Required:** No
Publication Lag Time: Varies   **Proofs Corrected By:** Editor
Reprints: 2   **Payment:** No
Authorship Restrictions: None

THE MANUSCRIPT:
Number of Copies: 1   **Length:** 500-750 words
Acknowledgment: No   **Critique Provided:** Never
Acceptance Lag Time: Not given   **Style:** Standard style sheet

Format: Typed, double-spaced, in article format.

REVIEW POLICY:
Refereed: Not given   **Acceptance Rate:** Not given
Reviewed By: Editor with input from staff

COPYRIGHT HELD BY:
First Publication: Not copyrighted   **Republication:** Not given

SUBSCRIPTION ADDRESS: *Focus on Indiana Libraries*, 1500 N. Delaware Street, Indianapolis, IN 46202

Frequency: Monthly , except July/   **Circulation:** 3,500
August issue
Cost: $15 individuals; $15 institutions; $15 others; $1.50 single issue

TELECOMMUNICATIONS: Editor: Phone: (317) 636-6613; Fax: (317) 634-9503

FOR REFERENCE

AFFILIATION: New York Metropolitan Reference and Research Library Agency (METRO)

SCOPE & CONTENT: As the official newsletter of METRO, *For Reference* is distributed to member libraries as a membership benefit. It keeps its readership informed on the activities in the region, statewide and nationally. Some frequently covered subjects are: resource sharing (group access, collective purchasing, interlibrary loan), electronic and nonprint technologies development, historic preservation, and hospital library programs. Contributors are mostly from the METRO staff, however, occasionally guest contributors are solicited from member libraries.

INDEXED: None

EDITOR: Pam Daniels

MANUSCRIPT ADDRESS: For Reference from METRO, 57 East 11th Street, New York, NY 10003

EDITORIAL POLICY:
Student Papers Accepted: Not given   **Abstract Required:** Not given
Publication Lag Time: Not given   **Proofs Corrected By:** Not given
Reprints: Not given   **Payment:** Not given
Authorship Restrictions: Yes,
  members only

THE MANUSCRIPT:
Number of Copies: Not given   **Length:** Not given
Acknowledgment: Not given   **Critique Provided:** Not given
Acceptance Lag Time: Not given   **Style:** Not given

Format: Not given.

REVIEW POLICY:
Refereed: Not given   **Acceptance Rate:** Not given
Reviewed By: Not given

COPYRIGHT HELD BY: .
First Publication: Not given   **Republication:** Not given

SUBSCRIPTION ADDRESS: 57 East 11th Street, New York, NY 10003

Frequency: Monthly   **Circulation:** About 350
Cost: $10; free to METRO members

TELECOMMUNICATIONS: Editor: Phone: (212) 228-2320; Fax: (212) 228-2598

FREE STATE LIBRARIES

AFFILIATION: None

SCOPE & CONTENT: *Free State Libraries* is a South African journal that provides information and stimulates debate on current public and school library issues. It frequently covers articles on: promotion of reading, information and reference, children's services, marketing and in-service training. Contributors are academicians and practicing librarians. This publication also includes book, video, and audio reviews and publishes theme issues.

INDEXED: None

EDITOR: J. Schimper

MANUSCRIPT ADDRESS: *Free State Libraries*, Private Bag X20606, Bloemfontein, South Africa 9300

EDITORIAL POLICY:
Student Papers Accepted: No	**Abstract Required:** 100-120
Publication Lag Time: 6 months	words
Reprints: 1	**Proofs Corrected By:** Editor
Authorship Restrictions: None	(generally)
	Payment: No

THE MANUSCRIPT:
Number of Copies: 1	**Length:** 1,500-2,000 words
Acknowledgment: Yes	**Critique Provided:** Not usually
Acceptance Lag Time: 3-6 months	**Style:** Standard style sheet

Format: A4 paper, typed and double-spaced.

REVIEW POLICY:
Refereed: Yes	**Acceptance Rate:** 80%
Reviewed By: Editorial board	

COPYRIGHT HELD BY:
First Publication: Journal	**Republication:** Journal

SUBSCRIPTION ADDRESS: Orange Free State Provincial Library Service, Private Bag X20606, Bloemfontein, South Africa 9300

Frequency: Quarterly	**Circulation:** 600
Cost: Free	

TELECOMMUNICATIONS: None

GEORGIA LIBRARIAN

AFFILIATION: Georgia Library Association

SCOPE & CONTENT: *Georgia Librarian* caters to a state-wide audience, and its contributors are primarily librarians living and working in Georgia. It provides information about the business and activities of the Georgia Library Association, as well as news of Georgia libraries and librarians. Articles of both a scholarly and popular nature are accepted for consideration. Book reviews are limited to those of interest to librarians in Georgia, or are written by authors residing in Georgia.

INDEXED: Lib.Lit.

EDITOR: Joanne Lincoln

MANUSCRIPT ADDRESS: *The Georgia Librarian*, Professional Library, Atlanta Public Schools, 2930 Forrest Hill Drive, SW, Atlanta, GA 30315

EDITORIAL POLICY:
Student Papers Accepted: Yes | Abstract Required: Not given
Publication Lag Time: Varies | Proofs Corrected By: Editor
Reprints: 1 copy of issue and more | Payment: No
upon request
Authorship Restrictions: Priority given to association members and Georgia librarians

THE MANUSCRIPT:
Number of Copies: 2 | Length: 5-10 pages
Acknowledgment: Yes | Critique Provided: Not usually
Acceptance Lag Time: 2-4 weeks | Style: *Chicago Manual of Style*

Format: Submit manuscripts double-spaced in duplicate on plain white paper measuring 8 1/2″ × 11″.

REVIEW POLICY:
Refereed: No | Acceptance Rate: 75%
Reviewed By: Editor and editorial board

COPYRIGHT HELD BY:
First Publication: Not copyrighted | Republication: Not copyrighted

SUBSCRIPTION ADDRESS: Joanne Lincoln, Editor, *The Georgia Librarian*, P.O. Box 39, Young Harris College, Young Harris, GA 30582

Frequency: Quarterly | **Circulation:** 1,250
Cost: $12.50 individuals and institutions; $20 foreign; free with membership in association

TELECOMMUNICATIONS: Phone: (404) 827-8725; Fax: (404) 669-2705

GOVERNMENT INFORMATION QUARTERLY: An International Journal of Policies, Resources, Services, and Practices

AFFILIATION: None

SCOPE & CONTENT: *Government Information Quarterly* is a cross-disciplinary journal that provides a forum for theoretical and philosophical analyses, the presentation of research findings and their practical applications, and a discussion of current policies and practices, as well as new developments at all levels of government. The journal presents valuable resource material to government officials and policy makers, journalists, lawyers, researchers, teachers and scholars, students, librarians, and those interested in the role of government information in society. The most frequently published articles focus on policy research and analysis. Subjects covered most often are information resources management, access to information, privacy, freedom of information and electronic information.

INDEXED: C.I.J.E., Curr.Cont., Inform.Hot., Leg.Info.Manage.Ind., Lib.Lit., LISA, P.A.I.S., SSCI

EDITOR: Peter Hernon

MANUSCRIPT ADDRESS: Graduate School of Library and Information Science, 300 The Fenway, Boston, MA 02115

EDITORIAL POLICY:
Student Papers Accepted: No
Publication Lag Time: 6 months
Reprints: 15
Authorship Restrictions: None

Abstract Required: Yes, up to 150 words
Proofs Corrected By: Author
Payment: No

THE MANUSCRIPT:
Number of Copies: 3
Acknowledgment: Yes
Acceptance Lag Time: 4-6 weeks

Length: 2,000-3,500 words
Critique Provided: Always
Style: *Chicago Manual of Style*

Format: Paper copy typed, double-spaced plus diskette. Figures must be camera ready, preferably drawn in India ink. If accepted, original or glossy print of figures is required.

REVIEW POLICY:
Refereed: Yes
Reviewed By: Blind refereed

Acceptance Rate: 45%

COPYRIGHT HELD BY:
First Publication: Publisher

Republication: Publisher

SUBSCRIPTION ADDRESS: *Government Information Quarterly,* 55 Old Post Road–No. 2, P.O. Box 1678, Greenwich, CT 06836-1678. (Europe and United Kingdom) 118 Pentonville Road, London N1 9JN, England

Frequency: Quarterly   **Circulation:** 1,200

Cost: $55 individuals, $75 foreign air mail individuals, $65 foreign surface mail individuals; $110 institutions, $130 foreign air mail institutions, $120 foreign surface mail

TELECOMMUNICATIONS: Editor: Phone: (617) 738-2223

GOVERNMENT PUBLICATIONS REVIEW:
An International Journal Of Issues And Information Resources

AFFILIATION: None

SCOPE & CONTENT: *Government Publications Review* provides a forum for the publication of articles that provide insight into the history, current practice, national policies, and new developments in the production, distribution, processing, and use of information in all formats and at all levels of government. Unsolicited articles are particularly welcomed. These articles, as well as invited papers, are subject to the refereeing process.

INDEXED: Amer.Hist.&Life, ASCA, Chem.Abstr., Curr.Cont./Soc.&Beh.Sci., ERIC, Hist.Abstr., Inform.Hot., Inform.Sci.Abstr., Lib.Lit., LISA, P.A.I.S.

EDITOR: Steven D. Zink

MANUSCRIPT ADDRESS: Government Publications Dept., University of Nevada Library, Reno, NV 89557

EDITORIAL POLICY:

Student Papers Accepted: Yes

Publication Lag Time: 6-9 months

Reprints: Yes

Authorship Restrictions: No

Abstract Required: Yes, 200 words or less

Proofs Corrected By: Author

Payment: No

THE MANUSCRIPT:

Number of Copies: 3

Acknowledgment: Yes

Acceptance Lag Time: Day of receipt

Length: 20 pages

Critique Provided: Always

Style: *Chicago Manual of Style*

Format: Manuscripts may be submitted in English, French, or German. All abstracts should be in English. Type all material double-spaced on white bond paper with 1 1/2" margins all around. Pages should be numbered, including title page. All figures and illustrations should be professionally drawn.

REVIEW POLICY:

Refereed: Yes

Reviewed By: Editorial board, editor, double-blind review, and outside experts.

Acceptance Rate: About 60%

COPYRIGHT HELD BY:

First Publication: Publisher

Republication: Publisher

SUBSCRIPTION ADDRESS: *Government Publications Review*, Pergamon Press, Inc., 660 White Plains Rd., Tarrytown, NY 10591-5153

Frequency: Bimonthly

Circulation: About 1,000

Cost: $80 individuals; $290 institutions; $49 single issue

TELECOMMUNICATIONS: Editor: Phone: (701) 784-6579; Fax: (702) 784-1751; Internet: stevenz@unr.edu; BITNET: STEVENZ@EQUINOX

GUYANA LIBRARY ASSOCIATION BULLETIN (GLA BULLETIN)

AFFILIATION: Guyana Library Association

SCOPE & CONTENT: *The Guyana Library Association Bulletin*, deals with all aspects of librarianship, documentation and information science, in libraries/information units. The *Bulletin* usually contains two full-length articles; conference reports; news about the Association; general news about libraries; and news on matters of interest to librarians. It seeks articles on current library developments on improving services in Guyana.

INDEXED: LISA

EDITOR: Karen Sills

MANUSCRIPT ADDRESS: GLA Bulletin, P.O. Box 10240, Georgetown, Guyana

EDITORIAL POLICY:
Student Papers Accepted: No   **Abstract Required:** No
Publication Lag Time: 2 months or more **Proofs Corrected By:** Editor
Reprints: Not given   **Payment:** No
Authorship Restrictions: No

THE MANUSCRIPT:
Number of Copies: 1   **Length:** Approx. 12 pages
Acknowledgment: Not given   **Critique Provided:** Always
Acceptance Lag Time: Not given   **Style:** Not given

Format: Typed, double-spaced on foolscap size paper ($17'' \times 13\ 1/2''$) with 1 1/2" margins on all sides.

REVIEW POLICY:
Refereed: Not given   **Acceptance Rate:** Not given
Reviewed By: Editorial board

COPYRIGHT HELD BY:
First Publication: Author   **Republication:** Journal

SUBSCRIPTION ADDRESS: Guyana Library Association, P.O. Box 10240, Georgetown, Guyana

Frequency: Two per year   **Circulation:** 55
Cost: $20 both individuals and institutions; $10 single issue

TELECOMMUNICATIONS: Phone: 62690 or 62699

HERALD OF LIBRARY SCIENCE

AFFILIATION: P. K. Endowment for Library and Information Science

SCOPE & CONTENT: The focus of this international journal is to keep the library profession and those connected with the dissemination of knowledge regularly informed of library development, library techniques, indexing methods, bibliographical and documentation changes, information retrieval devices, book production, book analysis, and the development of the universe of knowledge.

INDEXED: Indian Lib.Sci.Abstr., Inform.Sci.Abstr., LISA

EDITOR: P. N. Kaula

MANUSCRIPT ADDRESS: C-239 Indira Nagar, Lucknow-226016, India

EDITORIAL POLICY:

Student Papers Accepted: Yes

Publication Lag Time: Varies

Reprints: 15 copies

Authorship Restrictions: None

Abstract Required: Yes

Proofs Corrected By: Editor

Payment: Invited papers only

THE MANUSCRIPT:

Number of Copies: 2

Acknowledgment: Yes

Acceptance Lag Time: Varies

Length: Approx. 10 pages

Critique Provided: No

Style: Standard

Format: Standard

REVIEW POLICY:

Refereed: Yes

Reviewed By: Board of referees

Acceptance Rate: 70%

COPYRIGHT HELD BY:

First Publication: Journal

Republication: Journal

SUBSCRIPTION ADDRESS: C-239 Indira Nagar, Lucknow-226016, India

Frequency: Quarterly

Circulation: Not given

Cost: $63 individuals; $70 institutions; $70 others; $18 single issue

TELECOMMUNICATIONS: Phone: (India) 381497

IFLA JOURNAL

AFFILIATION: IFLA (International Federation of Library Associations and Institutions)

SCOPE & CONTENT: *IFLA Journal* serves the IFLA membership, the international library world and related fields by publishing articles, reports and news on the activities of IFLA, and on the topics included in its program as well as on topics dealing with the furtherance of library and information activities organized outside IFLA or in cooperation with IFLA. It covers contemporary library problems of international interest which in some way are, or may become, related to IFLA as an organization. Topics of national interest in general are not included unless they are part of a special theme issue. Contributors are IFLA officers, speakers at IFLA conferences, and experts on topics for theme issues. It does not include reviews.

INDEXED: LISA

EDITOR: Carol Henry

MANUSCRIPT ADDRESS: IFLA Headquarters, P.O. Box 95312, 2509 CH The Hague, Netherlands

EDITORIAL POLICY:

Student Papers Accepted: Yes
Publication Lag Time: 3-9 months
Reprints: 1 issue of journal
Authorship Restrictions: None

Abstract Required: 100-250 words
Proofs Corrected By: Editorial staff
Payment: No

THE MANUSCRIPT:

Number of Copies: 1
Acknowledgment: Yes
Acceptance Lag Time: 3 months

Length: 4-15 single-spaced pages
Critique Provided: Sometimes
Style: No specific requirements

Format: Double-spaced on one side of page only.

REVIEW POLICY:

Refereed: Yes
Reviewed By: Editorial board

Acceptance Rate: 10%

COPYRIGHT HELD BY:

First Publication: Publisher

Republication: Publisher

SUBSCRIPTION ADDRESS: K.G. Saur, Verlag, 120 Chanlon Rd., New Providence, NJ 07974

Frequency: Quarterly

Circulation: 4,000

Cost: DEM 149 plus postage for annual subscription for individuals, institutions and others; DEM 43 single issue. The currency exchange rate of U.S. dollars to German Marks on day of placing order should be used.

TELECOMMUNICATIONS: Editor: Phone: *31 (70) 3140 884; Fax: *31 (70) 3 834827

IFRT REPORT

AFFILIATION: Intellectual Freedom Round Table (IFRT) is a unit of the American Library Association

SCOPE & CONTENT: *IFRT Report* is an irregularly published newsletter. It includes news about current censorship controversies, American Library Association conferences and activities of the Round Table. Contributors to the newsletter are members, committee chairs, and the chair of the Intellectual Freedom Round Table.

INDEXED: Not given

EDITOR: Paul Vermouth

MANUSCRIPT ADDRESS: M.I.T. Room 145-222, Massachusetts Institute of Technology, Cambridge, MA 02139

EDITORIAL POLICY:

Student Papers Accepted: Not given	**Abstract Required:** Not given
Publication Lag Time: Not given	**Proofs Corrected By:** Not given
Reprints: Not given	**Payment:** Not given
Authorship Restrictions: Committee chairs and members	

THE MANUSCRIPT:

Number of Copies: Not given	**Length:** Not given
Acknowledgment: Not given	**Critique Provided:** Not given
Acceptance Lag Time: Not given	**Style:** Not given

Format: Not given

REVIEW POLICY:

Refereed: Not given	**Acceptance Rate:** Not given
Reviewed By: Not given	

COPYRIGHT HELD BY:

First Publication: Not given	**Republication:** Not given

SUBSCRIPTION ADDRESS: Anne E. Levinson, IFRT Staff Liaison, American Library Association, 50 E. Huron St., Chicago, IL 60611

Frequency: Irregular   **Circulation:** 2,219 (membership)
Cost: Free to members of IFRT

TELECOMMUNICATIONS: IFRT Liaison: Phone: (312) 280-4224

ILLINOIS LIBRARIES

AFFILIATION: Illinois State Library

SCOPE & CONTENT: *Illinois Libraries* provides information on state library programs to all types of libraries in Illinois and in national library communities. It also develops single topic issues on subjects of importance to the library profession. Most journal issues are thematic, and a special guest editor solicits contribution for articles. Frequently covered subjects include: reference, automation, management, library development, library buildings, technical services, and archives. Articles are mostly based on empirical research. As the official journal of the Illinois State Library, it also publishes information which meets state library obligations.

INDEXED: Lib.Lit.

EDITOR: Nancy Krah, associate editor

MANUSCRIPT ADDRESS: *Illinois Libraries*, Illinois State Library, 300 South Second Street, Room 515, Springfield, IL 62701-1796

EDITORIAL POLICY:
Student Papers Accepted: No
Publication Lag Time: Within 1 year
Reprints: Upon author's request
Authorship Restrictions: None

Abstract Required: No
Proofs Corrected By: Editor
and/or staff
Payment: No

THE MANUSCRIPT:
Number of Copies: 1
Acknowledgment: Yes
Acceptance Lag Time: 2-3 weeks

Length: 5-10 pages
Critique Provided: Not usually
Style: Standard style

Format: Articles should be typed, double-spaced on 8 1/2" × 11" white paper

REVIEW POLICY:
Refereed: Yes
Reviewed by: Editor with input from staff

Acceptance Rate: Not given

COPYRIGHT HELD BY:
First Publication: Not copyrighted

Republication: Publisher

SUBSCRIPTION ADDRESS: *Illinois Libraries*, Illinois State Library, 300 South Second Street, Room 515, Springfield, IL 62701-1796

Frequency: 6 issues annually
Cost: Free

Circulation: 7,000

TELECOMMUNICATIONS: Editor: Phone: (217) 782-5870; Fax (217) 785-4326

THE INDIAN ARCHIVES

AFFILIATION: National Archives of India

SCOPE & CONTENT: *The Indian Archives* is a publication of the National Archives of India. Its focus is archival studies and the preservation of manuscripts. Frequently covered subjects are records administration, preparation of reference media, editing of records, methods of preservation and repair of documents, and microfilming. Contributors are historians, archivists, and conservators.

INDEXED: None

EDITOR: Not given

MANUSCRIPT ADDRESS: *The Indian Archives,* National Archives of India, Janpath, New Delhi 110001, India

EDITORIAL POLICY:

Student Papers Accepted: No
Publication Lag Time: 6 months
Reprints: 10
Authorship Restrictions: No

Abstract Required: Not necessarily
Proofs Corrected By: Editor
Payment: (Rupee) 14.00 per 400 words, or equivalent currency

THE MANUSCRIPT:

Number of Copies: 2
Acknowledgment: Yes
Acceptance Lag Time: 1 month

Length: No word limit
Critique Provided: Not usually
Style: Standard style sheet

Format: Neatly typed, double-spaced on standard sheet. Complete notes and references should be collated and given at the end of the article.

REVIEW POLICY:

Refereed: Yes
Reviewed By: Experts recommended by the editor

Acceptance Rate: Not given

COPYRIGHT HELD BY:

First Publication: Publisher

Republication: Publisher

SUBSCRIPTION ADDRESS: Director General of Archives, National Archives of India, Janpath, New Delhi 110001, India

Frequency: Biannual
Cost: $6.84 others; $3.60 single issue (Cost subject to revision)

Circulation: About 300

TELECOMMUNICATIONS: Editor: Phone: (0)11 383436

INFORMATION DISPLAY

AFFILIATION: Society for Information Display

SCOPE & CONTENT: *Information Display* is edited for research and development management, and for engineers, designers, scientists, and ergonomists responsible for the design and development of display, computer graphics, and image processing systems. It includes state-of-the-art developments in electronic, electromechanical, and hard-copy display equipment. Contributors are scientists, engineers, university students and professors.

INDEXED: SRDS

EDITOR: Ken Werner

MANUSCRIPT ADDRESS: Palisades Institute for Research Services, 201 Varick Street, New York, NY 10014

EDITORIAL POLICY:

Student Papers Accepted: Not given   **Abstract Required:** Not given
Publication Lag Time: Varies   **Proofs Corrected By:** Author
Reprints: No limit   **Payment:** No
Authorship Restrictions: Not given

THE MANUSCRIPT:

Number of Copies: Not given   **Length:** Not given
Acknowledgment: Not given   **Critique Provided:** Not usually
Acceptance Lag Time: Varies   **Style:** Not given

Format: Not given.

REVIEW POLICY:

Refereed: No   **Acceptance Rate:** Not given
Reviewed By: Editor

COPYRIGHT HELD BY:

First Publication: Author   **Republication:** Journal

SUBSCRIPTION ADDRESS: *Information Display*, Society for Information Display, 8055 W. Manchester Ave. Suite 615, Usually del Rey, CA 90293

Frequency: Monthly   **Circulation:** 12,000
Cost: $36 domestic; $72 foreign; $5 single issue; free to members of the Society for Information Display

TELECOMMUNICATIONS: Not given

INFORMATION REPORTS & BIBLIOGRAPHIES

AFFILIATION: None

SCOPE & CONTENT: This publication captures the "grey" library literature and makes it part of the permanent literature. Contributors consist of university librarians, government librarians, and information specialists in industry. The reports and bibliographies cover state-of-the-art issues, current interests, new developments, and research briefs. Recent papers published include, "Chief Information Officers on Campus," "Productivity in the Information Society," and "When Can You Weed an Unused Book?"

INDEXED: Not given

EDITOR: Ivan Lyons

MANUSCRIPT ADDRESS: 465 West End Avenue, Suite 4B, New York, NY 10024

EDITORIAL POLICY:

Student Papers Accepted: No   **Abstract Required:** No
Publication Lag Time: 2-6 months   **Proofs Corrected By:** Editor
Reprints: 20   **Payment:** No
Authorship Restrictions: None

THE MANUSCRIPT:

Number of Copies: 2   **Length:** 32 pages maximum
Acknowledgment: Yes   **Critique Provided:** Never
Acceptance Lag Time: 2-6 months   **Style:** Standard style sheet

Format: Submit reports and bibliographies on 8 1/2″ × 11″ paper.

REVIEW POLICY:

Refereed: Yes   **Acceptance Rate:** 85%
Reviewed By: Blind refereed

COPYRIGHT HELD BY:

First Publication: Author   **Republication:** Publisher

SUBSCRIPTION ADDRESS: 465 West End Avenue, Suite 4B, New York, NY 10024

Frequency: Bimonthly   **Circulation:** Not given
Cost: $95 domestic; $125 foreign; $15 single issue

TELECOMMUNICATIONS: Editor: Fax: (212) 873-5587

INFORMATION SERVICES & USE

AFFILIATION: None

SCOPE & CONTENT: *Information Services & Use* was conceived as an information technology oriented publication with a wide scope of subject matter. International in terms of both audience and authorship, the journal is aimed at leaders in information management and applications in an attempt to keep them fully informed of fast-moving developments in fields such as: online systems, offline systems, database services, electronic publishing, library automation, education and training, and telecommunications. These areas are treated not only in general, but also in specific contexts. Applications to business and scientific fields are sought so that a balanced view is offered to the reader. This journal provides a lively forum for debate and a reliable source of information on the information industry. It also includes extensive news and calendar of events sections, as well as frequent conference reports.

INDEXED: ACM Comp.Rev., Contenta, Commun.Abstr., Comput.Cont., Comput.Lit.Ind., Curr.Cont./Soc. & Beh.Sci., Data Process.Dig., Eng.Ind., ERIC, Inform.Sci.Abstr., INSPEC, Lib.Lit., LISA, Manage.Cont., Sci.Abstr.

EDITOR: A.W. Ecias

MANUSCRIPT ADDRESS: 3408 Warden Drive, Philadelphia, PA 19129 U.S.

EDITORIAL POLICY:

Student Papers Accepted: No	**Abstract Required:** Yes
Publication Lag Time: 10-12 months	**Proofs Corrected By:** Author
Reprints: 25	**Payment:** No
Authorship Restrictions: None	

THE MANUSCRIPT:

Number of Copies: 2	**Length:** Varies
Acknowledgment: Yes	**Critique Provided:** Sometimes
Acceptance Lag Time: 4-6 months	**Style:** House style sheet available

Format: Not given.

REVIEW POLICY:

Refereed: Yes	**Acceptance Rate:** 70%
Reviewed By: Editor, blind refereed	

COPYRIGHT HELD BY:

First Publication: Publisher	**Republication:** Publisher

SUBSCRIPTION ADDRESS: Elsevier Science Publishers BV., P.O. Box 1991, 1000 BZ Amsterdam, The Netherlands or, Elsevier Science Publ. Co., P.O. Box 882, Madison Square Garden, New York, NY 10159

Frequency: Bimonthly   **Circulation:** Not given
Cost: U.S. price subject to exchange rate fluctuations

INFORMATION SYSTEMS MANAGEMENT

AFFILIATION: None

SCOPE & CONTENT: *Information Systems Management* publishes practical and timely articles that offer techniques and practice-proven solutions to major technical and managerial problems facing executives and staff members in the field. Each issue contains six to seven feature-length articles and six to eight columns, including an interview and book review section. Articles may focus on a specific subject critical to successful information systems management; past themes include education's role, project management, systems development, and economics.

INDEXED: Anbar, Data Process.Dig., Deadline

EDITOR: Karen Brogno

MANUSCRIPT ADDRESS: Auerbach Publications, One Penn Plaza, New York, NY 10119

EDITORIAL POLICY:

Student Papers Accepted: No

Publication Lag Time: 6-7 months

Reprints: No, but 2 copies of issue provided

Authorship Restrictions: None

Abstract Required: Yes, 75 words

Proofs Corrected By: Editor

Payment: $100 honorarium for columns only

THE MANUSCRIPT:

Number of Copies: 2

Acknowledgment: Yes

Acceptance Lag Time: 6-8 weeks

Length: 5,000 words for features, 2,000 for columns

Critique Provided: Not usually

Style: Guidelines available to authors

Format: Include 3.5" diskette of WordPerfect 5.0 if possible. Submit manuscript double spaced on one side only of 8 1/2" × 11" paper. Place art work at back of manuscript, not in text.

REVIEW POLICY:

Refereed: Yes, peer reviewed

Reviewed By: Editor with input from staff

Acceptance Rate: 60%

COPYRIGHT HELD BY:

First Publication: Publisher

Republication: Publisher

SUBSCRIPTION ADDRESS: *Information Systems Management*, Warren Gorham Lamont, 210 South St., Boston, MA 02111

Frequency: Quarterly

Cost: $110 individuals and institutions

Circulation: About 6,000

TELECOMMUNICATIONS: Editor: Phone: (212) 971-5277; Fax: (212) 971-5025

INFORMATION TECHNOLOGY AND LIBRARIES

AFFILIATION: Library and Information Technology Association, a division of the American Library Association

SCOPE & CONTENT: The aim of *Information Technology and Libraries* is to disseminate research and applications in the field of information technology as it relates to library and information science. Subjects most frequently covered are online catalogs, browsable screens, authority control, and non-Roman scripts for computers. Contributions are often solicited for special theme issues.

INDEXED: ABI Inform, Bus.Ind., C.I.J.E., Compumath, Comput.Cont., Comput.Lit.Ind., Comput.Rev., Curr.Cont., Educ.Ind., Inform.Sci.Abstr., Leg. Info.Manage.Ind., LHTN, Lib.Lit., LISA, Mag.Ind., Pers.Lit., PMR, Ref.Sour., Ref.Zh., Sci.Abstr., Soft.Abstr.Eng., Tr.&Ind.Ind.

EDITOR: Thomas W. Leonhardt

MANUSCRIPT ADDRESS: Bizzell Library, 401 W. Brooks, University of Oklahoma, Norman, OK 73019-0528

EDITORIAL POLICY:

Student Papers Accepted: No
Publication Lag Time: 3-6 months
Reprints: Available at cost
Authorship Restrictions: None

Abstract Required: Yes, 1-2 paragraphs
Proofs Corrected By: Author
Payment: No

THE MANUSCRIPT:

Number of Copies: 2
Acknowledgment: Yes
Acceptance Lag Time: 1 week or less

Length: Not given
Critique Provided: Always
Style: *Chicago Manual of Style*

Format: Double-spaced, including abstracts and notes.

REVIEW POLICY:

Refereed: Yes
Reviewed By: Blind refereed

Acceptance Rate: 60%

COPYRIGHT HELD BY:

First Publication: Publisher

Republication: Author

SUBSCRIPTION ADDRESS: *Information Technology and Libraries*, American Library Association Publishing Services, 50 East Huron Street, Chicago, IL 60611

Frequency: Quarterly
Cost: Not given

Circulation: About 8,000

TELECOMMUNICATIONS: Editor: Phone: (405) 325-2611; BITNET: QC6305@UOKMYVSA

INTERLENDING AND DOCUMENT SUPPLY

AFFILIATION: None

SCOPE & CONTENT: *Interlending and Document Supply* is an international journal that provides state-of-the-art coverage on a wide range of activities relating to document delivery and supply. It includes traditional approaches as well as the use of advanced technologies, both within and between countries. Contributors are prominent professionals engaged in interlending.

INDEXED: Inform.Abstr., Inform.Sci.Abstr., Lib.Lit., LISA, PASCAL

EDITOR: Andrew Swires

MANUSCRIPT ADDRESS: *Interlending and Document Supply*, British Library Document Supply Centre, Boston Spa, Wetherby, West Yorkshire LS23 7BQ, U.K.

EDITORIAL POLICY:
Student Papers Accepted: No
Publication Lag Time: Varies
Reprints: Available for a fee
Authorship Restrictions: Not given

Abstract Required: 100 words
Proofs Corrected By: Editor
Payment: No

THE MANUSCRIPT:
Number of Copies: 3
Acknowledgment: Yes
Acceptance Lag Time: 7 days

Length: 3,500 words
Critique Provided: Not usually
Style: "Instructions For Authors" available

Format: Typed, double-spaced on A4 paper with 1″ margins on all sides.

REVIEW POLICY:
Refereed: Yes
Reviewed By: Editorial board

Acceptance Rate: 50%

COPYRIGHT HELD BY:
First Publication: Publisher

Republication: Publisher

SUBSCRIPTION ADDRESS: Publication Sales Unit, British Library, Boston Spa, Wetherby, West Yorkshire LS23 7BQ, U.K.

Frequency: Quarterly
Cost: £31 in U.K.; £36 in..U.S; £9 single issue

Circulation: 1,000

TELECOMMUNICATIONS: Phone: (0) 937 546070; Fax: (0) 937 546236; Telex: 557381

INTERNATIONAL CATALOGING
AND BIBLIOGRAPHIC CONTROL (ICBC)

AFFILIATION: International Federation of Library Associations (IFLA)

SCOPE & CONTENT: *International Cataloging and Bibliographic Control* covers topics related to Universal Bibliographic Control and International MARC (UBCIM). As a unit of IFLA, it is of world-wide interest to librarians and information scientists.

INDEXED: LISA

EDITOR: Ms. Marie-France Plassard

MANUSCRIPT ADDRESS: IFLA UBCIM Programme c/o Deutsche Bibliothek, Zeppelinallee 4-8, D-6000 Frankfurt am Main 1, Federal Republic of Germany

EDITORIAL POLICY:
Student Papers Accepted: Yes	**Abstract Required:** No
Publication Lag Time: 6-12 months	**Proofs Corrected By:** Editor
Reprints: No	**Payment:** No
Authorship Restrictions: None	

THE MANUSCRIPT:
Number of Copies: 1	**Length:** 3,000-4,000 words
Acknowledgment: Yes	**Critique Provided:** Always
Acceptance Lag Time: 3 months	**Style:** Standard, A4

Format: Printed matter only.

REVIEW POLICY:
Refereed: Yes	**Acceptance Rate:** Not given
Reviewed By: Blind refereed	

COPYRIGHT HELD BY:
First Publication: Author and IFLA	**Republication:** Author/Journal

SUBSCRIPTION ADDRESS: Bailey Management Services, 127 Sandgate Road Folkestone, Kent, CT20 2BL, U.K.

Frequency: Quarterly	**Circulation:** About 800
Cost: $48 institutions	

TELECOMMUNICATIONS: Phone: +49-69-7410906; Fax: +49-69-7566476; Telex: 416 643 deu bi

INTERNATIONAL FORUM ON INFORMATION AND DOCUMENTATION

AFFILIATION: Federation Internationale D'Information Et De Documentation and VINITI

SCOPE & CONTENT: This journal is intended to cover the most important problems of information theory and practical activities that are of interest to information specialists all over the world. A wide range of subjects is covered: communication in science, conventional and advanced forms and ways of information presentation and dissemination, forecasting and planning of development trends for information and library services and systems (both national and international), theoretical fundamentals of information, classifications and information languages, information needs, training of information personnel, and information user education. Special "theme" issues, case studies, and conferences/workshops are also included.

INDEXED: Bull.Signal. (now: PASCAL), Inform.Abstr., Inform.Sci. Abstr., LISA

EDITOR: Prof. R.S. Giljarevskij

MANUSCRIPT ADDRESS: VINITI, Usievicha 20a, 125219, Moscow, Russia

EDITORIAL POLICY:

Student Papers Accepted: No

Abstract Required: 200-250 words

Publication Lag Time: About 5 months

Proofs Corrected By: Editor

Payment: No

Reprints: 10

Authorship Restrictions: No

THE MANUSCRIPT:

Number of Copies: 2

Length: 5,000 words maximum

Acknowledgment: Yes

Critique Provided: Always

Acceptance Lag Time: Approx. 1-2 months

Style: A4

Format: A4 paper.

REVIEW POLICY:

Refereed: No

Acceptance Rate: 90%

Reviewed By: Not given

COPYRIGHT HELD BY:

First Publication: Publisher

Republication: Publisher

SUBSCRIPTION ADDRESS: FID, Distribution Centre, Blackhorse Road, Letchworth, Hertfordshire, SG6 1HN, U.K.

Frequency: Quarterly

Circulation: 800

Cost: £46 in European Economic Community countries; $88 in all other countries

TELECOMMUNICATIONS: Telex: 411249; Fax: (0) 117-095-943-0060

INTERNATIONAL JOURNAL OF INFORMATION AND LIBRARY RESEARCH

AFFILIATION: None

SCOPE & CONTENT: This journal focuses on information and library systems and their users, information technology, man-machine interfaces, the architecture and environment of systems, information designs, media and communication studies, freedom of information, copyright, socio-legal and political aspects of information, transnational information flow, the economics of information and information services, funding, artificial intelligence, knowledge-based systems, information management, classification and indexing, information retrieval, traditional and innovative service delivery, general theory, and organizational and behavioral aspects of information systems. It is designed specifically for information professionals around the world who need to know how contemporary information research is shaping present and future information and library services.

INDEXED: Lib.Lit., LISA

EDITOR: Dr. Stephen Roberts

MANUSCRIPT ADDRESS: Department Of Information Management, Polytechnic of West London, St. Mary's Road, Ealing, London W5 5RF, England

EDITORIAL POLICY:

Student Papers Accepted: No   **Abstract Required:** Yes
Publication Lag Time: Not given   **Proofs Corrected By:** Not given
Reprints: 20   **Payment:** No
Authorship Restrictions: None

THE MANUSCRIPT:

Number of Copies: 2   **Length:** 5,000-7,000 words
Acknowledgment: Yes   **Critique Provided:** Not given
Acceptance Lag Time: Not given   **Style:** Available in journal
Format: Manuscript or diskette in ASCII format.

REVIEW POLICY:

Refereed: Yes   **Acceptance Rate:** Not given
Reviewed By: Editor and Editorial Board

COPYRIGHT HELD BY:

First Publication: Author/Publisher   **Republication:** Author/Publisher

SUBSCRIPTION ADDRESS: Taylor Graham Publishing, 500 Chesham House, 150 Regent Street, London, WIR 5FA, U.K.

Frequency: 3 per year   **Circulation:** Not given
Cost: $96 institutions; $35 single issue

TELECOMMUNICATIONS: Not given

INTERNATIONAL LEADS

AFFILIATION: International Relations Round Table of the American Library Association

SCOPE & CONTENT: To serve as a source of news about international library activities, the international work of the American Library Association and other organizations, and people and publications in the field. This publication closes the gaps in information exchange and protocol by reporting on world-wide issues.

INDEXED: Lib.Lit.

EDITOR: Robert P. Doyle

MANUSCRIPT ADDRESS: American Library Association, 50 East Huron Street, Chicago, IL 60611

EDITORIAL POLICY:
Student Papers Accepted: No   **Abstract Required:** No
Publication Lag Time: Not given   **Proofs Corrected By:** Editor
Reprints: Not given   **Payment:** No
Authorship Restrictions: None

THE MANUSCRIPT:
Number of Copies: 1   **Length:** Not given
Acknowledgment: Not given   **Critique Provided:** Not given
Acceptance Lag Time: Not given   **Style:** Not given

Format: No specific format.

REVIEW POLICY:
Refereed: No   **Acceptance Rate:** Not given
Reviewed By: Editor

COPYRIGHT HELD BY:
First Publication: Optional   **Republication:** Optional

SUBSCRIPTION ADDRESS: Robert P. Doyle, American Library Association, 50 East Huron Street, Chicago, IL 60611

Frequency: Quarterly   **Circulation:** 875
Cost: $12 individuals; free to members

TELECOMMUNICATIONS: Phone: (312) 280-3200; Fax: (312) 944-3897

INTERNATIONAL LIBRARY MOVEMENT

AFFILIATION: None

SCOPE & CONTENT: This journal covers a wide range of subjects in management and organization for both public and technical services related to the library movement in the world. Contributors are welcomed from all countries, especially third world professionals. Book reviews are included on all subjects. Case studies, new developments, and bibliographies are added specialties.

INDEXED: Not given

EDITOR: N.K. Bhagi

MANUSCRIPT ADDRESS: *International Library Movement*, P.B. No.1 (GPO), 214-Model Town, Ambala City 134003 India

EDITORIAL POLICY:
Student Papers Accepted: Yes   **Abstract Required:** No
Publication Lag Time: Varies   **Proofs Corrected By:** Editor
Reprints: 1 copy of journal   **Payment:** No
Authorship Restrictions: None

THE MANUSCRIPT:
Number of Copies: 2   **Length:** About 2,500 words
Acknowledgment: Yes   **Critique Provided:** Never
Acceptance Lag Time: 1 month   **Style:** Standard style available

Format: International standard size.

REVIEW POLICY:
Refereed: Not given   **Acceptance Rate:** Not given
Reviewed By: Editorial board

COPYRIGHT HELD BY:
First Publication: Author/Journal   **Republication:** Journal

SUBSCRIPTION ADDRESS: *International Library Movement*, P.B. No. 1 (GPO), 214-Model Town, Ambala City, 134003 India

Frequency: Quarterly   **Circulation:** 1,400
Cost: $125 individuals; $125 institutions; $100 others

TELECOMMUNICATIONS: Not given

INTERNATIONAL REVIEW OF CHILDREN'S LITERATURE AND LIBRARIANSHIP

AFFILIATION: Not given

SCOPE & CONTENT: The *International Review of Children's Literature and Librarianship* is designed to explore the range of issues of current concern to those working in the field of children's literature around the world. It covers the management of library services to children and adolescents, educational issues affecting library services, information technology, user education and promotion of services, staff education and training, collection development and management, critical assessments of children's and adolescent literature, book and media selection, and research in literature and library services for children and adolescents.

INDEXED: Con.Pg.Educ., Lib.Lit., LISA

EDITOR: Margaret Kinnell

MANUSCRIPT ADDRESS: Department of Information & Library Studies, University of Loughborough, Loughborough LE11 3TU, U.K.

EDITORIAL POLICY:
Student Papers Accepted: No
Publication Lag Time: Not given
Reprints: 20
Authorship Restrictions: None
Abstract Required: Yes
Proofs Corrected By: Not given
Payment: No

THE MANUSCRIPT:
Number of Copies: 2
Acknowledgment: Yes
Acceptance Lag Time: Not given
Length: 5,000-7,000 words
Critique Provided: Not given
Style: Available in all issues of journal

Format: Manuscript or diskette in ASCII format.

REVIEW POLICY:
Refereed: Yes
Reviewed By: Editor and Editorial Board
Acceptance Rate: Not given

COPYRIGHT HELD BY:
First Publication: Author/Publisher
Republication: Author/Publisher

SUBSCRIPTION ADDRESS: Taylor Graham Publishing, 500 Chesham House, 150 Regent Street, London WIR 5FA, U.K.

Frequency: 3 per year
Circulation: Not given
Cost: $88 institutions; $30 single issue

TELECOMMUNICATIONS: Not given

INTERNET RESEARCH: ELECTRONIC NETWORKING, APPLICATIONS AND POLICY

AFFILIATION: None

SCOPE & CONTENT: A cross-disciplinary journal, it provides coverage of an evolving and converging area of information and communication technology. It publishes research findings related to electronic networks, analyses of policy issues related to electronic networking, and descriptions of current and potential applications of electronic networking. It is intended for a wide audience that includes network users, administrators and policy makers in academic, commercial, library and government settings. Members of the editorial board are from international organizations.

INDEXED: ERIC, Lib.Lit., LISA, SCI, SSCI

EDITOR: Dr. Charles R. McClure

MANUSCRIPT ADDRESS: School of Information Studies, Syracuse University, Syracuse, NY 13244

EDITORIAL POLICY:
Student Papers Accepted: Yes   **Abstract Required:** Yes
Publication Lag Time: 3 months   **Proofs Corrected By:** Editor/
Reprints: 1 copy of journal   author
Authorship Restrictions: None   **Payment:** No

THE MANUSCRIPT:
Number of Copies: 3   **Length:** 20-25 pages
Acknowledgment: Yes   **Critique Provided:** Always
Acceptance Lag Time: 2 weeks   **Style:** APA

Format: Typed, double-spaced on one side of 8 1/2" × 11" white paper with margins of 1" on all sides. Number each page. "Contributor Guidelines" available.

REVIEW POLICY:
Refereed: Yes   **Acceptance Rate:** 60%
Reviewed By: Blind refereed or reviewed by editor with input from staff

COPYRIGHT HELD BY:
First Publication: Journal   **Republication:** Journal

SUBSCRIPTION ADDRESS: Meckler Publishing, 11 Ferry Lane West, Westport, CT 06880

Frequency: Quarterly   **Circulation:** 350
Cost: $95 individuals and institutions

TELECOMMUNICATIONS: Phone: (315) 443-2911; E-mail: Internet: cmcclure@suvm.acs.syr.edu.

JOURNAL OF ACADEMIC LIBRARIANSHIP (JAL)

AFFILIATION: None

SCOPE & CONTENT: The *Journal of Academic Librarianship* publishes articles that focus on all aspects of problems and issues germane to college and university libraries. Authors report on the results of research, express opinions, or present bibliographical essays. JAL also brings to the attention of practitioners in general, and book selectors in particular, information about hundreds of new and recently published books in librarianship, information science, management, and higher education. It is written to appeal to a wide audience covering a broad range of topics.

INDEXED: C.I.J.E., Inform.Sci.Abstr., Lib.Lit., LISA, SSCI

EDITOR: Richard M. Dougherty

MANUSCRIPT ADDRESS: Mountainside Publishing, P.O. Box 8330, Ann Arbor, MI 48107

EDITORIAL POLICY:
Student Papers Accepted: No	**Abstract Required:** Yes, 75-100
Publication Lag Time: 6-12 months	words
Reprints: 2-6 copies of issue	**Proofs Corrected By:** Author
Authorship Restrictions: None	**Payment:** No

THE MANUSCRIPT:
Number of Copies: 3	**Length:** 4,000 words
Acknowledgment: Yes	**Critique Provided:** Always
Acceptance Lag Time: 8-12 weeks	**Style:** *Chicago Manual of Style*

Format: Submit manuscripts typed, double-spaced, include page numbers.

REVIEW POLICY:
Refereed: Yes	**Acceptance Rate:** 25-30%
Reviewed By: Double-blind refereed	

COPYRIGHT HELD BY:
First Publication: Publisher	**Republication:** Journal

SUBSCRIPTION ADDRESS: *Journal of Academic Librarianship*, Mountainside Publishing, P.O. Box 8330, Ann Arbor, MI 48107

Frequency: Bimonthly	**Circulation:** 3,000

Cost: $29 individuals, $52 institutions, $10 single issue

TELECOMMUNICATIONS: Phone: (313) 662-3925; Fax: (313) 662-4450

JOURNAL OF BUSINESS & FINANCE LIBRARIANSHIP

AFFILIATION: None

SCOPE & CONTENT: As a relatively new journal, its goal is to provide interesting and informative articles concerning the creation, organization, retrieval, dissemination and use of business information. Articles focus on business information needs in special libraries, academic and public libraries, as well as business information centers and services outside the traditional library setting. Case studies, results of research, literature reviews, and description and evaluation of innovative programs, products and services are the types of articles most frequently included. Contributors are librarians, information specialists, and academicians. Book reviews are included.

INDEXED: Curr.Aw.Bull., Ind.Per.Art.Relat.Law, InformSci.Abstr. INSPEC, LISA, Ref.Zh.

EDITOR: William Fisher

MANUSCRIPT ADDRESS: Division of Library & Information Science, San Jose State University, San Jose, CA 95192-0029

EDITORIAL POLICY:
Student Papers Accepted: Not given
Publication Lag Time: Not given
Reprints: 10 plus 1 copy of issue
Authorship Restrictions: None

Abstract Required: Yes, 100-150 words
Proofs Corrected By: Editor
Payment: No

THE MANUSCRIPT:
Number of Copies: 3 (original & 2 copies)
Acknowledgment: Yes
Acceptance Lag Time: 6-8 weeks

Length: 10-15 typed pages
Critic Provided: Always
Style: APA

Format: "Instructions For Author" available.

REVIEW POLICY:
Refereed: Yes
Reviewed By: Blind refereed

Acceptance Rate: 70%

COPYRIGHT HELD BY:
First Publication: Publisher

Republication: Author

SUBSCRIPTION ADDRESS: *Journal of Business & Finance Librarianship*, The Haworth Press, 10 Alice Street, Binghamton, NY 13904-1580

Frequency: Quarterly
Cost: $24 individuals; $40 institutions

Circulation: Not available

TELECOMMUNICATIONS: Editor: Phone: (408) 924-2494

JOURNAL OF DOCUMENTATION

AFFILIATION: ASLIB, The Association for Information Management

SCOPE & CONTENT: The *Journal of Documentation* is a publication of the Association for Information Management. Its aim is to publish papers based on research or practice relating to the recording, organization, management, retrieval, dissemination and use of information in systems of all kinds. A wide range of critical book and literature reviews are also included. Contributors are transcontinental library information science researchers and professionals.

INDEXED: Inform.Sci.Abstr., LISA

EDITOR: Mrs. A.M. Adams, Assistant Editor

MANUSCRIPT ADDRESS: Queen's University, Science Library, Chlorine Gardens, Belfast, BT9 5EQ, Ireland

EDITORIAL POLICY:
Student Papers Accepted: No
Publication Lag Time: About 3 months
Reprints: 25
Authorship Restrictions: None

Abstract Required: About 200 words
Proofs Corrected By: Author
Payment: No

THE MANUSCRIPT:
Number of Copies: 2
Acknowledgment: Yes
Acceptance Lag Time: About 3 months

Length: 3,000-6,000 words
Critique Provided: Not usually
Style: Not given

Format: Follow notes for contributors published in each issue.

REVIEW POLICY:
Refereed: Yes
Reviewed By: Editor with input from staff, editorial board, and blind refereed

Acceptance Rate: Varies

COPYRIGHT HELD BY:
First Publication: Author/Publisher

Republication: Author/Publisher

SUBSCRIPTION ADDRESS: ASLIB, 20-24 Old Street, London EC1V 9AP, England

Frequency: Quarterly
Cost: £80 in the U.K.; £55 for ASLIB members; £90 other countries

Circulation: About 3,000

TELECOMMUNICATIONS: Not given

JOURNAL OF EDUCATION FOR LIBRARY AND INFORMATION SCIENCE

AFFILIATION: Association for Library and Information Science Education (ALISE)

SCOPE & CONTENT: As the official publication of ALISE, this scholarly journal serves as a forum for discussion and for presentation of research and issues within the field. The subjects are examined from an educational perspective. Most contributors are faculty in schools of library and information science and practitioners.

INDEXED: C.I.J.E.,Curr.Cont., Educ.Ind., Inform.Sci.Abstr., Lib.Lit., LISA, Res.High.Educ.Abstr., SSCI

EDITOR: Rosemary Ruhig DuMont

MANUSCRIPT ADDRESS: School of Library and Information Science, Kent State University, Kent, OH 44242

EDITORIAL POLICY:
Student Papers Accepted: No
Publication Lag Time: 1 year
Reprints: 3 copies of issue
Authorship Restrictions: None

Abstract Required: 150 words or less
Proofs Corrected By: Author
Payment: No

THE MANUSCRIPT:
Number of Copies: 3
Acknowledgment: Yes
Acceptance Lag Time: 2 months

Length: 3,000 words for articles
Critique Provided: Always
Style: *Chicago Manual of Style*

Format: Typed, double-spaced throughout on one side.

REVIEW POLICY:
Refereed: Yes
Reviewed By: Blind refereed

Acceptance Rate: Varies

COPYRIGHT HELD BY:
First Publication: Journal

Republication: Journal

SUBSCRIPTION ADDRESS: Patty Hardaway, *Journal of Education For Library and Information Science*, Publications Office, 4101 Lake Boone Trail, Suite 201, Raleigh, NC 27607-4916

Frequency: Quarterly
Cost: $50 individuals; $60 foreign; $20 single issue

Circulation: 1,700

TELECOMMUNICATIONS: Phone: (216) 672-2782; Fax: (216) 672-7965; BITNET: CSLIBSHP@KENTVM.KENT.EDU.

JOURNAL OF INFORMATION ETHICS

AFFILIATION: None

SCOPE & CONTENT: To provide a forum for material from widely varied perspectives emphasizing ethical issues in any area of information or knowledge production and dissemination, and to foster interdisciplinary approaches to ethics in all information fields and related areas, ranging from library science to computer security. Subjects most frequently covered include censorship, privacy issues, intellectual freedom, librarianship, computerization, and access issues. This journal also publishes book, film and video reviews as well as pro/con symposia or "debates" on issues.

INDEXED: None

EDITOR: Robert Hauptman

MANUSCRIPT ADDRESS: *Journal of Information Ethics*, Centennial Hall, St. Cloud State University, St. Cloud, MN 56301

EDITORIAL POLICY:

Student Papers Accepted: No

Publication Lag Time: 3-6 months

Reprints: Reviews 1; articles 2

Authorship Restrictions: None

Abstract Required: No

Proofs Corrected By: Editor

Payment: $35-50 honorarium upon publication

THE MANUSCRIPT:

Number of Copies: 2

Acknowledgment: Yes

Acceptance Lag Time: Few days to few weeks

Length: 2,000-2,500 words

Critique Provided: Sometimes

Style: House style sheet available

Format: Two double-spaced copies and IBM compatible diskette; WordPerfect if possible.

REVIEW POLICY:

Refereed: No

Reviewed By: Editor and editorial board

Acceptance Rate: Not given

COPYRIGHT HELD BY:

First Publication: Publisher

Republication: Publisher

SUBSCRIPTION ADDRESS: *Journal of Information Ethics*, McFarland & Co. Publishers, P.O. Box 611, Jefferson, NC 28640

Frequency: Semi-annually, spring & fall **Circulation:** Not given
Cost: $38 individuals, $38 institutions, $21 single issue

TELECOMMUNICATIONS: Editor: Phone: (612) 255-4822 for editorial information; For other information: Phone: (919) 246-4460; Fax (919) 246-5018

JOURNAL OF INFORMATION SCIENCE

AFFILIATION: Institute of Information Scientists

SCOPE & CONTENT: The *Journal of Information Science* is an international journal providing a publication vehicle for complete coverage of all topics of interest to those involved in the area. The audience includes managers and practitioners of information services, as well as those concerned with their analysis, design, implementation and evaluation, from the point of view either of theory or of practice. It will also be of interest to generators and users of information, as well as those in related fields such as management science and communication science.

INDEXED: AESIS, BPIA, Bus.Ind., Chem.Abstr., Comput.Cont., Compumath, Comput.Lit.Ind., Comput.Rev., Curr.Cont./Soc.&Beh.Sci., Eng.Ind., ERIC, Fluidex, Inform.Sci.Abstr., INSPEC, Intl.Civil Eng.Abstr., Lib.Lit., LISA, LHTN, Manage.Cont., Ref.Zh., Sci.Abstr., SCI, Soft.Abstr.Eng., SSCI, Tr.&Ind., World Text.Abstr.

EDITOR: Alan Gilchrist

MANUSCRIPT ADDRESS: Institute of Information Scientists, 44/45 Museum Street, London WC1A 1LY, U.K.

EDITORIAL POLICY:

Student Papers Accepted: No

Publication Lag Time: 3 1/2 to 5 1/2 months

Reprints: 25

Authorship Restrictions: None

Abstract Required: 150 words

Proofs Corrected By: Author

Payment: No

THE MANUSCRIPT:

Number of Copies: 3

Acknowledgment: Yes

Acceptance Lag Time: 5-6 weeks

Length: 5,000-10,000 words

Critique Provided: Always

Style: Standard style

Format: Type footnotes, references, and abstracts double-spaced, with wide margins. "Information for Authors" is available in journal. Footnotes should be brief and kept to a minimum.

REVIEW POLICY:

Refereed: Yes

Reviewed By: Blind refereed

Acceptance Rate: 66%

COPYRIGHT HELD BY:

First Publication: Publisher

Republication: Publisher

SUBSCRIPTION ADDRESS: Elsevier Science Publishers, P.O. Box 1991, BZ 1000, Amsterdam, Netherlands

Frequency: Bimonthly

Cost: Dutch florins 346

Circulation: About 3,500

TELECOMMUNICATIONS: Fax: (0) 273-203495

JOURNAL OF INTERLIBRARY LOAN & INFORMATION SUPPLY

AFFILIATION: None

SCOPE & CONTENT: As the first journal devoted to interlibrary loan procedures and problems, this publication focuses on the expanding roles of librarians. In addition to practice and research-based articles, it focuses on the broad spectrum of all library and information center functions that rely heavily on interlibrary loan and information supply in North America and abroad.

INDEXED: Curr.Aw.Bull., Educ.Ind., For.Lib.Inf.Serv., Inform.Sci.Abstr., LISA, Ref.Zh.

EDITOR: Leslie R. Morris

MANUSCRIPT ADDRESS: Director of Libraries, Niagara University Library, Niagara University, NY 14109

EDITORIAL POLICY:
Student Papers Accepted: Not given
Publication Lag Time: Not given
Reprints: 10 and 1 copy of issue
Authorship Restrictions: None

Abstract Required: About 100 words
Proofs Corrected By: Editor
Payment: No

THE MANUSCRIPT:
Number of Copies: 3
Acknowledgment: Yes
Acceptance Lag Time: 1-3 months

Length: 10-20 typed pages
Critique Provided: Sometimes
Style: APA

Format: Leave 1″ margin all four sides. Use clean, white, 8 1/2″ × 11″ bond paper.

REVIEW POLICY:
Refereed: Yes
Reviewed By: Blind refereed

Acceptance Rate: Not given

COPYRIGHT HELD BY:
First Publication: Publisher

Republication: Publisher

SUBSCRIPTION ADDRESS: *Journal of Interlibrary Loan & Information Supply*, The Haworth Press, 10 Alice Street, Binghamton, NY 13904-1580

Frequency: Quarterly
Circulation: 620
Cost: $18 individuals; $24 institutions and others

TELECOMMUNICATIONS: Phone: (716) 286-8002; Fax: (716) 286-8030; Internet: niagara@class.org

JOURNAL OF LIBRARIANSHIP AND INFORMATION SCIENCE (JOLIS)

AFFILIATION: None

SCOPE & CONTENT: This journal, with a new format, design, and aim, supersedes the *Journal of Librarianship* (1969-1990). Following its predecessor, it is an academic publication committed to a high standard of scholarship. Most articles reflect issues of concern in the United Kingdom, however, editors encourage an international dimension to the journal by inviting contributions from academics, librarians, and information scientists world-wide.

INDEXED: Inform.Abstr., Inform.Bib., Lib.Lit., LISA, Ref.Zh.

EDITOR: David Stoker

MANUSCRIPT ADDRESS: Bowker-Saur–JOLIS, 60 Grosvenor Street, London W1X 9DA, U.K.

EDITORIAL POLICY:

Student Papers Accepted: Yes   **Abstract Required:** No
Publication Lag Time: 9-18 months   **Proofs Corrected By:** Editor
Reprints: 20 plus 1 copy of journal   **Payment:** No
Authorship Restrictions: None

THE MANUSCRIPT:

Number of Copies: 2   **Length:** 4,000-8,000 words
Acknowledgment: Yes   **Critique Provided:** Sometimes
Acceptance Lag Time: 6-8 weeks   **Style:** Published on back cover of journal

Format: Two copies of typed, double-spaced manuscript or (preferably) an unformatted text file on either 5 1/2″ or 3 1/2″ IBM compatible diskette together with a printed version.

REVIEW POLICY:

Refereed: Yes   **Acceptance Rate:** About 65%
Reviewed By: Editorial board and/or subject specialists

COPYRIGHT HELD BY:

First Publication: Publisher   **Republication:** Publisher

SUBSCRIPTION ADDRESS: JOLIS, Bailey Management Services, 127 Sandgate Road, Folkestone, Kent CT20 2BL U.K.

Frequency: Quarterly   **Circulation:** Not given
Cost: $99 individuals and institutions

TELECOMMUNICATIONS: Phone: (0) 970 622178 or 623111 Ex 2178; Fax: (0) 970 622190; E-mail: DAS@UK.AC.ABER

JOURNAL OF LIBRARY ADMINISTRATION

AFFILIATION: None

SCOPE & CONTENT: The *Journal of Library Administration* is the primary source of information on all aspects of the effective management of libraries. Stressing the practical, this valuable journal provides information that administrators want and need to know in order to most efficiently and effectively manage their libraries. The journal seeks out the most modern advances being made in professional management and applies them to the library setting.

INDEXED: BPIA, Bull.Signal., Excerp.Med., Info.Manage.Ind., Lib.Lit., LISA, Manage.Cont., P.A.I.S., Pers.Lit., Tr.&Ind.Ind., Ref.Zh.

EDITOR: Sul H. Lee

MANUSCRIPT ADDRESS: Dean of University Libraries, University of Oklahoma, Norman, OK 73019

EDITORIAL POLICY:
Student Papers Accepted: Not given **Abstract Required:** No
Publication Lag Time: 5-6 months **Proofs Corrected By:** Editor
Reprints: Yes **Payment:** No
Authorship Restrictions: None

THE MANUSCRIPT:
Number of Copies: 3 **Length:** 25 pages
Acknowledgment: Yes **Critique Provided:** Not given
Acceptance Lag Time: 1-4 months **Style:** *Chicago Manual of Style*

Format: Type manuscript double-spaced; use 8 1/2" × 11" paper.

REVIEW POLICY:
Refereed: Yes **Acceptance Rate:** Not given
Reviewed By: Editorial board and
  anonymous specialist referees

COPYRIGHT HELD BY:
First Publication: Publisher **Republication:** Publisher

SUBSCRIPTION ADDRESS: The Haworth Press, 10 Alice Street, Binghamton, NY 13904-1580

Frequency: Quarterly **Circulation:** 1,112
Cost: $36 individuals; $90 institutions; $90 libraries

TELECOMMUNICATIONS: Phone: (800) 342-9678; Fax: (607) 722-1424

JOURNAL OF THE RUTGERS UNIVERSITY LIBRARY

AFFILIATION: None

SCOPE & CONTENT: Most of the contributors are library faculty from Rutgers University. Articles relate to materials held by Rutgers University libraries, and primarily include New Jersey history, book and library history, and bibliographies.

INDEXED: Hist.Abstr.

EDITOR: Professor Pamela Spence Richards

MANUSCRIPT ADDRESS: Rutgers University, School of Communication, 4 Huntington Street, New Brunswick, NJ 08903

EDITORIAL POLICY:

Student Papers Accepted: No	**Abstract Required:** No
Publication Lag Time: 6-12 months	**Proofs Corrected By:** Author
Reprints: 10	**Payment:** No
Authorship Restrictions: None	

THE MANUSCRIPT:

Number of Copies: 1	**Length:** 6,500 words
Acknowledgment: Yes	**Critique Provided:** Always
Acceptance Lag Time: 3 months	**Style:** MLA

Format: Typed, double-spaced with end notes.

REVIEW POLICY:

Refereed: Yes	**Acceptance Rate:** 50%
Reviewed By: Editorial board and blind refereed	

COPYRIGHT HELD BY:

First Publication: Publisher	**Republication:** Publisher

SUBSCRIPTION ADDRESS: *Journal of the Rutgers University Library*, Ms. Nancy Wiencek, Administration, Alexander Library, Rutgers University, New Brunswick, NJ 08903

Frequency: Biannually	**Circulation:** About 550
Cost: $25	

TELECOMMUNICATIONS: Not given

JOURNAL OF YOUTH SERVICES IN LIBRARIES
(Previous title: Top Of The News)

AFFILIATION: Association For Library Services To Children (ALSC) and Young Adult Library Services (YALSA)

SCOPE & CONTENT: As the official journal of ALSC and YALSA, it provides an informational link to professionals in the combined fields of librarianship. As a vehicle for continuing education for librarians working with children and young adults, it serves as a showcase for current practice and a spotlight for current programs. Each division reports on activities surrounding related news items. Subjects include all aspects of services, promotion, materials, collection development, and programs dealing with this youthful population.

INDEXED: Bk.Rev.Ind., C.I.J.E., Lib.Lit., LISA

EDITOR: Linda J. Wilson

MANUSCRIPT ADDRESS: Reference Department, University Libraries, Virginia Tech., P.O. Box 90001, Blacksburg, VA 24062-9001

EDITORIAL POLICY:
Student Papers Accepted: No	**Abstract Required:** No
Publication Lag Time: Varies	**Proofs Corrected By:** Editor
Reprints: 5	**Payment:** No
Authorship Restrictions: None	

THE MANUSCRIPT:
Number of Copies: 4	**Length:** Not given
Acknowledgment: Not given	**Critique Provided:** Sometimes
Acceptance Lag Time: Varies	**Style:** ALA Guidelines

Format: Not given.

REVIEW POLICY:
Refereed: Yes	**Acceptance Rate:** Varies
Reviewed By: Blind refereed	

COPYRIGHT HELD BY:
First Publication: Journal	**Republication:** Journal

SUBSCRIPTION ADDRESS: American Library Association, 50 East Huron St, Chicago, IL 60611

Frequency: Quarterly   **Circulation:** About 10,000
Cost: $40.00 individuals; $40.00 institutions; $50.00 foreign; $12.00 single issue

TELECOMMUNICATIONS: Not given

JUDAICA LIBRARIANSHIP
(Supersedes AJL Bulletin)

AFFILIATION: Association of Jewish Libraries

SCOPE & CONTENT: The focus of this publication is mainly on the Judaica library of any size, in any setting, and with any subject, language, or media specialty. It includes the organization and management of Judaica and Hebraic collections of all types, and welcomes manuscripts on all aspects of the Jewish library and book worlds. Papers delivered at conferences with unpublished proceedings are welcome, as are articles on all aspects of the acquisition, bibliographic access and retrieval of materials, especially those dealing with current developments.

INDEXED: ERIC, Geneal.Per.Ind., Ind.Artic.Jew.Stud., Ind.Jew.Per., Inform. Sci.Abstr., Intl.Bib.Zeit., Lib.Lit., LISA, M.L.A. Intl.Bib.

EDITOR: Bella Hass Weinberg

MANUSCRIPT ADDRESS: Div. of Library & Information Science, St. John's University, Grand Central and Utopia Parkway, Jamaica, NY 10028

EDITORIAL POLICY:

Student Papers Accepted: No	**Abstract Required:** No
Publication Lag Time: 1 to 1 1/2 years	**Proofs Corrected By:** Author
Reprints: One copy of issue	**Payment:** No
Authorship Restrictions: None	

THE MANUSCRIPT:

Number of Copies: 2	**Length:** Varies
Acknowledgment: Yes	**Critique Provided:** Always
Acceptance Lag Time: 3-6 months	**Style:** *Chicago Manual of Style*

Format: Typed, double-spaced (including tables and references) on 8 1/2" × 11" white paper with margins of at least one inch on all sides.

REVIEW POLICY:

Refereed: Yes	**Acceptance Rate:** 85-90%
Reviewed By: Editorial board and editor	(authorities in the field)

COPYRIGHT HELD BY:

First Publication: Journal	**Republication:** Journal

SUBSCRIPTION ADDRESS: Aviva Astrinsky, Vice President for membership, Annenberg Research Institute Library, 420 Walnut Street, Philadelphia, PA 19106

Frequency: 2 issues per volume   **Circulation:** 1,200-1,400

Cost: Subscriptions include membership. $25 individuals and institutions; $18 students and retirees; $25 single issue.

TELECOMMUNICATIONS: Editor: Send inquiries by mail only to manuscript address

LAW LIBRARY ASSOCIATION MARYLAND NEWS

AFFILIATION: Law Library Association of Maryland

SCOPE & CONTENT: This is a state publication designed to keep members of the Association informed of news and developments in libraries, especially law libraries. Many types of articles are welcome, but in keeping with its mission as a newsletter, most articles are brief and newsy rather than scholarly.

INDEXED: None

EDITOR: Maxine Grosshans

MANUSCRIPT ADDRESS: Marshall Law Library, 20 N. Paca Street, Baltimore, MD 21201

EDITORIAL POLICY:

Student Papers Accepted: Not given	**Abstract Required:** Not given
Publication Lag Time: Not given	**Proofs Corrected By:** Not given
Reprints: Not given	**Payment:** Not given
Authorship Restrictions: Not given	

THE MANUSCRIPT:

Number of Copies: Not given	**Length:** Not given
Acknowledgment: Not given	**Critique Provided:** Not given
Acceptance Lag Time: Not given	**Style:** Not given

Format: Not given

REVIEW POLICY:

Refereed: Not given	**Acceptance Rate:** Not given
Reviewed By: Not given	

COPYRIGHT HELD BY:

First Publication: Not given	**Republication:** Not given

SUBSCRIPTION ADDRESS: Maxine Grosshans, Marshall Law Library, 20 N. Paca Street, Baltimore, MD 21201

Frequency: Quarterly   **Circulation:** About 200
Cost: Included in chapter dues of $20 a year

TELECOMMUNICATIONS: Not given

LAW LIBRARY JOURNAL

AFFILIATION: American Association of Law Libraries

SCOPE & CONTENT: This publication includes articles in all fields of interest and concern to law librarians and others who work with legal materials. Topics focus on: law library collections, their acquisition and organization, services to users and instructions to legal research; the administration of law libraries: the design and construction of law libraries and the history of law libraries and legal materials. Recent article titles included "How to Develop a Marketing Plan for a Law Firm Library" "Electronic Resources for Patent Searching" and "The Civil Law in Canada."

INDEXED: Not given

EDITOR: Richard A. Danner

MANUSCRIPT ADDRESS: *Law Library Journal*, Duke University, School of Law Library, Durham, NC 27706

EDITORIAL POLICY:
Student Papers Accepted: Sometimes
Publication Lag Time: 8-12 months
Reprints: 2 copies of issue
Authorship Restrictions: None

Abstract Required: Yes, 50 words or less
Proofs Corrected By: Editor and author
Payment: No

THE MANUSCRIPT:
Number of Copies: 2
Acknowledgment: Yes
Acceptance Lag Time: About 8 weeks

Length: No limit
Critique Provided: Yes
Style: *Chicago Manual of Style*

Format: Double-spaced with 1 1/2″ margins on all sides. Upon acceptance, the editor may request a diskette from the author.

REVIEW POLICY:
Refereed: Not usually
Reviewed By: Editor

Acceptance Rate: 70%

COPYRIGHT HELD BY:
First Publication: Author

Republication: Author

SUBSCRIPTION ADDRESS: *Law Library Journal*, American Association of Law Libraries, 53 West Jackson Blvd., Chicago, IL 60604

Frequency: Quarterly   **Circulation:** 5,000
Cost: $50 for nonmember individuals and institutions; $12.50 for single issue

TELECOMMUNICATIONS: Phone: (919) 684-2847; Fax: (919) 684-8770

LEGAL REFERENCE SERVICES QUARTERLY

AFFILIATION: None

SCOPE & CONTENT: This important forum for daily problems and issues assists day-to-day work as it has been helping law librarians and members of the legal profession for nearly a decade. You will find articles that are serious, humorous, critical, or simply helpful to the working librarian. Annotated subject bibliographies, overviews of legal literature, reviews of commonly used tools, and the inclusion of reference problems unique to corporate law libraries, judicial libraries, and academic collections will keep you up-to-date on the continuously expanding volume of legal materials and their use in legal research.

INDEXED: Comput.&Info.Sys., Comput.Lit.Ind., Leg.Info.Manage.Ind., Leg. Per., Lib.Lit., LISA, Sci.Abstr.

EDITOR: Robert C. Berring

MANUSCRIPT ADDRESS: University of California, Boalt Hall, Berkeley, CA 94720

EDITORIAL POLICY:

Student Papers Accepted: Yes	**Abstract Required:** 100 words
Publication Lag Time: 6-12 months	**Proofs Corrected By:** Editor
Reprints: Yes	**Payment:** No
Authorship Restrictions: None	

THE MANUSCRIPT:

Number of Copies: 3	**Length:** Open
Acknowledgment: Yes	**Critique Provided:** Yes
Acceptance Lag Time: Varies	**Style:** APA, *Chicago Manual of Style* or AMA
	NOTE: Editor. See style manuals' abbreviations page.

Format: Typed, double-spaced on 8 1/2″ × 11″ paper.

REVIEW POLICY:

Refereed: Yes	**Acceptance Rate:** Varies
Reviewed By: Editorial board and specialist referees. "Instructions for Authors" available.	

COPYRIGHT HELD BY:

First Publication: Publisher	**Republication:** Publisher

SUBSCRIPTION ADDRESS: The Haworth Press, 10 Alice Street, Binghamton, NY 13904-1580

Frequency: Quarterly	**Circulation:** 915
Cost: $36 individuals; $90 institutions	

TELECOMMUNICATIONS: Phone: (800) 342-9678; Fax: (607) 722-1424

LIBRARIES & CULTURE

AFFILIATION: Library History Round Table of the American Library Association

SCOPE & CONTENT: An interdisciplinary journal, it explores the significance of collections of recorded knowledge–their creation, organization, preservation and utilization–in the context of cultural and social history, unlimited to time and space. This journal is intended for an international audience. Proceedings of international conferences are included, as well as articles of a regional and national interest dealing with libraries and collections, librarians and scholars. Subjects frequently covered are: archives, reading/literacy, history of libraries and collections, information science, librarians, preservation and special libraries.

INDEXED: Not given

EDITOR: Dr. Donald G. Davis, Jr.

MANUSCRIPT ADDRESS: *Libraries & Culture*, Graduate School of Library and Information Science, University of Texas at Austin, Austin, TX 78712-1276

EDITORIAL POLICY:

Student Papers Accepted: No   **Abstract Required:** 100 word limit
Publication Lag Time: 1 to 1 1/2 years
Reprints: 5 copies of issue   **Proofs Corrected By:** Editor
Authorship Restrictions: None   **Payment:** No

THE MANUSCRIPT:

Number of Copies: 3   **Length:** 8,000 words
Acknowledgment: Yes   **Critique Provided:** Always
Acceptance Lag Time: 2-3 months   **Style:** *Chicago Manual of Style*

Format: Double-spaced, one side only, footnotes at end of article. Submit stamped self-addressed return envelope. "Guidelines for Book Reviews" available from editor.

REVIEW POLICY:

Refereed: Yes   **Acceptance Rate:** 33%
Reviewed By: Editorial board and blind refereed

COPYRIGHT HELD BY:

First Publication: Publisher   **Republication:** Publisher

SUBSCRIPTION ADDRESS: Journals Dept., University of Texas Press, P.O. Box 7819, Austin, TX 78713

Frequency: Quarterly   **Circulation:** 900
Cost: $24 individuals; $36 institutions; $15 students; single issue: $7 individuals; $10 institutions

TELECOMMUNICATIONS: Editor: Phone: (512) 471-3806; Fax: (512) 471-3971; Internet: ddavis.gslis@utxvm.cc.utexas.edu or BITNET; LSCU250 @UTXVM

LIBRARY ACQUISITIONS: PRACTICE & THEORY (LAPT)

AFFILIATION: None

SCOPE & CONTENT: This journal provides a forum for the exchange of ideas and experiences among members of the library acquisitions, collection management, and bookselling communities internationally. It is a comprehensive publication designed to bring together many of the specializations within the broad areas of library acquisitions and collection management, including, but not limited to, books and serials in academic, public, school and special libraries; government publications, gifts and exchanges, microforms and other nonprint media, such as videodiscs and computer software, and other pertinent library automation projects. In reflecting the broad practical and theoretical foundations of the discipline, LAPT presents on-the-job experiences of librarians and booksellers as well as more theoretical treatment.

INDEXED: ASCA, Cam.Sci.Abstr., Chem.Abstr., CISA, Comput.&Info.Sys., Curr.Cont., Curr.Cont./Soc.&Beh.Sci., ECA, Inform.Sci.Abstr., IS-MEC, Lib.Lit., LISA, SSCI, SSSA

EDITOR: Carol Pitts Hawks

MANUSCRIPT ADDRESS: 5380K Coachman Road, Columbus, OH 43220

EDITORIAL POLICY:

Student Papers Accepted: Yes   **Abstract Required:** Yes 50-75
Publication Lag Time: 4-6 months   words
Reprints: 25   **Proofs Corrected By:** Author
Authorship Restrictions: None   **Payment:** No

THE MANUSCRIPT:

Number of Copies: 3   **Length:** 10 pages
Acknowledgment: Yes   **Critique Provided:** Always
Acceptance Lag Time: 8-10 weeks   **Style:** *Chicago Manual of Style*

Format: Typed, double-spaced throughout including tables, legends, and citations on one-sided bond 8 1/2″ × 11″ paper.

REVIEW POLICY:

Refereed: Yes   **Acceptance Rate:** 40%
Reviewed By: Editorial board and blind
  refereed

COPYRIGHT HELD BY:

First Publication: Publisher   **Republication:** Publisher

SUBSCRIPTION ADDRESS: *Library Acquisitions: Practice & Theory*, 660 White Plains Road, Tarrytown, NY 10591-5153

Frequency: Quarterly   **Circulation:** Not given
Cost: $125 institutions

TELECOMMUNICATIONS: Editor: Phone: (614) 292-6314; Fax: (614) 292-7859; Internet: hawks.1@osu.edu

LIBRARY ADMINISTRATION & MANAGEMENT

AFFILIATION: Library Administration & Management Association, a division of American Library Association

SCOPE & CONTENT: The subject matter is organized around four theme issues per year as determined by the editorial board in consultation with the editors. This information is disseminated within the division to alert potential contributors. Articles deal in some depth with library management issues that have a practical benefit to administrators, or they highlight a methodology or technique that has been successfully used to solve a problem.

INDEXED: C.I.J.E., Inform.Sci.Abstr., Lib.Lit.

EDITOR: Diane Graves

MANUSCRIPT ADDRESS: 4043 Wolf Rd., Western Springs, IL 60558

EDITORIAL POLICY:
Student Papers Accepted: Yes
Publication Lag Time: Varies,
  2 mos. to 2 years
Reprints: Not given
Authorship Restrictions: None

Abstract Required: Yes
Proofs Corrected By: Editor
Payment: No

THE MANUSCRIPT:
Number of Copies: 2
Acknowledgment: No
Acceptance Lag Time: 60 days

Length: 5,000 words
Critique Provided: Yes
Style: *Chicago Manual of Style*

Format: Posted annually in *Library Administration & Management.*

REVIEW POLICY:
Refereed: Yes
Reviewed By: Editor with input
  from professional colleagues

Acceptance Rate: 20% of
  unsolicited manuscripts

COPYRIGHT HELD BY:
First Publication: Publisher

Republication: Publisher

SUBSCRIPTION ADDRESS: *Library Administration & Management,* American Library Administration, 50 E. Huron Street, Chicago, IL 60611

Frequency: Quarterly
Circulation: 6,000
Cost: $45 individuals and institutions; $12 single issue

TELECOMMUNICATIONS: Not given

LIBRARY & ARCHIVAL SECURITY

AFFILIATION: None

SCOPE & CONTENT: *Library & Archival Security* provides vital information to librarians, scholars, and researchers concerned with security planning, policies, procedures, and strategies for both libraries and archives. Designed for those concerned with making their library a safer, more secure place, this important journal offers suggestions for dealing with crime and security problems while minimizing inconveniences to staff and patrons and maximizing the safety to staff, patrons, and the collection. An effort is made to describe the effective programs that are applicable to a wide variety of libraries and that are within the scope of most institutional budgets.

INDEXED: Comput.&Info.Sys., Inform.Sci.Abstr., Leg.Info.Manage.Ind., Lib.Lit., LISA

EDITOR: Carol Zall Lincoln, Alan Jay Lincoln

MANUSCRIPT ADDRESS: 12 Littlehale Road, Durham, NH 03824

EDITORIAL POLICY:
Student Papers Accepted: Yes   **Abstract Required:** 100 words
Publication Lag Time: 6-12 months   **Proofs Corrected By:** Editor
Reprints: 10   **Payment:** No
Authorship Restrictions: None

THE MANUSCRIPT:
Number of Copies: 4   **Length:** 12-25 pages
Acknowledgment: Yes   **Critique Provided:** Yes
Acceptance Lag Time: 3-6 months   **Style:** *Chicago Manual of Style*

Format: Typed, double-spaced on 8 1/2″ × 11″ paper.

REVIEW POLICY:
Refereed: Yes   **Acceptance Rate:** 30%
Reviewed By: Editorial board and
  anonymous specialist referees

COPYRIGHT HELD BY:
First Publication: Publisher   **Republication:** Publisher

SUBSCRIPTION ADDRESS: The Haworth Press, 10 Alice Street, Binghamton, NY 13904-1580

Frequency: Quarterly   **Circulation:** 440
Cost: $36 individuals; $90 institutions; $80 libraries

TELECOMMUNICATIONS: Editor: Phone: (603) 868-1085; Fax: (607) 22-1424

LIBRARY AND INFORMATION SCIENCE

AFFILIATION: Mita Society for Library and Information Science

SCOPE & CONTENT: *Library and Information Science* is an annual publication of the Mita Society affiliated with the School of Library and Information Science at Keio University in Tokyo. It is interested in scholarly and research papers, and technical reports not previously published.

INDEXED: Curr.Cont., Lib.Lit., LISA

EDITOR: Editorial Committee
Mita Society for Library and Information Science
c/o School of Library and Information Science
Keio University

MANUSCRIPT ADDRESS: 21545 Mita, Minato-Ku, Tokyo 108, JAPAN

EDITORIAL POLICY:

Student Papers Accepted: Not given
Publication Lag Time: Not given
Reprints: 20 + one copy of issue
Authorship Restrictions: None

Abstract Required: Yes
Proofs Corrected By: Editor
Payment: No

THE MANUSCRIPT:

Number of Copies: 2
Acknowledgment: Not given
Acceptance Lag Time: Not given

Length: Not given
Critique Provided: Not given
Style: See copy style in previous issues

Format: Typed, double-spaced. "Guidance for Contributors" available.

REVIEW POLICY:

Refereed: Not given
Reviewed By: Editorial committee

Acceptance Rate: Not given

COPYRIGHT HELD BY:

First Publication: Not given

Republication: Not given

SUBSCRIPTION ADDRESS: Mita Society for Library and Information Science, c/o School of Library and Information Science, Keio University, 21545 Mita, Minato-ku, Tokyo 108, JAPAN

Frequency: Annually
Cost: $20.00 (outside Japan)

Circulation: Not given

TELECOMMUNICATIONS: Phone: 03-3453-3920

LIBRARY & INFORMATION SCIENCE RESEARCH:
An International Journal

AFFILIATION: None

SCOPE & CONTENT: As a cross-disciplinary journal, it presents discussions related to the research process in library and information science, and also publishes research results and their practical applications. Subjects most frequently covered include bibliometrics, management, and information organization science. Contributors are generally academicians working within library and information science as well as those outside the profession. Reviews of books, computer programs, and dissertations are included.

INDEXED: C.I.J.E., Curr.Cont., Inform.Sci.Abstr., INSPEC, Lib.Lit., SSCI

EDITOR: Peter Hernon, and Candy Schwartz

MANUSCRIPT ADDRESS: Graduate School of Library & Information Science, Simmons College, 300 The Fenway, Boston, MA 02115-5898

EDITORIAL POLICY:
Student Papers Accepted: Yes
Publication Lag Time: 6-8 months
Reprints: 10 plus one copy of issue
Authorship Restrictions: None
Abstract Required: Yes, 150 words
Proofs Corrected By: Author
Payment: No

THE MANUSCRIPT:
Number of Copies: 4
Acknowledgment: Yes
Acceptance Lag Time: 8 weeks
Length: 2,000-3,500 words
Critique Provided: Always
Style: APA

Format: 8 1/2" × 11" paper and diskette (ASCII file); see "Instructions to Authors" in each issue.

REVIEW POLICY:
Refereed: Yes
Reviewed By: Blind refereed
Acceptance Rate: 45%

COPYRIGHT HELD BY:
First Publication: Publisher
Republication: Publisher

SUBSCRIPTION ADDRESS: Ablex Publishing Corp., 355 Chestnut Street, Norwood, NJ 07648

Frequency: Quarterly
Circulation: 1,000
Cost: $39.50 individuals; $85 institutions; $15 additional for overseas subscriptions

TELECOMMUNICATIONS: Editor: Phone: (617) 738-2223; Fax: (617) 738-2099; E-mail: BITNET: SCHWARTZ@BABSON.

LIBRARY HI TECH

AFFILIATION: None

SCOPE & CONTENT: *Library Hi Tech* offers a comprehensive view of the many facets of current developments in libraries today, from spreadsheet design to telecommunication systems. The articles, especially the case studies, have broad appeal to those practitioners interested in the state-of-the-art of technology in libraries as well as the specialists. A practical, informative journal, many articles include accompanying graphics.

INDEXED: C.I.J.E., Comput.&Info.Sys., Lib.Lit., LISA

EDITOR: C. Edward Wall

MANUSCRIPT ADDRESS: *Library Hi Tech*, Pierian Press, P.O. Box 1808, Ann Arbor, MI 48106

EDITORIAL POLICY:
Student Papers Accepted: Yes
Publication Lag Time: 3-6 months
Reprints: No
Authorship Restrictions: None. Authors should state their affiliation and telephone number.

Abstract Required: No, but appreciated
Proofs Corrected By: Editor and Author
Payment: Occasionally, an honorarium is given

THE MANUSCRIPT:
Number of Copies: 3 and diskette
Acknowledgment: Yes
Acceptance Lag Time: About 3 months

Length: 3-35 pages
Critique Provided: Not given
Style: *Chicago Manual of Style*

Format: "Guidelines on Style" available from editor.

REVIEW POLICY:
Refereed: Yes
Reviewed By: Double blind

Acceptance Rate: 50%

COPYRIGHT HELD BY:
First Publication: Journal

Republication: Journal

SUBSCRIPTION ADDRESS: *Library Hi Tech*, Pierian Press, P.O. Box 1808, Ann Arbor, MI 48106

Frequency: Quarterly
Cost: $40 individuals; $65 institutions; $14 for postage; $20 single issue

Circulation: 2,500

TELECOMMUNICATIONS: Phone: (313) 434-5530, or (800) 678-2435; Fax: (313) 434-6409

LIBRARY HI TECH NEWS

AFFILIATION: None

SCOPE & CONTENT: This monthly publication supplements *Library Hi Tech* by offering current awareness of new developments in library technology, vendor products, network news, new software and hardware, and people in technology. *Library Hi Tech News* features important timely articles and conference reports in each issue. A bibliography of current literature related to library automation is a regular feature.

INDEXED: Bk.Rev.Ind., Comput.Dtbs., Comput.Lit.Ind.

EDITOR: C. Edward Wall

MANUSCRIPT ADDRESS: P.O. Box 1808, Ann Arbor, MI 48106

EDITORIAL POLICY:
Student Papers Accepted: Yes	**Abstract Required:** Yes
Publication Lag Time: 5-12 months	**Proofs Corrected By:** Editor
Reprints: Yes	**Payment:** No
Authorship Restrictions: None	

THE MANUSCRIPT:
Number of Copies: 2	**Length:** Not given
Acknowledgment: Yes	**Critique Provided:** No
Acceptance Lag Time: 1-3 months	**Style:** *Chicago Manual of Style*

Format: Two paper copies and diskette.

REVIEW POLICY:
Refereed: No	**Acceptance Rate:** 40%
Reviewed By: Editor	

COPYRIGHT HELD BY:
First Publication: Publisher	**Republication:** Publisher

SUBSCRIPTION ADDRESS: Pierian Press, P.O. Box 1808, Ann Arbor, MI 48106

Frequency: 10 per year	**Circulation:** 3,000

Cost: $70 individuals; $95 institutions

TELECOMMUNICATIONS: Editor: Phone: (313) 434-5530; Fax: (313) 434-6409

LIBRARY HISTORY

AFFILIATION: Library Association of Great Britain, (Library History Group)

SCOPE & CONTENT: *Library History* mainly publishes articles and bibliographies, but not exclusively, about British library history. Special features include book reviews and guides to research in library history. Contributors are frequently librarians in academic institutions.

INDEXED: Br.Hum.Ind., Lib.Lit., LISA

EDITOR: Dr. K. A. Manley

MANUSCRIPT ADDRESS: Institute of Historical Research, University of London, Senate House, Malet St., London, WCIE 7HU, U.K.

EDITORIAL POLICY:
Student Papers Accepted: No
Publication Lag Time: 18-24 months
Reprints: Negotiable
Authorship Restrictions: None

Abstract Required: No
Proofs Corrected By: Editor
Payment: No

THE MANUSCRIPT:
Number of Copies: 2
Acknowledgment: Yes
Acceptance Lag Time: 2-3 months

Length: 5,000-8,000 words
Critique Provided: Always
Style: See copy style in previous issues

Format: Prefer diskette in WordPerfect, WordStar, or ASCII.

REVIEW POLICY:
Refereed: Yes, blind refereed
Reviewed By: Editor with input from staff

Acceptance Rate: 50%

COPYRIGHT HELD BY:
First Publication: Author & publisher   **Republication:** Journal

SUBSCRIPTION ADDRESS: c/o Mrs. Judith Harrison, The Reading Room, The British Library, Great Russell Street, London, WCIB 3DG, U.K.

Frequency: Annual, sometimes two per year
Circulation: Not given

Cost: $25 individuals; $25 institutions; $14 single issue; $25 double issue

TELECOMMUNICATIONS: Not given

LIBRARY HISTORY REVIEW

AFFILIATION: International Agency for Research in Library History

SCOPE & CONTENT: *Library History Review* provides the channel of communication for a world-wide network of people interested in establishing a library historiography of a high standard of scholarship. It aims to integrate research of historians of all epochs of librarianship and all aspects of library development and activity in the whole range of their cultural, scientific and social implications on an international plane. Contributions of original articles whose conclusions have been reached through a use of methods, criticism and knowledge of modern research in library history are respectfully invited.

INDEXED: Not given

EDITOR: Dr. Kuldip Kumar Roy

MANUSCRIPT ADDRESS: *Library History Review*, 55 Gariahat Road, P.O. Box 10210, Calcutta 700 019, India

EDITORIAL POLICY:
Student Papers Accepted: Yes   **Abstract Required:** Yes
Publication Lag Time: 6 months   **Proofs Corrected By:** Editor
Reprints: 25   **Payment:** No
Authorship Restrictions: None

THE MANUSCRIPT:
Number of Copies: 2   **Length:** 3,000 words
Acknowledgment: Yes   **Critique Provided:** Not usually
Acceptance Lag Time: 4-6 weeks   **Style:** Standard style sheet format

Format: No special requirements.

REVIEW POLICY:
Refereed: Yes   **Acceptance Rate:** About 80%
Reviewed By: Editorial board and editor
   with input from staff

COPYRIGHT HELD BY:
First Publication: Journal   **Republication:** Journal

SUBSCRIPTION ADDRESS: K.K. Roy (Private) Ltd., 55 Gariahat Road, P.O. Box 10210, Calcutta 700 019, India

Frequency: Quarterly   **Circulation:** 2,100
Cost: $45 for individuals, institutions, and others in U.S.; $12 single issue in U.S.; £22/in Europe and elsewhere

TELECOMMUNICATIONS: Not given

LIBRARY HOTLINE

AFFILIATION: None

SCOPE & CONTENT: *Library Hotline* is the weekly newsletter from *Library Journal* and *School Library Journal.* It features short, one or two paragraph news items focusing on events largely in public libraries throughout the country. A column on people in the news, a section on career opportunities and classified advertisements are featured items. Press releases, brief news items, and opinion pieces are accepted. Feature-length articles are not accepted.

INDEXED: Not given

EDITOR: Susan S. DiMattia, Editor

MANUSCRIPT ADDRESS: Cahners Publishing Company, 249 W. 17th Street, 6th Floor, New York, NY 10011

EDITORIAL POLICY:
Student Papers Accepted: Not given
Publication Lag Time: Not given
Reprints: Not given
Authorship Restrictions: Not given

Abstract Required: Not given
Proofs Corrected By: Not given
Payment: Not given

THE MANUSCRIPT:
Number of Copies: Not given
Acknowledgment: Not given
Acceptance Lag Time: Not given

Length: Not given
Critique Provided: Not given
Style: Not given

Format: Not given

REVIEW POLICY:
Refereed: Not given
Reviewed By: Not given

Acceptance Rate: Not given

COPYRIGHT HELD BY:
First Publication: Not given

Republication: Not given

SUBSCRIPTION ADDRESS: Not given

Frequency: Bimonthly
Cost: Not given

Circulation: Not given

TELECOMMUNICATIONS: Not given

THE LIBRARY IMAGINATION PAPER

AFFILIATION: None

SCOPE & CONTENT: The aim of this down-to-earth publication is to promote public relations education with tips and suggestions for public and school librarians. Articles are written by field experts on a wide range of public relations topics applied to media centers and libraries. Copyright-free clip-outs appear in each issue for use in libraries as promotional material. The *Library Imagination Paper* offers practical information and "how-to" pieces in a forthright manner.

INDEXED: Not given

EDITOR: Carol Bryan

MANUSCRIPT ADDRESS: 1000 Byus Drive, Charleston, WV 25311

EDITORIAL POLICY:
Student Papers Accepted: No
Publication Lag Time: Less than
  one year
Reprints: 3
Authorship Restrictions: None

Abstract Required: No
Proofs Corrected By: Editor
Payment: $25 or $50 depending
  on length; $5 for each photo used.

THE MANUSCRIPT:
Number of Copies: 1
Acknowledgment: Send stamped
  envelope
Acceptance Lag Time: 4-6 weeks

Length: Varies
Critique Provided: Never
Style: Not given

Format: No special requirements. Enclose self-addressed stamped envelope. Submit 50 word author credit/biography to include with article.

REVIEW POLICY:
Refereed: No
Reviewed By: Editor

Acceptance Rate: 13%

COPYRIGHT HELD BY:
First Publication: Publisher

Republication: Author

SUBSCRIPTION ADDRESS: *The Library Imagination Paper*, 1000 Byus Drive, Charleston, WV 25311

Frequency: Quarterly
Cost: $28 individuals; $32 foreign; $7 single issue

Circulation: 1,800

TELECOMMUNICATIONS: Not given

LIBRARY ISSUES: BRIEFINGS FOR FACULTY AND ADMINISTRATORS

AFFILIATION: None

SCOPE & CONTENT: *Library Issues* is a four-page newsletter designed to provide campus administrators and faculty members with short jargon-free articles discussing current problems and issues in academic libraries, and how these issues concern the campus as a whole. Frequent subjects include rising costs of serials, information technology, changing culture of campuses, and ownership of and access to information.

INDEXED: Not given

EDITOR: Richard M. Dougherty

MANUSCRIPT ADDRESS: Mountainside Publishing, P.O. Box 8330, Ann Arbor, MI 48107

EDITORIAL POLICY:
Student Papers Accepted: Not given
Publication Lag Time: Varies
Reprints: 3-6
Authorship Restrictions: None

Abstract Required: No
Proofs Corrected By: Author
Payment: Yes, $50-150

THE MANUSCRIPT:
Number of Copies: Not given
Acknowledgment: Not given
Acceptance Lag Time: Not given

Length: Varies
Critique Provided: Not given
Style: Standard style sheet

Format: Not given.

REVIEW POLICY:
Refereed: No
Reviewed By: Editor

Acceptance Rate: Not given

COPYRIGHT HELD BY:
First Publication: Publisher

Republication: Publisher

SUBSCRIPTION ADDRESS: Richard M. Dougherty, Mountainside Publishing, P.O. Box 8330, Ann Arbor, MI 48107

Frequency: Bimonthly
Circulation: 900
Cost: $35 individuals; $35 institutions; $6 single issue; additional $5 for airmail

TELECOMMUNICATIONS: Not given

LIBRARY JOURNAL

AFFILIATION: None

SCOPE & CONTENT: Although a response by *Library Journal* was not available, this publication has been included because of its significance in the library world. Foremost in current awareness, it provides news coverage of conferences, people, library "happenings," late bulletins, and a calendar of events. It devotes about one-half of each issue to reviews of all types of books, magazines, CD-ROM's, and audiovisual materials. Case studies in library management, articles, and reviews all provide publishing opportunities for authors.

INDEXED: Educ.Ind., Lib.Lit., LISA, Mag.Ind.

EDITOR: John N. Berry, III

MANUSCRIPT ADDRESS: *Library Journal*, 249 West 17th St., New York, NY 10011

EDITORIAL POLICY:
Student Papers Accepted: Not given   **Abstract Required:** Not given
Publication Lag Time: Not given   **Proofs Corrected By:** Not given
Reprints: Not given   **Payment:** Varies
Authorship Restrictions: Not given

THE MANUSCRIPT:
Number of Copies: Not given   **Length:** Not given
Acknowledgment: Not given   **Critique Provided:** Not given
Acceptance Lag Time: Not given   **Style:** Not given

Format: Not given.

REVIEW POLICY:
Refereed: No   **Acceptance Rate:** Not given
Reviewed By: Not given

COPYRIGHT HELD BY:
First Publication: Not given   **Republication:** Not given

SUBSCRIPTION ADDRESS: *Library Journal*, Box 1977, Marion, OH 43305-1977

Frequency: 21 times per year   **Circulation:** 24,000
Cost: $79 in U.S.; $99 in Canada; $138 foreign

TELECOMMUNICATIONS: Phone: (212) 463-6819; Fax: (212) 463-6734 or (212) 463-6890

LIBRARY MANAGEMENT

AFFILIATION: None

SCOPE & CONTENT: *Library Management* publishes articles of interest and value to senior managers. It strives to keep ahead of the rapid changes within the field. The journal concentrates on issues that affect the future of the information profession. The Editorial Advisory Board consists of 19 experts from 12 countries.

INDEXED: ABI Inform., Anbar, LISA

EDITOR: Professor Ken Bakewell

MANUSCRIPT ADDRESS: 9 Greenacre Road, Liverpool, L25 OLD, England

EDITORIAL POLICY:
Student Papers Accepted: Yes
Publication Lag Time: About 6 months
Reprints: 10 copies of issue
Authorship Restrictions: None

Abstract Required: About 150 words
Proofs Corrected By: Author
Payment: Possibly, by prior arrangement

THE MANUSCRIPT:
Number of Copies: 2
Acknowledgment: Yes
Acceptance Lag Time: About 1 month

Length: 2,000-4,000 words
Critique Provided: Always
Style: Not given

Format: "Notes for Contributor" available.

REVIEW POLICY:
Refereed: Yes
Reviewed By: Editor and Editorial Board

Acceptance Rate: Varies

COPYRIGHT HELD BY:
First Publication: Publisher

Republication: Publisher

SUBSCRIPTION ADDRESS: MCB University Press, 62 Toller Lane, Bradford, West Yorkshire, BD8 9BY, England

Frequency: Bimonthly
Circulation: Not given
Cost: $1,649.95 individuals and institutions; $274.95 single issue

TELECOMMUNICATIONS: Editor: Phone: Home: (0) 51 486 4137; Work: (0) 51 231 4218; Fax: (0) 51 258 1718

LIBRARY PERSONNEL NEWS

AFFILIATION: Office for Library Personnel Resources, American Library Association

SCOPE & CONTENT: *Library Personnel News* is a publication of the office of Library Personnel Resources. It provides news, short features and new developments from the field of personnel administration as well as library-related personnel topics. It covers a wide range of issues including human resources management, career and staff development, and employment legislation applicable to library personnel. Contributors are personnel officers, administrators, freelance writers, library and *Library Personnel News* staff. Editors are interested in short original, unpublished articles that express informed opinion in a personnel-related issue, results of a research project on personnel-related topic, or description of library policies, procedures, or programs in a particular personnel area.

INDEXED: Lib.Lit.

EDITOR: Margaret Myers and Jeniece Guy, Coeditors

MANUSCRIPT ADDRESS: *Library Personnel News*, ALA Office for Library Personnel Resources, 50 E. Huron St., Chicago, IL 60611

EDITORIAL POLICY:
Student Papers Accepted: Yes   **Abstract Required:** No
Publication Lag Time: 2-6 months   **Proofs Corrected By:** Editor
Reprints: 2-3   **Payment:** Not usually
Authorship Restrictions: None

THE MANUSCRIPT:
Number of Copies: 1   **Length:** 800-1,000 words
Acknowledgment: Yes   **Critique Provided:** Not usually
Acceptance Lag Time: 1-2 months   **Style:** *Chicago Manual of Style*

Format: "Guidelines for Authors" available.

REVIEW POLICY:
Refereed: No   **Acceptance Rate:** High
Reviewed By: Coeditors and staff

COPYRIGHT HELD BY:
First Publication: Publisher   **Republication:** Negotiable

SUBSCRIPTION ADDRESS: *Library Personnel News*, American Library Association, 50 East Huron Street, Chicago, IL 60611

Frequency: Bimonthly   **Circulation:** 850 to 1,000
Cost: $20 individuals; $20 institutions; $3.50 single issue

TELECOMMUNICATIONS: Fax: (312) 280-3256

THE LIBRARY QUARTERLY

AFFILIATION: School of Library and Information Science, Indiana University

SCOPE & CONTENT: *The Library Quarterly* welcomes submission of manuscripts of research and discussion. Articles are scholarly and focus on topics of interest to library educators in particular. Its audience is international. Recent article titles included "Women in Southern Library Education, 1905-1945," and "Teaching General Reference Work: The Complete Paradigm and Competing Schools of Thought, 1890-1990." Each issue contains about 16 book review essays written primarily by educators and scholars.

INDEXED: C.I.J.E., Curr.Cont./Soc.&Beh.Sci., Inform.Hot., Lib.Lit., LISA, P.A.I.S., SSCI

EDITOR: Stephen P. Harter

MANUSCRIPT ADDRESS: School of Library and Information Science, Indiana University, Bloomington, IN 47405

EDITORIAL POLICY:

Student Papers Accepted: Yes
Publication Lag Time: 6 months
Reprints: 10 copies of issue, or a 1 year subscription or renewal
Authorship Restrictions: None

Abstract Required: 100-150 words
Proofs Corrected By: Editor and author
Payment: No

THE MANUSCRIPT:

Number of Copies: 1
Acknowledgment: Yes
Acceptance Lag Time: 1-2 months

Length: No maximum length
Critique Provided: Yes
Style: *Chicago Manual of Style*

Format: Double-spaced with right and left margins of at least 1 1/2" each.

REVIEW POLICY:

Refereed: Yes
Reviewed By: Subject specialists

Acceptance Rate: About 30%

COPYRIGHT HELD BY:

First Publication: Journal

Republication: Journal

SUBSCRIPTION ADDRESS: *The Library Quarterly*, The University of Chicago Press, 5720 So. Woodlawn Avenue, Chicago, IL 60637

Frequency: Quarterly   **Circulation:** 2,500

Cost: U.S. $26 individuals; $40 institutions; $20 students. Single issue: $10 institutions; $6.50 individuals. Canada: add 7% GST to subscription price. Outside U.S. add $3 for postage.

TELECOMMUNICATIONS: Editor: Phone: (812) 855-5113; Fax: (812) 855-6166

LIBRARY RESOURCES & TECHNICAL SERVICES

AFFILIATION: Association for Library Collections & Technical Services, a division of the American Library Association

SCOPE & CONTENT: The aim of the journal is to support the theoretical, intellectual, practical, and scholarly aspects of collection management and development, acquisitions, and technical services by publishing articles, book reviews, editorials, and correspondence in response to the same. Articles on technology, management, and education are appropriate to the journal when the application of these is to issues of interest to practitioners and researchers working in collection development and technical services. The scope of the articles published in LRTS is also guided by the "Missions and Priorities Statement" adopted by the ALCTS Board of Directors in 1990.

INDEXED: Bk.Rev.Dig., Bk.Rev.Ind., CALL, C.I.J.E., Hosp.Lit.Ind., Lib.Lit., LISA, Rev.of Revs., SCI

EDITOR: Richard P. Smiraglia

MANUSCRIPT ADDRESS: *Library Resources & Technical Services*, Palmer School of Library & Information Science, Long Island University–C. W. Post Campus, Brookville, NY 11548

EDITORIAL POLICY:

Student Papers Accepted: Yes	**Abstract Required:** Yes
Publication Lag Time: 3-9 months	**Proofs Corrected By:** Author
Reprints: 2 copies of issue with article	**Payment:** No
Authorship Restrictions: None	

THE MANUSCRIPT:

Number of Copies: 3	**Length:** 4,000-6,000 words
Acknowledgment: Yes	**Critique Provided:** Sometimes
Acceptance Lag Time: 10 weeks	**Style:** *Chicago Manual of Style*

Format: Typed, double-spaced on 8 1/2″ × 11″ nonerasable paper. "Instructions For Authors" appear on pp. 253-254 of April 1992 issue of LRTS.

REVIEW POLICY:

Refereed: Yes	**Acceptance Rate:** 20%
Reviewed By: Double blind	

COPYRIGHT HELD BY:

First Publication: Publisher	**Republication:** Publisher

SUBSCRIPTION ADDRESS: *Library Resources & Technical Services*, Subscriptions, American Library Association, 50 East Huron Street, Chicago, IL 60611

Frequency: Quarterly	**Circulation:** 8,200

Cost: $45 to nonmembers in U.S.; $55 to nonmembers in Canada and other foreign countries; $14 single copy.

TELECOMMUNICATIONS: Not given

LIBRARY REVIEW

AFFILIATION: None

SCOPE & CONTENT: *Library Review* offers an independent medium for the expression of ideas, opinions, reviews or analysis of any topic whether central to, or concerned with librarianship or information transfer and communication. The emphasis is on an international review of the library, information and book worlds, combining scholarly and technical analysis with discussions of current and future trends. Contributions may comprise: previously unpublished research-based papers; news or reviews of current developments; descriptions of practical projects or innovations; surveys of the documentation (both print and nonprint) on particular subject areas and literature surveys.

INDEXED: Abstr.Engl.Stud., Bk.Rev.Ind., Inform.Abstr., Lib.Lit., LISA, Ref. Sour.

EDITOR: S. James, The Library

MANUSCRIPT ADDRESS: Paisley College, High Street Paisley, Renfrewshire, Scotland, PA1 2BE, U.K.

EDITORIAL POLICY:

Student Papers Accepted: Yes	**Abstract Required:** About 150 words
Publication Lag Time: Varies	
Reprints: 3, more upon request	**Proofs Corrected By:** Author
Authorship Restrictions: None	**Payment:** Varies

THE MANUSCRIPT:

Number of Copies: 3	**Length:** 2,500-4,500 words
Acknowledgment: Yes	**Critique Provided:** Always
Acceptance Lag Time: 3 weeks maximum	**Style:** Not given

Format: Submit article typed, double-spaced with wide margins. IBM PC diskettes (WordPerfect) 3 1/2″ are useful.

REVIEW POLICY:

Refereed: Yes	**Acceptance Rate:** 80%
Reviewed By: Subject specialists	

COPYRIGHT HELD BY:

First Publication: Publisher	**Republication:** Publisher

SUBSCRIPTION ADDRESS: MCB University Press Limited, 62 Toller Lane, Bradford, West Yorkshire, England BD8 9BY

Frequency: 6 per year	**Circulation:** Not given

Cost: $799.95 individuals and institutions; $135 single issue

TELECOMMUNICATIONS: Editor: Phone: (041) 848 3750 Fax: (041) 887 0812

LIBRARY SCIENCE WITH A SLANT TO DOCUMENTATION AND INFORMATION STUDIES

AFFILIATION: Sarada Ranganathan Endowment for Library Science (SRELS)

SCOPE & CONTENT: This is an international journal designed to develop, promote and coordinate the science and practice of librarianship. It is concerned primarily with the publication of original papers and scholarly review articles, case studies, and conference reports covering the research and development of technologies, hardware and management systems. Contributors should focus on the results of research, and reports of significant developments in the practice of librarianship which are of interest to the profession. Topics include: classification, cataloging, computer-based information systems and state-of-the-art technology, bibliometrics, organization and administration of libraries, and education of librarians.

INDEXED: LISA

EDITOR: Professor A. Neelameghan, The Secretary

MANUSCRIPT ADDRESS: Sarada Ranganathan Endowment For Library Science, 432, 18th Main Rd, 10th Cross, J.P. Nagar II Phase, Bangalore 560 078 India

EDITORIAL POLICY:

Student Papers Accepted: Yes	**Abstract Required:** Yes
Publication Lag Time: 3-6 months	**Proofs Corrected By:** Editor
Reprints: 10	**Payment:** Not given
Authorship Restrictions: Not given	

THE MANUSCRIPT:

Number of Copies: 2	**Length:** 5,000-6,000 words
Acknowledgment: Yes	**Critique Provided:** Not usually
Acceptance Lag Time: Not given	**Style:** High standard of English

Format: Double-spaced, typed on one side of the paper and wide left margin. Inclusion of a 5 1/4″ IBM compatible disk with the typed manuscript is encouraged. "Guidelines to Contributors" available.

REVIEW POLICY:

Refereed: Not given	**Acceptance Rate:** Not given
Reviewed By: Editor	

COPYRIGHT HELD BY:

First Publication: Publisher	**Republication:** Publisher

SUBSCRIPTION ADDRESS: The Secretary, Sarada Ranganathan Endowment for Library Science, 432, 18th Main Road, 10th Cross, J.P. Nagar II Phase, Bangalore 560 078, India

Frequency: Quarterly	**Circulation:** 500

Cost: $100 individuals and institutions; $25 single issue

TELECOMMUNICATIONS: Not given

LIBRARY SOFTWARE REVIEW (LSR)

AFFILIATION: None

SCOPE & CONTENT: LSR is interested in original contributions concerning the selection, integration, applications, development efforts, end-user experience, and evaluation of computers, peripherals, and software. Articles focus on current awareness of the field, and new developments with a minimum of technical jargon. The "Software Review" column offers detailed evaluative summaries. Each issue also has lengthy book reviews of about 500 words on topics relevant to the technological explosion.

INDEXED: Cam.Sci.Abstr., Comput.Dtbs., Comput.Lit.Ind., Consum.Ind., LAMP, Leg.Info.Manage.Ind., Inform.Tech.Rev., Lib.Hi.Tech.Biblio., Lib.Lit., LHTN, Microcomp.Ind., Software Rev.File

EDITOR: Marshall Breeding

MANUSCRIPT ADDRESS: *Library Software Review*, 419 21st Ave. South, Nashville, TN 37240

EDITORIAL POLICY:

Student Papers Accepted: Yes

Publication Lag Time: About 3 months

Reprints: 1 copy of issue

Authorship Restrictions: None

Abstract Required: Preferred, not required

Proofs Corrected By: Editor and author

Payment: Honorariums offered on occasion

THE MANUSCRIPT:

Number of Copies: One, plus diskette

Acknowledgment: Yes

Acceptance Lag Time: 1 month

Length: Varies

Critique Provided: Generally

Style: *Chicago Manual of Style*

Format: Double-spaced paper copy with diskette in IBM or Macintosh format or in ASCII. Contact editor for copy of "Word Processing Guidelines."

REVIEW POLICY:

Refereed: No

Acceptance Rate: 80%

Reviewed By: Editor with input from board

COPYRIGHT HELD BY:

First Publication: Publisher

Republication: Publisher

SUBSCRIPTION ADDRESS: *Library Software Review*, Meckler Corporation, 11 Ferry Lane West, Westport, CT 06880

Frequency: Bimonthly

Circulation: About 1,500

Cost: $115 for both individuals and institutions in U.S.; $125 to Canada, Central and South America

TELECOMMUNICATIONS: Editor: Phone: (615) 343-6094; Fax: (615) 343-0394; BITNET: BREEDIMM@VUCTR.VAX; Internet: breedimm@ctrvax.vanderbilt.edu

LIBRARY TIMES INTERNATIONAL

AFFILIATION: None

SCOPE & CONTENT: *Library Times International* provides summaries of the news in all countries covering the world of library and information science. Serving as an informational network, contributors encompass a wide international base of librarians, library educators, and publishers. Special features are news items, new developments, bibliographies and book reviews. The international flavor of this publication reinforces the boundless perimeters of information.

INDEXED: None

EDITOR: Dr. R. N. Sharma

MANUSCRIPT ADDRESS: *Library Times International*, P.O. Box 15661, Evansville, IN 47716

EDITORIAL POLICY:
Student Papers Accepted: No   **Abstract Required:** No
Publication Lag Time: 2 months   **Proofs Corrected By:** Editor
Reprints: 2   **Payment:** No
Authorship Restrictions: Not given

THE MANUSCRIPT:
Number of Copies: 2   **Length:** 2,000 words
Acknowledgment: Yes   **Critique Provided:** Always
Acceptance Lag Time: 4-6 weeks   **Style:** *Chicago Manual of Style*

Format: Not given

REVIEW POLICY:
Refereed: Yes   **Acceptance Rate:** 20-30%
Reviewed By: Editor and editorial board

COPYRIGHT HELD BY:
First Publication: Publisher   **Republication:** Publisher

SUBSCRIPTION ADDRESS: *Library Times International*, 8128 Briarwood Drive, Evansville, IN 47715

Frequency: Quarterly   **Circulation:** 1,200-1,500
Cost: $18 individuals; $25 institutions; $25 foreign; $6.25 single issue

TELECOMMUNICATIONS: Editor: Phone: (812) 473-2420

LIBRARY TRENDS

AFFILIATION: Graduate School Of Library and Information Science, University Of Illinois

SCOPE & CONTENT: *Library Trends*, a thematic journal, focuses on current trends in all areas of library practice. Each issue addresses a single theme, exploring topics of interest primarily to practicing librarians and information scientists and secondarily to educators and students. Examples of themes include: "Ethics and the Dissemination of Information," and "Off-Campus Library Programs in Higher Education." Articles are formal and in-depth. Readers are encouraged to submit their ideas for a theme to the editor.

INDEXED: C.I.J.E., Curr.Cont., Leg.Info.Manage.Ind., Lib.Lit., LISA, Mag.Ind., Mid.East: Abstr.& Ind., P.A.I.S., Pers.Lit., SCI, Sci.Abstr., SSCI

EDITOR: F.W. Lancaster

MANUSCRIPT ADDRESS: Graduate School of Library and Information Science, University of Illinois, Urbana, IL 61801

EDITORIAL POLICY:
Student Papers Accepted: No
Publication Lag Time: Not given
Reprints: 5 copies of issue
Authorship Restrictions: Unsolicited manuscripts are not accepted

Abstract Required: Not given
Proofs Corrected By: Author
Payment: No

THE MANUSCRIPT:
Number of Copies: Not given
Acknowledgment: Not given
Acceptance Lag Time: Not given

Length: Not given
Critique Provided: Not given
Style: Not given

Format: Not given.

REVIEW POLICY:
Refereed: Yes
Reviewed By: Editor

Acceptance Rate: 100%

COPYRIGHT HELD BY:
First Publication: Publisher

Republication: Publisher

SUBSCRIPTION ADDRESS: *Library Trends*, University of Illinois Press, 54 East Gregory Drive, Champaign, IL 61820

Frequency: Quarterly   **Circulation:** 3,200
Cost: $60 individuals; $60 institutions; $65 foreign; $18 single issue

TELECOMMUNICATIONS: Not given

LITA NEWSLETTER

AFFILIATION: Library & Information Technology Association, a division of the American Library Association

SCOPE & CONTENT: The *LITA Newsletter* supports the interest of its membership with news items and articles covering current events within LITA and the American Library Association. It includes a wide range of subjects focusing on computerization and all aspects of information technology pertinent to librarians. Most contributors are members of LITA.

INDEXED: Not given

EDITOR: Walt Crawford c/o RLG

MANUSCRIPT ADDRESS: 1200 Villa Street, Mountain View, CA 94041-1100

EDITORIAL POLICY:
Student Papers Accepted: No
Publication Lag Time: 2-4 weeks
Reprints: None
Authorship Restrictions: Normally members only

Abstract Required: No
Proofs Corrected By: Editor
Payment: No

THE MANUSCRIPT:
Number of Copies: 1
Acknowledgment: Yes
Acceptance Lag Time: 1 day

Length: 500-1,500 words
Critique Provided: No
Style: None

Format: Electronic transmission preferred.

REVIEW POLICY:
Refereed: No
Reviewed By: Editor

Acceptance Rate: 90% if applicable

COPYRIGHT HELD BY:
First Publication: Material not copyrighted

Republication: Author

SUBSCRIPTION ADDRESS: *LITA Newsletter*, Subscription Department, American Library Association, 50 East Huron Street, Chicago, IL 60611

Frequency: Quarterly   **Circulation:** 5,400
Cost: $25 individuals; $25 institutions; $30 Canada and Mexico; $40 foreign; $8 single issue

TELECOMMUNICATIONS: Phone: (415) 691-2227; Fax: (415) 964-0943; Internet: br.wcc@rlg.stanford.edu; BITNET:BR.WCC@RLG.

LUCKNOW LIBRARIAN
(Formerly NIL)

AFFILIATION: U.P. Library Association, Lucknow Branch

SCOPE & CONTENT: *Lucknow Librarian* publishes papers dealing with all aspects of librarianship, documentation, information work, and service in India and elsewhere.

INDEXED: ILSA, G. Indian Per.Lit., Lib.Lit., LISA

EDITOR: Mr. S.N. Agarwal

MANUSCRIPT ADDRESS: U.P. Library Association, Post Box No. 446, Lucknow 226001, India

EDITORIAL POLICY:
Student Papers Accepted: Yes
Publication Lag Time: 6-8 months
Reprints: Yes
Authorship Restrictions: None

Abstract Required: Yes, no fixed length requirement
Proofs Corrected By: Editor
Payment: No

THE MANUSCRIPT:
Number of Copies: 2
Acknowledgment: Yes
Acceptance Lag Time: 6 weeks

Length: 1,500 words
Critique Provided: Upon request
Style: Indian standard

Format: A4 size paper.

REVIEW POLICY:
Refereed: Yes
Reviewed By: Editorial board

Acceptance Rate: Approx. 70%

COPYRIGHT HELD BY:
First Publication: Publisher

Republication: Journal, publisher

SUBSCRIPTION ADDRESS: Circulation Manager, *Lucknow Librarian*, U.P. Library Association, Post Box No. 446, Lucknow 226001, India

Frequency: Quarterly
Cost: $20 individuals; $40 institutions

Circulation: Not given

TELECOMMUNICATIONS: Phone: 235596 (Lucknow, India)

MEDICAL LIBRARY ASSOCIATION. BULLETIN (BMLA)

AFFILIATION: Medical Library Association

SCOPE & CONTENT: The aim is to publish literature on health sciences librarianship, biomedical communication, medical informatics, and the history of these fields. Areas of interest include administration, organization, and services; interlibrary relationships and cooperation; education and other developments that affect the profession; use of information and new applications of information theory and technology.

INDEXED: Bibl.Hist.Med., CINAHL, Curr.Aware.Bio.Sci., Curr.Work Hist. Med., Hosp.Lit.Ind., Ind.Med., Ind.Den.Lit., Int.Nurs.Ind., Inform.Sci.Abstr., Intl.Phar.Abstr., Lib.Lit, LISA, SCI

EDITOR: Naomi C. Broering

MANUSCRIPT ADDRESS: Bulletin of the Medical Library Assoc., Georgetown University Medical Center Library, 3900 Reservoir Road, N.W., Washington, D.C. 20007

EDITORIAL POLICY:
Student Papers Accepted: Yes   **Abstract Required:** Yes, about
Publication Lag Time: 8-12 months   250 words
Reprints: Available at nominal fee   **Proofs Corrected By:** Author
Authorship Restrictions: None   **Payment:** No

THE MANUSCRIPT:
Number of Copies: 5   **Length:** 3,000 words
Acknowledgment: Yes   **Critique Provided:** Yes
Acceptance Lag Time: 3-4 months   **Style:** See copy style in previous
                                                    issues

Format: Typed, double-spaced including title page, tables, captions, and references. Diskettes in DOS or "Mac" formats acceptable.

REVIEW POLICY:
Refereed: Yes   **Acceptance Rate:** 35-40%
Reviewed By: Double-blind review process

COPYRIGHT HELD BY:
First Publication: Publisher   **Republication:** Publisher

SUBSCRIPTION ADDRESS: Medical Library Association, Suite 300, Six North Michigan Ave., Chicago, Il 60602

Frequency: Quarterly   **Circulation:** 5,000-6,000
Cost: $130 individuals; $39.50 single issue

TELECOMMUNICATIONS: Editor: Phone: 202-687-1187; Fax: 202-687-1862

MEDICAL REFERENCE SERVICES QUARTERLY

AFFILIATION: None

SCOPE & CONTENT: *Medical Reference Services Quarterly* publishes practice-oriented articles pertaining to health science reference librarianship. Articles tend to present the practical aspects of public services, the subject most frequently covered. Book reviews, letters, and bibliographies are also included.

INDEXED: Abstr.HealthCare Manage.Stud., Biol.Abstr., CINAHL, Excerp. Med., Hosp.Lit.Ind., Inform.Sci.Abstr., Leg.Info.Manage.Ind., Lib.Lit., LISA, Sci.Abstr.

EDITOR: M. Sandra Wood

MANUSCRIPT ADDRESS: George T. Harrell Library, Milton S. Hershey Medical Center, Pennsylvania State University–Box 850, Hershey, PA 17033

EDITORIAL POLICY:
Student Papers Accepted: No   **Abstract Required:** Yes, 100 words
Publication Lag Time: 9-10 months   **Proofs Corrected By:** Author
Reprints: 10 plus 1 copy of entire issue   **Payment:** No
Authorship Restrictions: None

THE MANUSCRIPT:
Number of Copies: 3   **Length:** 15 pages
Acknowledgment: Yes   **Critique Provided:** Always
Acceptance Lag Time: 2 days   **Style:** *Chicago Manual of Style*

Format: Typed, double-spaced.

REVIEW POLICY:
Refereed: Yes   **Acceptance Rate:** About 60%
Reviewed By: Editorial board
  and blind refereed

COPYRIGHT HELD BY:
First Publication: Publisher   **Republication:** Publisher

SUBSCRIPTION ADDRESS: *Medical Reference Services Quarterly*, The Haworth Press, 10 Alice Street, Binghamton, NY 13904-1580

Frequency: Quarterly   **Circulation:** Not given
Cost: $36 individuals; $90 institutions and others.

TELECOMMUNICATIONS: Editor: Phone: (717) 531-8630; Fax: (717) 531-8635

MICROCOMPUTERS FOR INFORMATION MANAGEMENT

AFFILIATION: None

SCOPE & CONTENT: This journal is devoted exclusively to microcomputer applications for library and information professionals. Articles report innovative applications of microcomputer uses for information managers in all types of libraries and information centers, and reflect the most current and significant trends, issues, and problems. The journal is international in coverage and provides both a practical and research forum for information in this area. Contributors are library and information specialists all over the world who are interested in microcomputer applications.

INDEXED: C.I.J.E., Lib.Lit., LISA, Microcomp.Ind., SSCI

EDITOR: Dr. Ching-Chih Chen

MANUSCRIPT ADDRESS: Simmons College, Graduate School of Library Science, 300 The Fenway, Boston, MA 02115-5878

EDITORIAL POLICY:
Student Papers Accepted: No
Publication Lag Time: 2 months
Reprints: Not given
Authorship Restrictions: None

Abstract Required: 250 words or less
Proofs Coprrected By: Author
Payment: No

THE MANUSCRIPT:
Number of Copies: 2
Acknowledgment: Yes
Acceptance Lag Time: 2 weeks

Length: 3,000 words
Critique Provided: Sometimes
Style: Not given

Format: "Guidelines to Authors" available from editor.

REVIEW POLICY:
Refereed: Yes
Reviewed By: Editor with input from experts

Acceptance Rate: Varies

COPYRIGHT HELD BY:
First Publication: Journal/publisher   **Republication:** Journal/publisher

SUBSCRIPTION ADDRESS: *Microcomputers for Information Management*, Ablex Publishing Corporation, 355 Chestnut Street, Norwood, NJ 07648-9975

Frequency: Quarterly   **Circulation:** Not given
Cost: $32.50 individuals; $80 institutions

TELECOMMUNICATIONS: Not given

MICROFORM REVIEW

AFFILIATION: None

SCOPE & CONTENT: The purpose of *Microform Review* is to evaluate scholarly micropublications for libraries and educational institutions. It also reviews major microform collections. *Microform Review* provides articles on microforms management, preservation microfilming, new preservation technologies, and bibliographic control of microforms. Contributors are librarians, archivists, conservation/preservation staff, and micropublishers (editors).

INDEXED: C.I.J.E., Inform.Sci.Abstr., Leg.Info.Manage.Ind., LHTN, Lib.Lit., LISA, Sci.Abstr.

EDITOR: Susan Marie Szasz

MANUSCRIPT ADDRESS: Reference Department, John M. Olin Library, Cornell University, Ithaca, NY 14853

EDITORIAL POLICY:

Student Papers Accepted: No
Publication Lag Time: Varies
Reprints: 1 copy of issue
Authorship Restrictions: None

Abstract Required: Preferred, not required
Proofs Corrected By: Editor
Payment: $75 single author; $40 joint authors

THE MANUSCRIPT:

Number of Copies: 2
Acknowledgment: Yes
Acceptance Lag Time: 3-6 months

Length: Will accept 3,500 words
Critique Provided: Sometimes
Style: No formal style available

Format: Hard copy; diskette (in addition) preferred, IBM compatible. Endnotes rather than footnotes are used.

REVIEW POLICY:

Refereed: No
Reviewed By: Editor with input from editorial board

Acceptance Rate: 90%

COPYRIGHT HELD BY:

First Publication: Publisher

Republication: Publisher

SUBSCRIPTION ADDRESS: R.R. Bowker, 121 Charlon Road, New Providence, NJ 07974

Frequency: Quarterly
Cost: $125 individuals and institutions

Circulation: 1,500

TELECOMMUNICATIONS: Editor: Phone: Office: (607) 255-9493 or 255-3319; Home: (607) 257-0810; Fax: (607) 257-1025; BITNET: SZA@CORNELL

MUSIC LIBRARY ASSOCIATION. NOTES

AFFILIATION: Music Library Association

SCOPE & CONTENT: *Notes* provides music librarians and musicologists with scholarly articles in the areas of music bibliography, music librarianship, and certain aspects of music history. It provides a broadly-based record of publications in music: extensive reviews of scholarly books, scholarly and historical editions of music as well as publications of contemporary concert music, listings of recently published music books, scores, music software, music publishers catalog, new music periodicals, and an index to reviews of compact discs.

INDEXED: Art&Hum.Cit.Ind., Bk.Rev.Dig., Bk.Rev.Ind., G.Perf.Arts, Lib.Lit., LISA, Music Art.Guide, Music Ind.

EDITOR: Daniel Zager

MANUSCRIPT ADDRESS: Conservatory of Music Library, Oberlin College, Oberlin, OH 44074

EDITORIAL POLICY:

Student Papers Accepted: No   **Abstract Required:** No
Publication Lag Time: Up to 12 months   **Proofs Corrected By:** Author
Reprints: 20   **Payment:** No
Authorship Restrictions: None

THE MANUSCRIPT:

Number of Copies: 1   **Length:** Not given
Acknowledgment: Yes   **Critique Provided:** Sometimes
Acceptance Lag Time: 8 weeks   **Style:** *Chicago Manual of Style*

Format: Manuscript should be submitted on 8 1/2″ × 11″ paper, double-spaced. Diskette submission only after an article has been accepted, and author and editor have agreed on final text.

REVIEW POLICY:

Refereed: At editor's discretion   **Acceptance Rate:** 50%
Reviewed By: Editor

COPYRIGHT HELD BY:

First Publication: Publisher   **Republication:** Publisher

SUBSCRIPTION ADDRESS: Business office, Music Library Association, Inc., P.O. Box 487, Canton, MA 02021

Frequency: Quarterly   **Circulation:** 2,750
Cost: $50 individuals; $65 institutions; students and retirees $25; without membership: $45 individuals; $60 institutions. $15 single issues. Extra for foreign addresses.

TELECOMMUNICATIONS: Editor: Phone: (216) 775-8280; Internet: pzager@ocvaxa.cc.oberlin.edu

MUSIC REFERENCE SERVICES QUARTERLY

AFFILIATION: None

SCOPE & CONTENT: *Music Reference Services Quarterly* is a new journal with a broad spectrum serving the entire range of interest of music librarians. The coverage of this publication will include administration, collection development, cataloging, online services, and bibliographies. It is dedicated primarily to providing articles on topics of interest for the music reference librarian.

INDEXED: Not given

EDITOR: William Studwell

MANUSCRIPT ADDRESS: Northern Illinois University Libraries, Dekalb, IL 60115-2868

EDITORIAL POLICY:
Student Papers Accepted: No   **Abstract Required:** Yes
Publication Lag Time: Varies   **Proofs Corrected By:** Editor
Reprints: Yes–senior authors   **Payment:** No
Authorship Restrictions: None

THE MANUSCRIPT:
Number of Copies: 1 paper with diskette   **Length:** Not given
Acknowledgment: Yes   **Critique Provided:** Sometimes
Acceptance Lag Time: Not given   **Style:** "Instructions for Authors"
                                                available

Format: Typed, double-spaced on 8 1/2″ × 11″ paper.

REVIEW POLICY:
Refereed: Yes   **Acceptance Rate:** Varies
Reviewed By: Editorial board
  and specialist referees

COPYRIGHT HELD BY:
First Publication: Publisher   **Republication:** Publisher

SUBSCRIPTION ADDRESS: The Haworth Press, 10 Alice Street, Binghamton, NY 13904-1580

Frequency: Quarterly   **Circulation:** Not given
Cost: $18 individuals; $24 institutions; $24 libraries

TELECOMMUNICATIONS: Phone: (815) 753-9856; Fax: (815) 753-2003

NATIONAL LIBRARIAN
(Formerly NLA Newsletter)

AFFILIATION: National Librarians Association

SCOPE & CONTENT: This newsletter, sponsored by the National Librarians Association publishes articles relating directly to the professional concerns of librarians. Subjects most frequently covered are the professional concerns of public and technical services, management, computerization, archives, reference and preservation. Commentaries, bibliographies and book reviews are added features.

INDEXED: LISA

EDITOR: Peter Dollard

MANUSCRIPT ADDRESS: P.O. Box 486, Alma, MI 48801

EDITORIAL POLICY:
Student Papers Accepted: No	**Abstract Required:** No
Publication Lag Time: 6 months	**Proofs Corrected By:** Not given
Reprints: 10	**Payment:** No
Authorship Restrictions: No	

THE MANUSCRIPT:
Number of Copies: 2	**Length:** 1,500 words
Acknowledgment: Yes	**Critique Provided:** Sometimes
Acceptance Lag Time: 2-3 months	**Style:** Any reasonable style will be accepted

Format: Double-spaced, typed with side margins.

REVIEW POLICY:
Refereed: No	**Acceptance Rate:** 75%
Reviewed By: Editor	

COPYRIGHT HELD BY:
First Publication: Author	**Republication:** Author

SUBSCRIPTION ADDRESS: Peter Dollard, P.O. Box 486, Alma, MI 48801

Frequency: Quarterly	**Circulation:** 600

Cost: $20 individuals; $15 institutions; $4 others

TELECOMMUNICATIONS: Editor: Fax (517) 463-8694; E-mail: Dollard@alma.edu

NEW JERSEY LIBRARIES

AFFILIATION: New Jersey Libraries Association

SCOPE & CONTENT: *New Jersey Libraries* publishes articles on a variety of topics: programming outreach, social issues, library architecture, personnel, education, preservation, and management as well as other subjects of interest to public and technical service librarians. Articles are typically general or practical in nature. Special features include columns covering regional news, reference, research and technology, and theme issues. There are no reviews. Contributors are primarily New Jersey librarians.

INDEXED: Lib.Lit.

EDITOR: Eleanor M. Clarke

MANUSCRIPT ADDRESS: Manchester Branch of the Ocean County Library, 21 Colonial Drive, Lakehurst, NJ 08733

EDITORIAL POLICY:

Student Papers Accepted: No	**Abstract Required:** Yes, short
Publication Lag Time: 3-6 months	**Proofs Corrected By:** Editor
Reprints: 2	and/or staff
Authorship Restrictions: None	**Payment:** No

THE MANUSCRIPT:

Number of Copies: 1	**Length:** 1200-1500
Acknowledgment: No	**Critique Provided:** Sometimes
Acceptance Lag Time: 2-3 months	**Style:** *Chicago Manual of Style* or Turabian

Format: Not available.

REVIEW POLICY:

Refereed: No	**Acceptance Rate:** 90%
Reviewed By: Editor with input from staff	

COPYRIGHT HELD BY:

First Publication: Publisher	**Republication:** Publisher

SUBSCRIPTION ADDRESS: New Jersey Library Assoc., P.O. Box 1534, Trenton, NJ 08677

Frequency: Quarterly **Circulation:** 1,800
Cost: $12 individuals; $10.80 institutions

TELECOMMUNICATIONS: Editor: Phone: (908) 657-2317 or (908) 657-0124; Fax: same as phone numbers.

NEWSLETTER ON INTELLECTUAL FREEDOM

AFFILIATION: American Library Association

SCOPE & CONTENT: The *Newsletter on Intellectual Freedom* reports on censorship incidents throughout the United States. It publishes original articles and reviews of recent books on censorship that provide a guide to the history of the First Amendment. It includes summaries of recent court rulings on freedom of speech, the press, and of inquiry. It lists important developments in federal and state laws affecting librarians, educators, authors, students, journalists and artists.

INDEXED: Not given

EDITOR: Judith F. Krugg

MANUSCRIPT ADDRESS: *Newsletter on Intellectual Freedom,* ALA, 50 East Huron Street, Chicago, IL 60610

EDITORIAL POLICY:
Student Papers Accepted: No   **Abstract Required:** Not given
Publication Lag Time: 6 weeks   **Proofs Corrected By:** Editor
Reprints: 1   **Payment:** No
Authorship Restrictions: Not given

THE MANUSCRIPT:
Number of Copies: Not given   **Length:** Not given
Acknowledgment: Yes   **Critique Provided:** Not usually
Acceptance Lag Time: 2-3 months **Style:** House style sheet available

Format: Not given.

REVIEW POLICY:
Refereed: No   **Acceptance Rate:** Not given
Reviewed By: Editor

COPYRIGHT HELD BY:
First Publication: Journal/Publisher   **Republication:** Journal/Publisher

SUBSCRIPTION ADDRESS: *Newsletter on Intellectual Freedom,* American Library Association, 50 Huron Street, Chicago, IL 60610

Frequency: Bimonthly   **Circulation:** 2,500
Cost: $30 individuals and institutions; $40 foreign; $6 single issue.

TELECOMMUNICATIONS: Editor: Phone: (312) 280-4223; Fax (312) 440-9374

NORTH CAROLINA LIBRARIES

AFFILIATION: North Carolina Library Association

SCOPE & CONTENT: *North Carolina Libraries* is the official publication of the North Carolina Library Association. Each issue is thematic and attempts to cover all aspects of librarianship that are related to the theme topic. A new feature is a column for unsolicited non-thematic articles. Its aim is to publish articles of relevance and quality. It includes material reviews and bibliographies. While NCL welcomes and solicits articles from contributors nationwide, the journal is primarily a forum for North Carolina librarians.

INDEXED: Lib.Lit.

EDITOR: Frances B. Bradburn

MANUSCRIPT ADDRESS: J.Y. Joyner Library, East Carolina Library, Greenville, NC 27858-4353

EDITORIAL POLICY:
Student Papers Accepted: No
Publication Lag Time: Varies
Reprints: 3 copies of issue
Authorship Restrictions: Primarily
   North Carolina librarians

Abstract Required: No
Proofs Corrected By: Author
Payment: $25

THE MANUSCRIPT:
Number of Copies: 3
Acknowledgment: Yes
Acceptance Lag Time: 2-3 months

Length: 8,000-10,000 words
Critique Provided: Sometimes
Style: *Chicago Manual Of Style*

Format: "Instructions For Authors" available.

REVIEW POLICY:
Refereed: Yes
Reviewed By: Editorial board
   and blind refereed

Acceptance Rate: 50%

COPYRIGHT HELD BY:
First Publication: Journal

Republication: Journal

SUBSCRIPTION ADDRESS: Frances B. Bradburn, J.Y. Joyner Library, East Carolina University, Greenville, NC 27858-4353

Frequency: Quarterly
Cost: $32 individuals and institutions; $10 single issue

Circulation: 2,500

TELECOMMUNICATIONS: Editor: (919) 757-6076; Fax: (919) 757-6618

OHIO MEDIA SPECTRUM

AFFILIATION: Ohio Educational Library/Media Association

SCOPE & CONTENT: The aim of the *Ohio Media Spectrum* is to provide information, especially of a practical nature, to its readership. The school library/media center and its operation are the central focus along with trends, ideas and issues related to them. Contributors are library/media specialists serving kindergarten through twelfth grade and higher education as well as educational technologists in higher education. The International Children's Literature column will cease with the fall 1992 issue.

INDEXED: Lib.Lit.

EDITOR: Ed Newren

MANUSCRIPT ADDRESS: Dept. of Teacher Education, Ed. Media & Tech. Group, Miami University, Oxford, OH 45056

EDITORIAL POLICY:
Student Papers Accepted: Yes
Publication Lag Time: 5-10 months
Reprints: 1 copy of issue
Authorship Restrictions: None

Abstract Required: Yes, one to lines
Proofs Corrected By: Editor
Payment: No

THE MANUSCRIPT:
Number of Copies: 2 typed or 1 plus diskette
Acknowledgment: Yes
Acceptance Lag Time: 2-4 weeks

Length: 5-8 pages
Critique Provided: Not usually
Style: APA

Format: Use double spacing, main headings on left margin, subheading centered, spell out numbers under ten. Authors are encouraged to send photographs and graphics that directly relate to articles.

REVIEW POLICY:
Refereed: Yes
Reviewed By: Blind refereed

Acceptance Rate: 80%

COPYRIGHT HELD BY:
First Publication: Journal

Republication: Journal/Association

SUBSCRIPTION ADDRESS: Ohio Educational Library Media Association, 67 Jefferson Avenue, Columbus, OH 43215

Frequency: Quarterly
Circulation: 1,500
Cost: $40 individuals and institutions; $6 single issue plus $1.50 postage and handling

TELECOMMUNICATIONS: Not given

THE ONE PERSON LIBRARY:
A Newsletter for Librarians and Management

AFFILIATION: None

SCOPE & CONTENT: This newsletter offers management support for librarians who either work alone, or with minimum staff support. It uses case studies effectively to explore a wide range of subjects, and encourages the submission of solutions from its readership. Articles that express editorial opinions and commentaries are frequent. It includes interviews, news items, and reviews of books, videos, and computer programs.

INDEXED: Not given

EDITOR: Andrew Berner or Guy St.Clair

MANUSCRIPT ADDRESS: OPL Resources Ltd., Murray Hill Station, P.O. Box 948, New York, NY 10156

EDITORIAL POLICY:

Student Papers Accepted: Yes   **Abstract Required:** 50-75 words
Publication Lag Time: Varies   **Proofs Corrected By:** Editor
Reprints: Usually 5-10   **Payment:** About $50 to $100
Authorship Restrictions: None

THE MANUSCRIPT:

Number of Copies: 1   **Length:** 750 to 1,000 words
Acknowledgment: Yes   **Critique Provided:** Never
Acceptance Lag Time: 2-3 weeks   **Style:** *Chicago Manual of Style* or
                                        New York Times Manual of Style and Usage

Format: Double-spaced manuscript.

REVIEW POLICY:

Refereed: No   **Acceptance Rate:** About 50%
Reviewed By: Editor & editorial board

COPYRIGHT HELD BY:

First Publication: Publisher   **Republication:** Publisher

SUBSCRIPTION ADDRESS: OPL Resources Ltd., Murray Hill Station, P.O. Box 948, New York, NY 10156

Frequency: Monthly   **Circulation:** 2,500
Cost: $70 for each: individuals, institutions & others; $12 single issue

TELECOMMUNICATIONS: Phone or Fax: (212) 683-6285

ONLINE

AFFILIATION: None

SCOPE & CONTENT: *Online* covers the range of online topics including online searching tips and techniques for online searchers. It seeks a balanced mix of industry and technology coverage with practical, how-to articles, and articles on online management topics. It covers online systems, enhancements to the systems, and microcomputer's hardware and software as they are used for online searching and management of online search services.

INDEXED: B.P.I., CINAHL, ERIC, Inform.Sci.Abstr., INSPEC, Lib.Lit., LISA, Mag.Ind., Microcomp.Ind., Predi.F&S Ind.U.S., PROMT, SSCI, Tr.&Ind.Ind.

EDITOR: Nancy Garman

MANUSCRIPT ADDRESS: P.O. Box 17507, Fort Mitchell, KY 41017

EDITORIAL POLICY:

Student Papers Accepted: No
Publication Lag Time: 4-6 months
Reprints: 10-20
Authorship Restrictions: None

Abstract Required: No
Proofs Corrected By: Author
Payment: Yes

THE MANUSCRIPT:

Number of Copies: 2
Acknowledgment: Yes
Acceptance Lag Time: 1 month

Length: 2,000-3,000 words
Critique Provided: Sometimes
Style: House style sheet available to prospective authors

Format: Two paper copies plus one copy on diskette. To enhance the likelihood of acceptance, potential authors should call to discuss ideas before submitting an article.

REVIEW POLICY:

Refereed: No
Reviewed By: Editorial board and editor with input from staff, and other outside experts

Acceptance Rate: 50% if unsolicited

COPYRIGHT HELD BY:

First Publication: Publisher
Republication: Publisher

SUBSCRIPTION ADDRESS: *Online*, 462 Danbury Road, Wilton, CT 06897-2126

Frequency: Bimonthly
Cost: $99 for individuals

Circulation: 5,500

TELECOMMUNICATIONS: Editor: Phone: (606) 331-6345; E-mail: CLASS. ONLINEGAR; Internet: ngarman@tso.uc.edu

ORANA: JOURNAL OF SCHOOL AND CHILDREN'S LIBRARIANSHIP
(Formerly Children's Libraries Newsletter)

AFFILIATION: Australian Library and Information Association

SCOPE & CONTENT: Covering topics of general interest, this journal aims to educate, inform and advise about school and children's librarianship in Australia. It provides current awareness of the literature, and acts as a medium for the exchange of ideas among practitioners specializing in children's and young adult's librarianship. Contributors are library faculty, practitioners in schools, teachers, and writers of children's books.

INDEXED: ALISA, APAIS, Aus.Educ.Ind, Child.Lit.Abstr.

EDITOR: Robert Sharman

MANUSCRIPT ADDRESS: 9 Lawley Road, Lesmurdie, Western Australia 6076 Australia

EDITORIAL POLICY:
Student Papers Accepted: No	**Abstract Required:** About 40-50
Publication Lag Time: 6 months	words
Reprints: None	**Proofs Corrected By:** Editor
Authorship Restrictions: None	**Payment:** None

THE MANUSCRIPT:
Number of Copies: 2	**Length:** 3,500 words
Acknowledgment: Yes	**Critique Provided:** Always
Acceptance Lag Time: 3 months	**Style:** Varies

Format: Typed, 1 1/2" spacing on A4 paper or in machine readable form (3 1/2" diskette, formatted in Microsoft Word for the Macintosh).

REVIEW POLICY:
Refereed: Yes	**Acceptance Rate:** 50%
Reviewed By: Blind refereed	

COPYRIGHT HELD BY:
First Publication: Author/Journal	**Republication:** Author

SUBSCRIPTION ADDRESS: Robert Sharman, 9 Lawley Road, Lesmurdie, Western Australia 6076 Australia

Frequency: Quarterly **Circulation:** 900
Cost: $25 individuals; $25 institutions; $25 others; $5 single issue

TELECOMMUNICATIONS: Editor: Phone and Fax: Australia (09) 291 7220

PAKISTAN LIBRARY BULLETIN

AFFILIATION: None

SCOPE & CONTENT: This journal serves to introduce librarianship in Pakistan to others worldwide. It publishes articles on the promotion and development in Pakistan. Contributors are Library & Information Science professionals. Articles cover a wide range of subjects. Book reviews are included.

INDEXED: Amer.Hist. & Life, Inform.Sci.Abstr., Lib.Lit.

EDITOR: Raees Ahmad Samdani

MANUSCRIPT ADDRESS: Library Promotion Bureau, P.O. Box 8421, University of Karachi Campus, Karachi-75270, Pakistan

EDITORIAL POLICY:

Student Papers Accepted: Yes	**Abstract Required:** No
Publication Lag Time: 6 months	**Proofs Corrected By:** Editor
Reprints: Yes	**Payment:** No
Authorship Restrictions: None	

THE MANUSCRIPT:

Number of Copies: Two	**Length:** 2,500 - 3,000 words
Acknowledgment: Yes	**Critique Provided:** Sometimes
Acceptance Lag Time: 6 months	**Style:** Standard style sheet

Format: Neatly typed on one side of paper.

REVIEW POLICY:

Refereed: Yes	**Acceptance Rate:** 70%
Reviewed By: Editorial board	

COPYRIGHT HELD BY:

First Publication: Journal	**Republication:** Journal

SUBSCRIPTION ADDRESS: Library Promotion Bureau, P.O. Box 8421, University of Karachi Campus, Karachi-75270, Pakistan

Frequency: Quarterly   **Circulation:** 500
Cost: $60.00 individuals; $80.00 institutions; $15 single issue

TELECOMMUNICATIONS: Not given

PERSONNEL TRAINING AND EDUCATION: A Journal for Library and Information Workers

AFFILIATION: Library Association: Personnel, Training and Education Group

SCOPE & CONTENT: As an international publication, it covers all aspects of personnel management, training, and education for librarianship. Contributors are librarians and library school faculty who frequently publish the results of empirical research and case studies in this journal.

INDEXED: C.I.J.E., Inform.Sci.Abstr., Lib.Lit., LISA, Ref.Zh.

EDITOR: Mr. H. Nicholson

MANUSCRIPT ADDRESS: BLPES, 10 Portugal Street, London WC2A 2HD, United Kingdom

EDITORIAL POLICY:
Student Papers Accepted: Yes   **Abstract Required:** No
Publication Lag Time: 2-3 months   **Proofs Corrected By:** Editor
Reprints: 1 copy of issue   **Payment:** No
Authorship Restrictions: None

THE MANUSCRIPT:
Number of Copies: 1   **Length:** 2,000-5,000 words
Acknowledgment: Yes   **Critique Provided:** Not given
Acceptance Lag Time: 4-6 months   **Style:** Not given

Format: Double-spaced and typed on one side of A4 paper with references at end of article.

REVIEW POLICY:
Refereed: No   **Acceptance Rate:** Not given
Reviewed By: Editorial board

COPYRIGHT HELD BY:
First Publication: Not given   **Republication:** Not given

SUBSCRIPTION ADDRESS: Mr. P.M. Noon, Deputy Librarian, Staffordshire Polytechnic, College Road, Stoke on Trent ST42DE, United Kingdom

Frequency: 3 per year   **Circulation:** 1,000
Cost: £35 individuals and institutions

TELECOMMUNICATIONS: Not given

PLA BULLETIN

AFFILIATION: Pennsylvania Library Association

SCOPE & CONTENT: As a state publication, it serves as a communication vehicle for Pennsylvania Library Association members on matters of current news, trends, events and general information. Contributors are librarians, administrators, and trustees as well as other organizations.

INDEXED: Not given

EDITOR: Margaret S. Bauer, CAE

MANUSCRIPT ADDRESS: Pennsylvania Library Association, 3107 N. Front Street, Harrisburg, PA 17110

EDITORIAL POLICY:

Student Papers Accepted: No	**Abstract Required:** No
Publication Lag Time: 1 month	**Proofs Corrected By:** Editor
Reprints: No	**Payment:** None
Authorship Restrictions: None	

THE MANUSCRIPT:

Number of Copies: 1	**Length:** 500 words
Acknowledgment: No	**Critique Provided:** Not usually
Acceptance Lag Time: 1 month	**Style:** *Chicago Manual of Style*

Format: Typed, double-spaced in WordPerfect 5.0 on 5 1/4″ diskette or PageMaker 4.0 on 5 1/4″ diskette.

REVIEW POLICY:

Refereed: No	**Acceptance Rate:** 75%
Reviewed By: Editor and editorial board	

COPYRIGHT HELD BY:

First Publication: Journal	**Republication:** Journal

SUBSCRIPTION ADDRESS: Pennsylvania Library Association, 3107 N. Front St., Harrisburg, PA 17110

Frequency: Monthly	**Circulation:** 2,300

Cost: $40 individuals and institutions; $4 single issue

TELECOMMUNICATIONS: Editor: Fax: (717) 233-3121

POPULAR CULTURE IN LIBRARIES

AFFILIATION: Not given

SCOPE & CONTENT: This new journal encompasses the full breadth of the popular culture field. Future topics include mass media (including radio, television, the recorded sound industry, motion pictures, video, periodicals, newspapers, broadsides, posters, etc.), the literature, fads and mass consciousness movements (civil rights, women's suffrage, etc.) It will also include peer-reviewed academic papers along with invited editor-reviewed feature papers and a selective resource guide of book and media reviews.

INDEXED: Not given

EDITOR: Frank W. Hoffman

MANUSCRIPT ADDRESS: School of Library Science, Sam Houston State University, Huntsville, TX 77341-2418

EDITORIAL POLICY:
Student Papers Accepted: Yes　　　**Abstract Required:** 100 words
Publication Lag Time: Varies　　　**Proofs Corrected By:** Editor
Reprints: Varies　　　　　　　　**Payment:** No
Authorship Restrictions: None

THE MANUSCRIPT:
Number of Copies: 3　　　　　　**Length:** 5-50 pages
Acknowledgment: Yes　　　　　**Critique Provided:** Not given
Acceptance Lag Time: Not given　**Style:** APA

Format: Typed, double-spaced on 8 1/2″ × 11″ bond paper with 1″ margins on all sides.

REVIEW POLICY:
Refereed: Yes　　　　　　　　**Acceptance Rate:** Not given
Reviewed By: Editorial board and
　anonymous specialist referees

COPYRIGHT HELD BY:
First Publication: Publisher　　**Republication:** Publisher

SUBSCRIPTION ADDRESS: The Haworth Press, 10 Alice Street, Binghamton, NY 13904-1580

Frequency: Quarterly　　　　　**Circulation:** Not given
Cost: $18 individuals; $24 institutions; $24 libraries

TELECOMMUNICATIONS: Not given

PRIMARY SOURCES & ORIGINAL WORKS

AFFILIATION: None

SCOPE & CONTENT: *Primary Sources & Original Works* is the only journal devoted entirely to research, documentation, and curatorship of primary sources and original works in archives, museums, and special library collections. Although existing journals for archivists, museum professionals, and librarians deal with managing and accessing rare materials of different types and formats, there is no cross-institutional and interdisciplinary journal until now that specifically treats the most critical material to all researchers in any field of knowledge: primary sources, which includes original works, documentation, artifacts, records, and historical evidence of any kind. *Primary Sources & Original Works* is intended to fill this void by publishing feature articles, reports, reviews, columns, mini forums, collector and collection profiles, plus special issues that discuss current topics and challenges the handling of primary sources in any kind of institution.

INDEXED: Hum.Ind., Inform.Sci.Abstr., LHTN, Lib.Lit., LISA, Sci.Abstr., Soc.Work Res.& Abstr.

EDITOR: Lawrence J. Mc Crank

MANUSCRIPT ADDRESS: Abigail Timme Library, Admin., Ferris State University, Big Rapids, MI 49307

EDITORIAL POLICY:

Student Papers Accepted: No	**Abstract Required:** 1 paragraph
Publication Lag Time: 6-12 months	**Proofs Corrected By:** Author
Reprints: 3-5	**Payment:** No
Authorship Restrictions: None	

THE MANUSCRIPT:

Number of Copies: 3	**Length:** 3,000-4,000 words
Acknowledgment: Not given	**Critique Provided:** Always
Acceptance Lag Time: 1-2 months	**Style:** APA

Format: Typed, double-spaced on 8 1/2″ × 11″ paper.

REVIEW POLICY:

Refereed: Yes	**Acceptance Rate:** 50%
Reviewed By: Editor and editorial board	unsolicited; 90% solicited

COPYRIGHT HELD BY:

First Publication: Publisher	**Republication:** Publisher

SUBSCRIPTION ADDRESS: The Haworth Press, 10 Alice Street, Binghamton, NY 13904-1580

Frequency: Quarterly	**Circulation:** Over 400

Cost: $25 individuals; $45 institutions; $45 libraries; $25 special issues

TELECOMMUNICATIONS: Phone: (616) 592-3727; Fax: (616) 592-2662

PROGRAM: AUTOMATED LIBRARY & INFORMATION SYSTEMS

AFFILIATION: ASLIB, The Association for Information Management

SCOPE & CONTENT: This international journal is published by the Association for Information Management and serves a global audience. The major contributors are working librarians and information scientists and library school teachers. Special features published are case studies, new developments, special "theme" issues, and conference or workshop proceedings. Contributors are librarians, information scientists and library school teachers.

INDEXED: INSPEC, LISA, SCI, SSCI

EDITOR: Lucy A. Tedd

MANUSCRIPT ADDRESS: Llys Blodau, Iorwerth Avenue, Aberystwyth SY23 1EW, Wales, UK

EDITORIAL POLICY:
Student Papers Accepted: No   **Abstract Required:** Yes
Publication Lag Time: 3-6 months   **Proofs Corrected By:** Author
Reprints: 10   **Payment:** No
Authorship Restrictions: No

THE MANUSCRIPT:
Number of Copies: 3   **Length:** 3,000-4,000 words
Acknowledgment: Yes   **Critique Provided:** Never
Acceptance Lag Time: 3 weeks to   **Style:** "Notes for Contributors"
   3 months   available

Format: Double-spaced on A4 paper with diskette.

REVIEW POLICY:
Refereed: Yes   **Acceptance Rate:** 70%
Reviewed By: Editorial board and referees

COPYRIGHT HELD BY:
First Publication: Author/Publisher   **Republication:** Author/Publisher

SUBSCRIPTION ADDRESS: Publication Sales Department, ASLIB, The Association for Information Management, 20-24 Old Street, London, EC1V 9AP, U.K.

Frequency: Quarterly   **Circulation:** About 1,200
Cost: £95 individual

TELECOMMUNICATIONS: ASLIB: Phone: (0) 71 253 4488; Editor's Phone: (0) 970 611518; Fax: (0) 71 430 0514

PUBLIC LIBRARIES

AFFILIATION: Public Library Association; a division of the American Library Association

SCOPE & CONTENT: *Public Libraries* is the official journal of the Public Library Association. There are generally four feature articles providing information on current issues of concern, as well as descriptive and evaluative contributions on services, systems, accountability, and the state-of-the-art to name a few. It has broad appeal to public libraries nationally, and includes such features as news from the Public Library Association, reviews and brief descriptions of innovative ideas developed in libraries.

INDEXED: C.I.J.E., Lib.Lit., LISA

EDITOR: Ellen Altman

MANUSCRIPT ADDRESS: Feature Editor, 1936 E. Belmont Drive, Tempe, AZ 85284

EDITORIAL POLICY:

Student Papers Accepted: Yes	**Abstract Required:** Yes
Publication Lag Time: 4-6 months	**Proofs Corrected By:** Contributor
Reprints: 2 copies of issues	and editor
Authorship Restrictions: None	**Payment:** No

THE MANUSCRIPT:

Number of Copies: 3	**Length:** 10-15 pages
Acknowledgment: Yes	**Critique Provided:** For provisionally
Acceptance Lag Time: 3 weeks	accepted articles
	Style: *Chicago Manual of Style*

Format: Typed, double-spaced. "Instructions to Authors" published in Jan/Feb issue of *Public Libraries* annually.

REVIEW POLICY:

Refereed: Yes	**Acceptance Rate:** Not available
Reviewed By: Editor and outside reviewers	

COPYRIGHT HELD BY:

First Publication: ALA/Author	**Republication:** ALA/Author

SUBSCRIPTION ADDRESS: *Public Libraries,* Customer Services Dept., American Library Association, 50 E. Huron St., Chicago, IL 60611

Frequency: 6 issues per year	**Circulation:** 8,000

Cost: $10 single issue; $35 membership fee includes subscription; $50 nonmembers in U.S.; $60 foreign countries

TELECOMMUNICATIONS: Editor: Phone: (602) 621-3565; Fax: (602) 621-3279

PUBLIC LIBRARY QUARTERLY

AFFILIATION: None

SCOPE & CONTENT: *Public Library Quarterly* combines both scholarly articles with primary information on all aspects of public libraries. It covers such topics as public library administration and management, community relationships and programs, technology, architecture, finances, politics, and the evaluation of and accountability for public libraries. It has broad appeal especially for public librarians, administrators, and others affiliated with or interested in public libraries.

INDEXED: Cam.Sci.Abstr., Comput.&Info.Sys., Curr.Aw.Bull., For.Lib.Inf. Serv., Ind.Per.Art.Relat.Law, Inform.Sci.Abstr., Lib.Lit., LISA

EDITOR: Richard L. Waters

MANUSCRIPT ADDRESS: *Public Library Quarterly*, 2903 Pennsylvania Drive, Denton, TX 76205-8309

EDITORIAL POLICY:
Student Papers Accepted: No   **Abstract Required:** Yes, 100 words
Publication Lag Time: 4-6 months   **Proofs Corrected By:** Author
Reprints: 10 copies of article   **Payment:** No
Authorship Restrictions: None

THE MANUSCRIPT:
Number of Copies: 3   **Length:** 8-14 pages theoretical;
Acknowledgment: Yes   4-6 practice oriented
Acceptance Lag Time: 1-2 months   **Critique provided:** Not usually
                                         Style: *Chicago Manual of Style*

Format: Typed, double-spaced on 8 1/2" × 11" white bond paper with 1" margins on all sides. After approval of manuscript, submit it in printed format and floppy diskette.

REVIEW POLICY:
Refereed: Yes   **Acceptance Rate:** 75%
Reviewed By: Blind refereed

COPYRIGHT HELD BY:
First Publication: Publisher   **Republication:** Publisher

SUBSCRIPTION ADDRESS: *Public Library Quarterly*, Subscription Dept., The Haworth Press, 10 Alice St., Binghamton, NY 13904-1580

Frequency: Quarterly   **Circulation:** 609
Cost: $36 individuals; $85 institutions; 25% above current subscription rate for single issue; 30% above U.S. rate for Canada; 40% above U.S. rate for others

TELECOMMUNICATIONS: Not given

PUBLIC SERVICES QUARTERLY

AFFILIATION: None

SCOPE & CONTENT: The new *Public Services Quarterly* is the first journal to specifically address the rapidly growing areas that involve direct interaction of librarians with the library's users. It will publish research and practical articles that aim to enhance the relationship between the library/information center and its clientele. This includes academic, public, and special libraries of all types. The public services librarian, of course, is intended as a primary reader of the new journal, but the scope goes far beyond this to cover the newly evolving role of providing access services to information in any format, regardless of whether the source material is owned, reproduced, or borrowed by the host library.

INDEXED: Not given

EDITOR: Virgil Blake, PhD

MANUSCRIPT ADDRESS: Library and Information Science, City University of New York, 38 Beryl Street, South River, New Jersey 08882

EDITORIAL POLICY:
Student Papers Accepted: No   **Abstract Required:** 100 words
Publication Lag Time: Varies   **Proofs Corrected By:** Editor
Reprints: Varies   **Payment:** No
Authorship Restrictions: None

THE MANUSCRIPT:
Number of Copies: 3   **Length:** 5-50 pages
Acknowledgment: Not given   **Critique Provided:** Not given
Acceptance Lag Time: Not given   **Style:** APA

Format: Typed, double-spaced on 8 1/2" × 11" paper and diskette.

REVIEW POLICY:
Refereed: Yes   **Acceptance Rate:** Not given
Reviewed By: Editorial board and
   specialist referees

COPYRIGHT HELD BY:
First Publication: Publisher   **Republication:** Publisher

SUBSCRIPTION ADDRESS: The Haworth Press, 10 Alice Street, Binghamton, NY 13904-1580

Frequency: Quarterly   **Circulation:** Not given
Cost: $18 individuals; $24 institutions; $24 libraries

TELECOMMUNICATIONS: Editor: Office Phone: 1-718-997-3787

RARE BOOKS AND MANUSCRIPTS LIBRARIANSHIP

AFFILIATION: Association of College and Research Libraries (ACRL); a division of the American Library Association

SCOPE & CONTENT: The aim of this journal is to publish articles on the theory, practice and application of rare book, manuscript, and special collections librarianship. The subjects range from administration of modern manuscript collections and bibliographic control to in-depth theoretical and empirical research. This publication serves as an information network for this distinct area of librarianship.

INDEXED: Lib.Lit., M.L.A. Int.Bib.

EDITOR: Alice Schreyer

MANUSCRIPT ADDRESS: University of Chicago Library, 1100 East 57th Street, Chicago, IL 60637

EDITORIAL POLICY:
Student Papers Accepted: No   **Abstract Required:** No
Publication Lag Time: 6-8 weeks   **Proofs Corrected By:** Author
Reprints: 5 copies of issue   **Payment:** No
Authorship Restrictions: None

THE MANUSCRIPT:
Number of Copies: 3   **Length:** 4,000 to 6,000 words
Acknowledgment: Yes   **Critique Provided:** Always
Acceptance Lag Time: 6 weeks to   **Style:** *Chicago Manual of Style*
    to 2 months

Format: Double-spaced, with author's name on cover sheet.

REVIEW POLICY:
Refereed: Yes   **Acceptance Rate:** 40-50%
Reviewed By: Editorial board
    and blind refereed

COPYRIGHT HELD BY:
First Publication: Publisher   **Republication:** Publisher

SUBSCRIPTION ADDRESS: *Rare Books and Manuscripts Librarianship*, Subscription Dept., American Library Association, 50 East Huron Street, Chicago, IL 60611

Frequency: Biannually   **Circulation:** 500
Cost: $25 individuals; $30 institutions; $40 foreign; $12.50 single issue

TELECOMMUNICATIONS: Not given

RASD UPDATE

AFFILIATION: Reference and Adult Services Division of the American Library Association

SCOPE & CONTENT: As the official newsletter of Reference and Adult Services Division, *RASD Update* provides current news to its membership about RASD Board actions, state and regional events, conference programs, and RASD committee, section and discussion group activities. It includes short bibliographical review articles and opinion pieces on current library issues. Contributors are usually RASD members.

INDEXED: Not given

EDITOR: Jane P. Kleiner

MANUSCRIPT ADDRESS: The LSU Libraries, Louisiana State University, Baton Rouge, LA 70803

EDITORIAL POLICY:

Student Papers Accepted: No	**Abstract Required:** No
Publication Lag Time: 3-4 months	**Proofs Corrected By:** Editor
Reprints: None	**Payment:** No

Authorship Restrictions: None, but preference given to RASD members

THE MANUSCRIPT:

Number of Copies: 1	**Length:** Not given
Acknowledgment: No	**Critique Provided:** Explanation
Acceptance Lag Time: Not given	for rejection given
	Style: House style sheet available

Format: Hard copy with WordPerfect diskette version preferred.

REVIEW POLICY:

Refereed: No	**Acceptance Rate:** High
Reviewed By: Editor	

COPYRIGHT HELD BY:

First Publication: Optional	**Republication:** Optional

SUBSCRIPTION ADDRESS: *RASD Update*, Subscription Dept., American Library Association, 50 East Huron Street, Chicago, IL 60611

Frequency: Quarterly	**Circulation:** 5,600

Cost: $15 individuals and institutions; $4 single issue

TELECOMMUNICATIONS: Editor: Phone: (504) 388-4016; Fax: (504) 388-6992; BITNET: NOTJPK@LSUVM

THE REFERENCE LIBRARIAN

AFFILIATION: None

SCOPE & CONTENT: Each issue of *The Reference Librarian* focuses on a single topic of current concern to reference librarians, allowing exhaustive treatment of the subject. Authors are experts familiar with both the theoretical and practical aspects of the problem being considered. This refereed journal is edited by Bill Katz and an editorial board of outstanding international experts in the field. The editor seeks authors who have unique, imaginative, and useful points of view about the topics under discussion.

INDEXED: Cam.Sci.Abstr., C.I.J.E., Curr.Aw.Abstr., Educ.Admin.Abstr., For.Lib.Inf.Serv., Ind.Per.Ar.Relat.Law, Inform.Sci.Abstr., INSPEC., Lib.Lit., LISA, Sage Pub.Admin.Abstr.

EDITOR: Bill Katz

MANUSCRIPT ADDRESS: School of Library and Information Science, State University of New York at Albany, Albany, NY 12230

EDITORIAL POLICY:

Student Papers Accepted: No
Publication Lag Time: 8-12 months
Reprints: Senior authors only

Abstract Required: Yes, 100-150 words
Proofs Corrected By: Editor
Payment: No

Authorship Restrictions: Submit name, position, qualifications, and briefly explain focus of proposed article and its length. Under no circumstances should a manuscript be submitted without an inquiry first.

THE MANUSCRIPT:

Number of Copies: 2
Acknowledgment: Yes
Acceptance Lag Time: Not given

Length: 10-15 typed pages
Critique Provided: Yes
Style: "Instructions for Authors" available

Format: Not given.

REVIEW POLICY:

Refereed: Yes
Reviewed By: Editor and editorial board

Acceptance Rate: Not given

COPYRIGHT HELD BY:

First Publication: Publisher

Republication: Author

SUBSCRIPTION ADDRESS: *The Reference Librarian,* The Haworth Press, 10 Alice St., Binghamton, NY 13904-1580

Frequency: Two issues per academic year **Circulation:** Not given
Cost: In U.S., Canada, and Mexico: $40 individuals; $95 institutions; current rate plus 25% surcharge for single issue

TELECOMMUNICATIONS: The Haworth Press: Phone: (607) 722-5857

REFERENCE SERVICES REVIEW

AFFILIATION: None

SCOPE & CONTENT: *Reference Services Review* is a quarterly journal dedicated to automation of reference services, the evaluation of reference sources, and advancement of reference functions in libraries. RSR prepares its readers to embrace emerging technologies. It also contains valuable bibliographies and articles on print publications that will help librarians address the information needs of current library users. Readers of RSR include reference, acquisitions, and public services librarians, as well as managers of information, database, and online services.

INDEXED: Abstr.Engl.Stud., Bibl.Ind., Bk.Rev.Ind., C.I.J.E., LHTN, Lib. Lit., LISA

EDITOR: Dr. Ilene F. Rockman, Interim Dean

MANUSCRIPT ADDRESS: Associate of Library Services, Kennedy Library, California Polytechnic State University, San Luis Obispo, CA 93407

EDITORIAL POLICY:

Student Papers Accepted: Yes   **Abstract Required:** Yes
Publication Lag Time: 6-12 months   **Proofs Corrected By:** Editor
Reprints: 2 copies of journal   **Payment:** No
Authorship Restrictions: None

THE MANUSCRIPT:

Number of Copies: 2   **Length:** Not given
Acknowledgment: Yes   **Critique Provided:** Yes
Acceptance Lag Time: 2-3 months   **Style:** *Chicago Manual of Style*

Format: Two print copies with machine readable format, IBM compatible microcomputer.

REVIEW POLICY:

Refereed: Yes   **Acceptance Rate:** 40%
Reviewed By: Editor and editorial board

COPYRIGHT HELD BY:

First Publication: Publisher   **Republication:** Publisher

SUBSCRIPTION ADDRESS: Pierian Press, P.O. Box 1808, Ann Arbor, MI 48106

Frequency: Quarterly   **Circulation:** 2,000
Cost: $40 individuals; $65 institutions; Foreign: $54 individuals; $79 institutions

TELECOMMUNICATIONS: Editor: Phone: (313) 434-5530; Fax: (313) 434-6409

RESEARCH STRATEGIES:
A Journal of Library Concepts and Instruction

AFFILIATION: None

SCOPE & CONTENT: *Research Strategies* publishes articles that focus on conceptual models for bibliographic instruction (BI), theoretical underpinnings of knowledge generation and discipline structure, applications of learning theory to the library environment, and the relationship of BI to other instruction programs that could have wider applicability. It also reviews books from librarianship, information science, and higher education that are relevant to bibliographical instruction, and selected articles from journals in all disciplines dealing with the library research process.

INDEXED: C.I.J.E., LHTN, Lib.Lit., LISA

EDITOR: Barbara Wittkopf

MANUSCRIPT ADDRESS: *Research Strategies*, P.O. Box 25144, Baton Rouge, LA 70894

EDITORIAL POLICY:
Student Papers Accepted: Yes
Publication Lag Time: 4-6 months
Reprints: 6 copies of issue
Authorship Restrictions: None

Abstract Required: 75 to 100 words, double-spaced
Proofs Corrected By: Author
Payment: No

THE MANUSCRIPT:
Number of Copies: 2 originals
Acknowledgment: Yes
Acceptance Lag Time: 2-4 months

Length: 4,000 words
Critique Provided: Always
Style: *Chicago Manual of Style*

Format: Typed, double-spaced on standard white paper. Type footnotes, double-spaced, on separate sheets, never in body of the text.

REVIEW POLICY:
Refereed: Yes
Reviewed By: Blind refereed

Acceptance Rate: About 60%

COPYRIGHT HELD BY:
First Publication: Journal

Republication: Journal

SUBSCRIPTION ADDRESS: *Research Strategies*, Mountainside Publishing, P.O. Box 8330, Ann Arbor, MI 48107

Frequency: Quarterly

Circulation: 1,000

Cost: $28 individuals; $40 institutions; $10 others; Foreign: $33 individuals; $45 institutions; $12 single issue

TELECOMMUNICATIONS: Business Office: Phone: (313) 662-3925; Fax: (313) 662-4450 Editorial Office: Phone: (504) 388-8264; Fax: (504) 388-6992

RESOURCE SHARING & INFORMATION NETWORKS

AFFILIATION: None

SCOPE & CONTENT: *Resource Sharing & Information Networks* focuses on topics appropriate to local, state, regional, national, and international networks and their associated activities, such as interlibrary loan, cooperative collection development, document delivery including telefacsimile, and transborder data flow. It has a strong international focus that appeals to contributors worldwide.

INDEXED: ACM, C.I.J.E., Comput.&Info.Sys., Comput.Lit.Ind., Excerp. Med., Ind.Per.Art.Relat.Law, Inform.Sci.Abstr., INSPEC, LISA, P.A.I.S., Ref.Zh., RIE

EDITOR: Robert P. Holly

MANUSCRIPT ADDRESS: 134 Purdy Library, Wayne State University, Detroit, MI 48202

EDITORIAL POLICY:
Student Papers Accepted: Yes
Publication Lag Time: 12-24 months
Reprints: Varies
Authorship Restrictions: None

Abstract Required: Yes, 100-300 words
Proofs Corrected By: Editor
Payment: No

THE MANUSCRIPT:
Number of Copies: 1 plus copy on diskette
Acknowledgment: Yes
Acceptance Lag Time: 1-3 months

Length: 1,500-6,000 words
Critique Provided: Always
Style: Varies

Format: Use clean white 8 1/2″ × 11″ bond paper, include footnotes. "Instruction for Authors" available.

REVIEW POLICY:
Refereed: Yes
Reviewed By: Editor and editorial board

Acceptance Rate: 90%

COPYRIGHT HELD BY:
First Publication: Publisher
Republication: Publisher

SUBSCRIPTION ADDRESS: The Haworth Press, 10 Alice Street, Binghamton, NY 13904-1580

Frequency: Biannually
Circulation: 350
Cost: $32 individuals; $85 institutions; $85 others

TELECOMMUNICATIONS: Editor: Phone: (313) 577-4021; Fax: (313) 577-5525; BITNET: RHOLLEY@WAYNEST1

RQ

AFFILIATION: Reference and Adult Services Division (RASD) of the American Library Association

SCOPE & CONTENT: *RQ* is the official journal of the Reference and Adult Services Division of the American Library Association. Its aim is to disseminate information of interest to reference librarians, bibliographers, adult service librarians, those in collection development and selection, and others interested in public services. The scope of the journal includes all aspects of library service to adults, and reference service and collection development at every level and for all types of libraries.

INDEXED: Bibl.Ind., Bk.Rev.Ind., C.I.J.E., Curr.Bk.Rev.Cit., Curr.Cont., Inform.Sci.Abstr., Lib.Lit., LISA, Mag.Ind., P.A.I.S., PMR, Ref.Zh., SSCI

EDITOR: Connie Van Fleet & Danny P. Wallace

MANUSCRIPT ADDRESS: Louisiana State University, School of Library & Information Science, 267 Coates Hall, Baton Rouge, LA 70803-3290

EDITORIAL POLICY:

Student Papers Accepted: No
Publication Lag Time: 6 months
Reprints: None
Authorship Restrictions: None

Abstract Required: Brief, double spaced
Proofs Corrected By: Author
Payment: No

THE MANUSCRIPT:

Number of Copies: 3
Acknowledgment: Yes
Acceptance Lag Time: 6 weeks

Length: 4,000-6,000 words
Critique Provided: Yes
Style: *Chicago Manual of Style*

Format: Typed, double-spaced on 8 1/2" × 11" paper with citations on separate paper. "Instructions For Authors" available in *RQ*.

REVIEW POLICY:

Refereed: Yes
Reviewed By: Double blind

Acceptance Rate: 60%

COPYRIGHT HELD BY:

First Publication: Publisher

Republication: Publisher

SUBSCRIPTION ADDRESS: *RQ*, Subscription Department, American Library Association, 50 East Huron Street, Chicago, IL 60611

Frequency: Quarterly

Circulation: 7,500

Cost: $42 to nonmembers of RASD in the U.S., Canada, and Mexico, $52 other foreign countries, $12 for single issue. Membership in RASD includes subscription to RQ.

TELECOMMUNICATIONS: Editors: Phone: (504) 388-3158; Fax: (504) 388-1465

SCHOOL LIBRARY JOURNAL:
The Magazine of Children's, Young Adult & School Librarians

AFFILIATION: None

SCOPE & CONTENT: This journal provides a one-stop source of news, information and development for librarians serving children and adolescents in schools and public libraries. It includes suggestions and ideas for enhancing library services to children ranging from book selection to library management. Contributors are librarians serving children and adolescents in school and public libraries as well as faculty in education and library schools.

INDEXED: Access, ERIC, Lib.Lit.

EDITOR: Lillian N. Gerhardt

MANUSCRIPT ADDRESS: *School Library Journal*, 249 West 17th Street, New York, NY 10011

EDITORIAL POLICY:
Student Papers Accepted: Yes   **Abstract Required:** No
Publication Lag Time: 2 months   **Proofs Corrected By:** Editor
Reprints: 3 copies   **Payment:** Features average $30,
Authorship Restrictions: None   1 page column $100

THE MANUSCRIPT:
Number of Copies: 1   **Length:** 3,000 words
Acknowledgment: Yes   **Critique Provided:** No
Acceptance Lag Time: 3 months   **Style:** *Chicago Manual of Style*

Format: Type manuscript, double-spaced, no longer than 15 pages.

REVIEW POLICY:
Refereed: Yes   **Acceptance Rate:** 20-25%
Reviewed By: Editor with input from staff

COPYRIGHT HELD BY:
First Publication: Journal   **Republication:** Author and journal

SUBSCRIPTION ADDRESS: *School Library Journal*, P.O. Box 1978, Marion, OH 43305-1978

Frequency: Monthly   **Circulation:** 42,000
Cost: $63 individuals; $63 institutions; $5.75 single issue

TELECOMMUNICATIONS: Editor: Phone: (212) 463-6759; Fax: (212) 463-6734

SCHOOL LIBRARY MEDIA ACTIVITIES MONTHLY

AFFILIATION: None

SCOPE & CONTENT: This is a national publication that promotes instructional activities for library media, and research skills for all curriculum areas. It includes areas such as reference skills, production and computer skills, daily instructional activities and lesson plans. It publishes reviews of computer programs. Major contributors are library school media specialists and educators.

INDEXED: ERIC, Lib.Lit.

EDITOR: Paula Montgomery

MANUSCRIPT ADDRESS: *School Library Media Activities Monthly*, 17 East Henrietta Street, Baltimore, MD 21230

EDITORIAL POLICY:
Student Papers Accepted: Yes
Publication Lag Time: 3-7 months
Reprints: 3, author may request more
Authorship Restrictions: None

Abstract Required: No
Proofs Corrected By: Author
Payment: Yes, for feature articles

THE MANUSCRIPT:
Number of Copies: 2
Acknowledgment: Yes
Acceptance Lag Time: 1-2 months

Length: 1,000 words
Critique Provided: Always
Style: *Chicago Manual of Style*

Format: Type manuscript, double-spaced. Specific format for columns published in each issue.

REVIEW POLICY:
Refereed: Yes
Reviewed By: Editor with input
from staff

Acceptance Rate: 50-70%

COPYRIGHT HELD BY:
First Publication: Publisher

Republication: Publisher

SUBSCRIPTION ADDRESS: *School Library Media Activities Monthly*, 17 East Henrietta Street, Baltimore, MD 21230

Frequency: Monthly
Cost: $44 individuals; $44 institutions; $44 other

Circulation: 11,000

TELECOMMUNICATIONS: Editor: Phone: (410) 685-8621

SCHOOL LIBRARY MEDIA QUARTERLY

AFFILIATION: American Association of School Librarians, a division of the American Library Association

SCOPE & CONTENT: The official journal of the American Association of School Librarians is read by library media specialists, supervisors, library educators, and others concerned with the development of school library media programs and services in elementary and secondary schools. Its aim is to publish substantive articles to inform, inspire, motivate and assist school library media practitioners in integrating theories and practice.

INDEXED: Bk.Rev.Ind., C.I.J.E., Curr.Cont./Soc.&Beh.Sci., Excep.Child Educ.Abstr., Inform.Sci.Abstr., Lib.Lit., Media Rev.Dig., Ref.Serv.Rev.

EDITOR: Mary Kay Biagini

MANUSCRIPT ADDRESS: School of Library & Information Science, University of Pittsburgh, Room 505, SLIS Building, 135 N. Bellefield Ave., Pittsburgh, PA 15260

EDITORIAL POLICY:
Student Papers Accepted: Yes
Publication Lag Time: 6-12 months
Reprints: 1 copy of issue
Authorship Restrictions: None

Abstract Required: About 250 words
Proofs Corrected By: Author
Payment: No

THE MANUSCRIPT:
Number of Copies: 2
Acknowledgment: Yes
Acceptance Lag Time: Within 12 weeks

Length: 4,000-6,000 words
Critique Provided: Always
Style: *Chicago Manual of Style*

Format: Authors of accepted articles will be asked to provide a diskette with an IBM DOS or MacIntosh DOS ASCII file. "Instructions To Authors" available.

REVIEW POLICY:
Refereed: Yes
Reviewed By: Blind refereed

Acceptance Rate: Less than 50%

COPYRIGHT HELD BY:
First Publication: Journal

Republication: Journal

SUBSCRIPTION ADDRESS: *School Library Media Quarterly*, Subscription Dept., American Library Association, 50 East Huron Street, Chicago, IL 60611

Frequency: Quarterly

Circulation: 8,779

Cost: $40 individuals, in U.S., Canada, Mexico and Spain, $50 other foreign countries. $12 single issue; $20 to association members

TELECOMMUNICATIONS: Editor: Phone: (412) 624-5230; Fax: (412) 624-5231; E-mail: mkb@icarus.lis.pitt.edu

SCIENCE & TECHNOLOGY LIBRARIES

AFFILIATION: None

SCOPE & CONTENT: The objective of *Science & Technology Libraries* is to provide a forum for discussion of topics relevant to the management, operation, collections, services, and staffing of all types of specialized libraries in the science and technology field. Special features include "New Reference Works In Science & Technology" and "Sci-Tech Online."

INDEXED: Biol.Abstr., Bull.Signal., Chem.Abstr., Comput.&Info.Sys., Eng. Ind., Excerp.Med., Inform.Sci.Abstr., Lib.Lit., LISA, P.A.I.S., Ref.Zh., Sci.Abstr.

EDITOR: Cynthia Steinke

MANUSCRIPT ADDRESS: 499 Wilson Library, Institute of Technology Libraries, University of Minnesota, Minneapolis, MN 55455

EDITORIAL POLICY:
Student Papers Accepted: Yes   **Abstract Required:** 100 words
Publication Lag Time: Varies   **Proofs Corrected By:** Editor
Reprints: Varies   **Payment:** No
Authorship Restrictions: None

THE MANUSCRIPT:
Number of Copies: 3   **Length:** 12-20 pages
Acknowledgment: Yes   **Critique Provided:** Not given
Acceptance Lag Time: Not given   **Style:** APA

Format: Typed, double-spaced on 8 1/2" × 11" paper and diskette copy. "Instructions For Authors" available.

REVIEW POLICY:
Refereed: Yes   **Acceptance Rate:** Varies
Reviewed By: Editorial board and
  specialist referees

COPYRIGHT HELD BY:
First Publication: Publisher   **Republication:** Publisher

SUBSCRIPTION ADDRESS: The Haworth Press, 10 Alice Street, Binghamton, NY 13904-1580

Frequency: Quarterly   **Circulation:** 661
Cost: $36 individuals; $115 institutions; $115 libraries

TELECOMMUNICATIONS: Not given

THE SERIALS LIBRARIAN

AFFILIATION: None

SCOPE & CONTENT: *The Serials Librarian* publishes studies and reports on all aspects of serials work in libraries of all kinds and sizes, and examines serials developments in other areas insofar as these affect libraries. Special attention is given to the topics of control methods, use of the computer, and costs. Other articles regularly cover such areas as serials management, cataloging, automation, collection evaluation and development, copyright, periodicals history, cooperative developments and document delivery.

INDEXED: Amer.Hist.&Life, ASCA, Bull.Signal., Chem.Abstr., Comput.& Info.Sys., Excerp.Med., Inform.Sci.Abstr., Leg.Info.Manage.Ind., LHTN, Lib. Lit., LISA, SSCI

EDITOR: Peter Gellatly

MANUSCRIPT ADDRESS: The Haworth Press, 10 Alice Street, Binghamton, NY 13904-1580

EDITORIAL POLICY:
Student Papers Accepted: Occasionally
Publication Lag Time: 3-6 months
Reprints: 10 and 1 copy of issue
Authorship Restrictions: None

Abstract Required: 100 words or less
Proofs Corrected By: Editor
Payment: Varies

THE MANUSCRIPT:
Number of Copies: 2 plus original
Acknowledgment: Yes
Acceptance Lag Time: 1-2 months

Length: 3,000-4,000 words
Critique Provided: Sometimes
Style: *Chicago Manual of Style*

Format: Typed, double-spaced on 8 1/2″ × 11″ bond paper. "Instructions for Authors" available.

REVIEW POLICY:
Refereed: Yes
Reviewed By: Editor with input from staff, editorial board, and blind refereed

Acceptance Rate: About 65-70%

COPYRIGHT HELD BY:
First Publication: Publisher

Republication: Publisher

SUBSCRIPTION ADDRESS: The Haworth Press, 10 Alice Street, Binghamton, NY 13904-1580

Frequency: Quarterly
Cost: $35 individuals; $105 institutions; $105 libraries

Circulation: About 1,200

TELECOMMUNICATIONS: Not given

SERIALS REVIEW

AFFILIATION: None

SCOPE & CONTENT: *Serials Review* contains practical information on the management and administration of serial departments including automation, cataloging, and union lists. An important additional feature is reviews of periodicals published in certain selected subject areas such as endangered species or feminist journals. Much of the information contained in these reviews is not available in any other source.

INDEXED: Bibl.Ind., Bk.Rev.Ind., Inform.Sci.Abstr., Lib.Lit.

EDITOR: Cindy Hepfer

MANUSCRIPT ADDRESS: Serials Dept., Health Sciences Library, SUNY at Buffalo, Buffalo, NY 14214

EDITORIAL POLICY:

Student Papers Accepted: Yes	**Abstract Required:** Yes
Publication Lag Time: 6-12 months	**Proofs Corrected By:** Editor
Reprints: 2 copies of journal	**Payment:** No
Authorship Restrictions: None	

THE MANUSCRIPT:

Number of Copies: 3	**Length:** Not given
Acknowledgment: Yes	**Critique Provided:** Yes
Acceptance Lag Time: 1-2 months	**Style:** *Chicago Manual of Style*

Format: Prepare manuscripts on 3 1/2″ or 5 1/4″ diskette which can be used on an IBM (or compatible) microcomputer, using a popular word processing program.

REVIEW POLICY:

Refereed: Yes	**Acceptance Rate:** 40%
Reviewed By: Blind refereed	

COPYRIGHT HELD BY:

First Publication: Publisher	**Republication:** Publisher

SUBSCRIPTION ADDRESS: Pierian Press, P.O. Box 1808, Ann Arbor, MI 48106

Frequency: Quarterly	**Circulation:** 2,000

Cost: $40 individuals; $65 institutions; $20 single issue; Foreign: $54 individuals; $79 institutions

TELECOMMUNICATIONS: Editor: Phone: (716) 831-2139; Fax: (716) 835-4891 or 831-2211; BITNET: HSLCINDY@UBVM; Internet: hslcindy@ubvm.cc.buffalo.edu.

SHOW-ME LIBRARIES

AFFILIATION: Missouri State Library

SCOPE & CONTENT: *Show-Me Libraries* serves as a local news and information resource for Missouri librarians. It attempts to cover all aspects of library service for public, academic, and special libraries. Occasionally, articles relating to school librarianship are published. The wide range of subject areas for which articles are solicited reflect the journal's aim to reach its diverse readership of librarians, students, legislators, educators, and others. Contributors are primarily from Missouri. Unsolicited manuscripts are welcome.

INDEXED: Lib.Lit., Oz.Per.Ind.

EDITOR: Madeline Matson

MANUSCRIPT ADDRESS: Missouri State Library, P.O. Box 387, Jefferson City, MO 65102

EDITORIAL POLICY:
Student Papers Accepted: No	**Abstract Required:** No
Publication Lag Time: 3 months	**Proofs Corrected By:** Editor
Reprints: 3 copies of issue	**Payment:** Not given

Authorship Restrictions: Primarily Missouri professionals

THE MANUSCRIPT:
Number of Copies: 1	**Length:** 4-20 pages
Acknowledgment: Yes	**Critique Provided:** Sometimes
Acceptance Lag Time: 1 month	**Style:** Not given

Format: Typed, double-spaced on 8 1/2″ × 11″ white paper, with a minimum 1″ margin on all sides. Put name and address of author on first page and author's name at top right of succeeding pages.

REVIEW POLICY:
Refereed: No	**Acceptance Rate:** Not given
Reviewed by: Editor with input from staff	

COPYRIGHT HELD BY:
First Publication: Author (not copyrighted)	**Republication:** Author

SUBSCRIPTION ADDRESS: *Show Me Libraries*, Missouri State Library, P.O. Box 387, Jefferson City, MO 65102

Frequency: Quarterly   **Circulation:** 2,100
Cost: $10 individuals; $20 foreign; $2.50 single issue

TELECOMMUNICATIONS: Editor: Phone: (314) 751-2680; Fax: (314) 751-3612

THE SOURDOUGH

AFFILIATION: Alaska Library Association

SCOPE & CONTENT: As a state publication, *The Sourdough* serves as a conduit of news and general information about libraries in Alaska. It also serves to promote interest and support for libraries to the Alaskan legislature, and keeps volunteer librarians working in remote locations of Alaska informed of significant developments in the world of librarianship. Book, video, and film reviews are included.

INDEXED: Lib.Lit.

EDITOR: William Galbraith

MANUSCRIPT ADDRESS: Alaska Library Association, P.O. Box 81084, Fairbanks, AK 99708

EDITORIAL POLICY:
Student Papers Accepted: Not given   **Abstract Required:** No
Publication Lag Time: 3-4 months   **Proofs Corrected By:** Editor
Reprints: Not given   **Payment:** No
Authorship Restrictions: None

THE MANUSCRIPT:
Number of Copies: 1   **Length:** 250-500 words
Acknowledgment: No   **Critique Provided:** No
Acceptance Lag Time: 1-2 months   **Style:** Not given

Format: Not given.

REVIEW POLICY:
Refereed: No   **Acceptance Rate:** Not given
Reviewed By: Editor

COPYRIGHT HELD BY:
First Publication: Author   **Republication:** Author

SUBSCRIPTION ADDRESS: *The Sourdough*, Alaska Library Association, P.O. Box 81084, Fairbanks, AK 99708

Frequency: Quarterly   **Circulation:** Approximately 600
Cost: $15 individuals and institutions; $5 single issue

TELECOMMUNICATIONS: Editor: (907) 459-1027; (907) 479-4522

THE SOUTHEASTERN LIBRARIAN

AFFILIATION: Southeastern Library Association (SELA)

SCOPE & CONTENT: *The Southeastern Librarian* is the official publication of SELA, an 11-state regional association. It disseminates information about association activities, serves as a historical record of the association, shares information about activities in each member state, publishes thought-provoking articles concerning library services, provides continuing education through articles published, and serves as a forum for scholarly articles related to the southeastern library community. Most contributors are library professionals from the southeast.

INDEXED: Lib.Lit., UMI

EDITOR: Elizabeth Curry

MANUSCRIPT ADDRESS: SEFLIN Executive Director, Southeastern Library Association Headquarters, P.O. Box 987, Tucker, GA 30085

EDITORIAL POLICY:

Student Papers Accepted: No	**Abstract Required:** No
Publication Lag Time: 3 months	**Proofs Corrected By:** Editor
Reprints: 2	**Payment:** No

Authorship Restrictions: At editor's discretion; emphasis on articles and themes from association groups.

THE MANUSCRIPT:

Number of Copies: 2	**Length:** 8-10 pages
Acknowledgment: Yes	**Critique Provided:** Never
Acceptance Lag Time: 3-6 months	**Style:** *Chicago Manual of Style*

Format: Type text and references double-spaced on plain 8 1/2" × 11" paper. The name, position, and professional address of the author should appear in the bottom left-hand corner of a separate title page.

REVIEW POLICY:

Refereed: No	**Acceptance Rate:** About 65%
Reviewed By: Editorial board and editor with input from staff.	

COPYRIGHT HELD BY:

First Publication: Author	**Republication:** Author

SUBSCRIPTION ADDRESS: Southeastern Library Association Headquarters, P.O. Box 987, Tucker, GA 30085

Frequency: Quarterly	**Circulation:** 1,700

Cost: $35 individuals; $35 institutions; $3.50 single issue

TELECOMMUNICATIONS: Editor: Phone: (305) 357-7318; Fax: (305) 357-6998

SPECIAL LIBRARIES

AFFILIATION: Special Libraries Association

SCOPE & CONTENT: The focus of *Special Libraries* is on new and developing areas of librarianship and information technology. Subjects covered include informative papers on the administration, organization, and operation of special libraries and information centers, and reports of research in librarianship, documentation, and information science and technology. Full-length articles, brief reports, and letters to the editor are appropriate contributions. Papers are accepted from members of the SLA and nonmembers.

INDEXED: Bk.Rev.Ind., Cam.Sci.Abstr., CINAHL, Comput.Cont., Hist. Abstr., Hosp.Lit.Ind., Inform.Sci.Abstr., INSPEC, Intl.Bib.Bk.Rev., Intl.Bib. Per.Rev., Lib.Lit., LISA, Manage.Ind., P.A.I.S., SCI

EDITOR: Maria C. Barry

MANUSCRIPT ADDRESS: Special Libraries Association, 1700 18th Street, NW, Washington, DC 20009-2508

EDITORIAL POLICY:

Student Papers Accepted: Yes   **Abstract Required:** 100 words or less
Publication Lag Time: 2-10 months   **Proofs Corrected By:** Editor and
Reprints: 2 copies of issue   author
Authorship Restrictions: None   **Payment:** No

THE MANUSCRIPT:

Number of Copies: Original and   **Length:** In words: 1,000-5,000
   2 copies   (articles); 1,000 (reports)
Acknowledgment: Yes   **Critique provided:** Not given
Acceptance Lag Time: 8 weeks minimum   **Style:** *Chicago Manual of Style*

Format: Submit manuscript on 3 1/2" diskette for Apple MacIntosh or printed on an IBM 5219 printer or any printer with monospaced characters or typewritten on white paper, one side only. Instructions for authors appear in *Special Libraries.*

REVIEW POLICY:

Refereed: Yes   **Acceptance Rate:** 20%
Reviewed By: Blind reviewed

COPYRIGHT HELD BY:

First Publication: Publisher   **Republication:** Publisher

SUBSCRIPTION ADDRESS: *Special Libraries*, 1700 18th Street, NW, Washington, DC 20009-2508

Frequency: Quarterly   **Circulation:** 15,000

Cost: $95 for a standard subscription (includes *Specialist*, *Special Libraries*, and *Who's Who in Special Libraries*); $100 foreign; $10 single issue.

TELECOMMUNICATIONS: Editor: Phone: (202) 234-4700; Fax: (202) 265-9317

SPECIAL LIBRARIES ASSOCIATION.
GEOGRAPHY AND MAP DIVISION. BULLETIN

AFFILIATION: Special Libraries Association, Geography and Map Division

SCOPE & CONTENT: The aim of the *Bulletin* is to provide articles about map libraries and geography to a national audience of professionals working in this specialized area, and to discuss topics of interest to map librarians. It includes bibliographies, map cataloging, case studies, new developments in the field, news items, new products and detailed reviews. Contributors are primarily geographers and map librarians.

INDEXED: Geo.Abstr., Lib.Lit., LISA, Ref.Sour.

EDITOR: Joanne M. Perry, Map Librarian

MANUSCRIPT ADDRESS: Kerr Library-121, Oregon State University, Corvallis, OR 97331

EDITORIAL POLICY:
Student Papers Accepted: No
Publication Lag Time: 6 months
Reprints: 2
Authorship Restrictions: None

Abstract Required: Yes, 125 words
Proofs Corrected By: Not given
Payment: No

THE MANUSCRIPT:
Number of Copies: 1
Acknowledgment: Yes
Acceptance Lag Time: Not given

Length: Not given
Critique Provided: Not given
Style: Not given

Format: One copy typed and one on diskette in WordPerfect.

REVIEW POLICY:
Refereed: No
Reviewed By: Not given

Acceptance Rate: 95%

COPYRIGHT HELD BY:
First Publication: Publisher

Republication: Publisher

SUBSCRIPTION ADDRESS: 406 East Smith Street, Topton, PA 19562

Frequency: Quarterly
Cost: $25 individuals; $22.50 institutions; Foreign: $30 individuals; $27 institutions

Circulation: 850

TELECOMMUNICATIONS: Not given

SPEC: SYSTEMS & PROCEDURES EXCHANGE CENTER (SPEC KITS)

AFFILIATION: Association of Research Libraries/Office of Management Services

SCOPE & CONTENT: The goals of the SPEC program are to identify expertise and encourage its exchange among library professionals, promoting experimentation, innovation and improved performance in the field of library management. Each SPEC kit is authored individually and deals with a different topic of interest to many types of libraries, including but not limited to: management issues, collections, access, personnel, interlibrary loan, and training.

INDEXED: Not given

EDITOR: C. Brigid Welch

MANUSCRIPT ADDRESS: Office of Management Services, 1527 New Hampshire Avenue, NW, Washington DC 20036

EDITORIAL POLICY:

Student Papers Accepted: No	**Abstract Required:** Send proposal
Publication Lag Time: About 4 months	**Proofs Corrected By:** Author
Reprints: 2 copies of kit	**Payment:** $200 honorarium

Authorship Restrictions: A topic is selected from proposals. Upon approval, a survey is designed and sent to membership.

THE MANUSCRIPT:

Number of Copies: Not applicable	**Length:** 150 pages per kit
Acknowledgment: Yes	**Critique Provided:** Not given
Acceptance Lag Time: About 4 months	**Style:** Varies

Format: Flyer, tabulations and reading list on diskette in WordPerfect 5.1.

REVIEW POLICY:

Refereed: No	**Acceptance Rate:** Not given
Reviewed By: Editor	

COPYRIGHT HELD BY:

First Publication: Publisher	**Republication:** Publisher

SUBSCRIPTION ADDRESS: Customer Service Department/Office of Management Services, 1527 New Hampshire Avenue, NW, Washington DC 20036, Orders & Checks Dept. 0692, Wash. DC 20073-0692

Frequency: Yearly; 7/8 & 11/12 combined issues   **Circulation:** 475 institutions

Cost: $140 ARL members; $210 non-members & Canada; $325 foreign; $33 single issue

TELECOMMUNICATIONS: Office of Management Services: Phone: (202) 232-8656; Fax:(202) 462-7849

TECHNICALITIES

AFFILIATION: None

SCOPE & CONTENT: *Technicalities* is an information-sharing publication for the library and information science professional in technical services. All aspects are explored: acquisitions, cataloging, serials, and library automation. It includes commentaries and letters, new developments, news items, new products, reviews, and profiles of vendors. Contributors are practicing librarians.

INDEXED: Lib.Lit., LISA

EDITOR: Brian Alley

MANUSCRIPT ADDRESS: *Technicalities*, 2057 So. Glenwood Avenue, Springfield, IL 62704

EDITORIAL POLICY:
Student Papers Accepted: No   **Abstract Required:** No
Publication Lag Time: 1-2 months   **Proofs Corrected By:** Editor
Reprints: 2 copies of issue   **Payment:** None
Authorship Restrictions: Not given

THE MANUSCRIPT:
Number of Copies: 1   **Length:** 2,000 words
Acknowledgment: Yes   **Critique Provided:** Sometimes
Acceptance Lag Time: 1 month   **Style:** Not given
  maximum

Format: Prefer hard copy plus ASCII file on diskette.

REVIEW POLICY:
Refereed: No   **Acceptance Rate:** 50%
Reviewed By: Editor

COPYRIGHT HELD BY:
First Publication: Publisher   **Republication:** Publisher

SUBSCRIPTION ADDRESS: *Technicalities*, Media Periodicals Division, Westport Publishers, 2444 'O' Street, Suite 202, Lincoln, NE 68510-1185

Frequency: Monthly   **Circulation:** 1,000
Cost: $47 individuals and institutions; $5 single issue

TELECOMMUNICATIONS: Editor: Phone: (217) 786-6597; Fax: (217) 786-6208; Internet: alley@eagle.sangamon.edu

TECHNICAL SERVICES QUARTERLY

AFFILIATION: None

SCOPE & CONTENT: *Technical Services Quarterly* keeps its readers informed of current developments and future trends in computers, automation, and advanced technologies in the technical operations of libraries and information centers. Technology is having a phenomenal impact on technical services–it is changing the way traditional technical services activities are conducted, and even the role and concept of technical services itself. *Technical Services Quarterly* plays an important role of support by publishing up-to-the-minute information that technical services professionals and paraprofessionals need to ease transitional changes and take full advantage of automated systems that ultimately make collections more accessible to users.

INDEXED: C.I.J.E., Comput.Cont., Inform.Sci.Abstr., Leg.Info.Manage.-Ind., Lib.Lit., LISA, Ref.Zh., Sci.Abstr.

EDITOR: Gary Pitkin

MANUSCRIPT ADDRESS: Director, Michener Library, University of Northern Colorado, Greeley, CO 80639

EDITORIAL POLICY:
Student Papers Accepted: Not given   **Abstract Required:** 100 words
Publication Lag Time: Varies   **Proofs Corrected By:** Editor
Reprints: Yes–senior authors   **Payment:** No
Authorship Restrictions: None

THE MANUSCRIPT:
Number of Copies: 3   **Length:** 20 pages
Acknowledgment: Yes   **Critique Provided:** Yes
Acceptance Lag Time: 2-4 months   **Style:** *Chicago Manual of Style*
Format: Typed, double-spaced on 8 1/2" × 11" paper and diskette copy. "Instruction for Authors" available.

REVIEW POLICY:
Refereed: Yes   **Acceptance Rate:** 30%
Reviewed By: Editorial board and
specialist referees

COPYRIGHT HELD BY:
First Publication: Publisher   **Republication:** Publisher

SUBSCRIPTION ADDRESS: The Haworth Press, 10 Alice Street, Binghamton, NY 13904-1580

Frequency: Quarterly   **Circulation:** 721
Cost: $36 individuals; $75 institutions; $75 libraries

TELECOMMUNICATIONS: Not given

THE UNABASHED LIBRARIAN,
The "How I Run My Library Good" Letter

AFFILIATION: None

SCOPE & CONTENT: The *Unabashed Librarian* has practical down-to-earth ideas geared for the public librarian in particular. Most of the articles are adapted from, or are actual reproductions from library publications. They include bibliographies complete with graphics, flyers, and newsletters. This publication is a successful blend of information, presented in a straight-forward style interspersed with humorous, light-hearted pieces.

INDEXED: Lib.Lit.

EDITOR: Marvin H. Scilken

MANUSCRIPT ADDRESS: P.O. Box 2631, New York, NY 10116

EDITORIAL POLICY:
Student Papers Accepted: Yes
Publication Lag Time: Varies
Reprints: 4 copies of entire issue
Authorship Restrictions: Not given

Abstract Required: Not given
Proofs Corrected By: Editor
Payment: No

THE MANUSCRIPT:
Number of Copies: 1
Acknowledgment: No
Acceptance Lag Time: Varies

Length: Not given
Critique Provided: Sometimes
Style: Not given

Format: Prefer typed manuscripts.

REVIEW POLICY:
Refereed: No
Reviewed By: Not given

Acceptance Rate: Not given

COPYRIGHT HELD BY:
First Publication: Not given

Republication: Not given

SUBSCRIPTION ADDRESS: Marvin H. Scilken, P.O. Box 2631, New York, NY 10116

Frequency: Quarterly
Circulation: Not given
Cost: $30 individuals, institutions, and other; $7.50 single issue

TELECOMMUNICATIONS: Fax: (212) 691-3807

URBAN ACADEMIC LIBRARIAN

AFFILIATION: Library Association of the City University of New York

SCOPE & CONTENT: In 1992, the *Urban Academic Librarian* completed 20 years of publishing on topics of interest to the academic librarian in an urban environment. The journal is affiliated with the City University of New York, one of the largest urban educational systems nationally. Many articles focus on major issues confronting urban libraries, especially those in New York. Contributors are both librarians and nonlibrarians.

INDEXED: High.Educ.Abstr., Lib.Lit., LISA

EDITOR: Robert Laurich

MANUSCRIPT ADDRESS: Hunter College Library, 695 Park Avenue, New York, NY 10021

EDITORIAL POLICY:

Student Papers Accepted: No	**Abstract Required:** 50-100 words
Publication Lag Time: Several months	**Proofs Corrected By:** Editor
Reprints: 1 copy of issue	**Payment:** None
Authorship Restrictions: None	

THE MANUSCRIPT:

Number of Copies: 3	**Length:** 2,000-3,000 words
Acknowledgment: Yes	**Critique Provided:** Not usually
Acceptance Lag Time: Several weeks	**Style:** *MLA Handbook*

Format: Title and affiliation of the author should accompany the manuscript.

REVIEW POLICY:

Refereed: Yes	**Acceptance Rate:** Not given
Reviewed By: Blind refereed	

COPYRIGHT HELD BY:

First Publication: Author	**Republication:** Author

SUBSCRIPTION ADDRESS: K. Meier, Hunter College Library, 695 Park Avenue, New York, NY 10021

Frequency: Biannually	**Circulation:** About 500

Cost: $10 individuals; $12 institutions; $15 outside U.S.; $8 single issue

TELECOMMUNICATIONS: K. Meier: Phone: (212) 772-4168

WESTERN ASSOCIATION OF MAP LIBRARIANS. INFORMATION BULLETIN

AFFILIATION: Western Association Map Libraries

SCOPE & CONTENT: This is a specialized publication of particular value to librarians and others involved with Western collections of maps. Subjects covered are limited to those that focus on aspects of map librarianship, geography or cartography. Contributors are librarians, geographers, map collectors, and cartographers. It publishes reviews of books, computer programs, and maps.

INDEXED: Lib.Lit.

EDITOR: Mary L. Lansgaard

MANUSCRIPT ADDRESS: Map and Imagery Lab, Library, University of California, Santa Barbara, CA 93106

EDITORIAL POLICY:

Student Papers Accepted: No   **Abstract Required:** Yes, 150 words
Publication Lag Time: 6 months   **Proofs Corrected By:** Editor
Reprints: None, except upon request   **Payment:** None
Authorship Restrictions: None

THE MANUSCRIPT:

Number of Copies: 1   **Length:** 2,000 words
Acknowledgment: Yes   **Critique Provided:** Always
Acceptance Lag Time: 1 month   **Style:** *Chicago Manual of Style*

Format: A word (IBM) or ASCII file on diskette if possible, otherwise typed.

REVIEW POLICY:

Refereed: No   **Acceptance Rate:** 90%
Reviewed By: Editor

COPYRIGHT HELD BY:

First Publication: Publisher   **Republication:** Publisher

SUBSCRIPTION ADDRESS: Western Association Map Libraries, P.O. Box 1667, Provo, Utah 84603

Frequency: 3 per year   **Circulation:** Approx. 250
Cost: $20 individuals; $25 institutions U.S.; $28 Canada; $30 others; single issue costs 1/3 of subscription

TELECOMMUNICATIONS: Editor: Phone: (805) 893-4049; Fax: (805) 893-4676; E-mail: BITNET: LB08MLL@UCSBVM.

WILSON LIBRARY BULLETIN

AFFILIATION: None

SCOPE & CONTENT: The WLB offers a wide variety of informative articles on subjects of interest to librarianship in general. The wide scope of topics covered, and their appeal to every level and for all types of libraries contribute to essential reading for those interested in professional issues. About half of the contents are devoted to feature articles and shorter commentaries; the second half include sections covering reviews in: Audio/Video, Technology, Books & Periodicals.

INDEXED: Amer.Hist.&Life, Bk.Rev.Ind., Educ.Ind., Hist.Abstr., Lib.Lit., LISA, Pop.Per.Ind.

EDITOR: Linda Mark, Acting Editor

MANUSCRIPT ADDRESS: H.W. Wilson Company, 950 University Avenue, Bronx, NY 10452

EDITORIAL POLICY:

Student Papers Accepted: Yes	**Abstract Required:** Yes
Publication Lag Time: 6 to 12 months	**Proofs Corrected By:** Editor
Reprints: 2 copies of issue	**Payment:** Yes
Authorship Restrictions: None	

THE MANUSCRIPT:

Number of Copies: 2	**Length:** 1,800-3,500 words
Acknowledgment: Yes	**Critique Provided:** Sometimes
Acceptance Lag Time: 6 to 12 months	**Style:** *Chicago Manual of Style*

Format: House style sheet available to authors upon request.

REVIEW POLICY:

Refereed: No	**Acceptance Rate:** 20-25%
Reviewed by: Editor with input from staff	

COPYRIGHT HELD BY:

First Publication: Journal	**Republication:** Journal

SUBSCRIPTION ADDRESS: *Wilson Library Bulletin*, The H.W. Wilson Company, 950 University Ave., Bronx, NY 10452

Frequency: Monthly, except July/August   **Circulation:** 12,000

Cost: $50 in U.S. and Canada; $56 foreign; $8 single copy in U.S. and Canada

TELECOMMUNICATIONS: H.W. Wilson Co. Phone: (800) 367-6770 and (212) 588-8400; Fax: (212) 681-1511

WLW JOURNAL

AFFILIATION: None

SCOPE & CONTENT: *WLW Journal* provides information to promote the development, education, and empowerment of women in librarianship for North America. Contributors are national and international professionals interested in women's social, economic, and developmental issues. Articles are encouraged that focus on topics such as sexual harassment in libraries, union experiences, physical and psychological stress as it relates to automated library procedures, flextime, services to the elderly or issues of concern in a profession in which women are predominant.

INDEXED: Not at this time

EDITOR: Audrey Eaglen

MANUSCRIPT ADDRESS: *WLW Journal,* 7055 Oakes Road, Breckville, OH 44141

EDITORIAL POLICY:
Student Papers Accepted: No   **Abstract Required:** No
Publication Lag Time: 3-6 months   **Proofs Corrected By:** Editor
Reprints: 1 copy of issue   **Payment:** $50 for two-page article
Authorship Restrictions: None

THE MANUSCRIPT:
Number of Copies: 1   **Length:** 1,500 words
Acknowledgment: Yes   **Critique Provided:** Not usually
Acceptance Lag Time: 1-2 weeks   **Style:** *Chicago Manual of Style*

Format: Use 8 1/2″ × 11″ paper double-spaced with diskette in WordPerfect.

REVIEW POLICY:
Refereed: No   **Acceptance Rate:** 90% based on
Reviewed By: Editor   solicited manuscripts

COPYRIGHT HELD BY:
First Publication: Publisher   **Republication:** Publisher

SUBSCRIPTION ADDRESS: *WLW Journal,* McFarland & Co., Box 611, Jefferson, NC 28640

Frequency: Quarterly   **Circulation:** About 300
Cost: $18 individuals; $22 foreign; $9 single issue

TELECOMMUNICATIONS: Phone: (919) 246-4460; Fax: (919) 246-5018

Electronic Journals and Newsletters

ACQNET

AFFILIATION: None

SCOPE & CONTENT: *ACQNET*, the Acquisitions Librarians Electronic Network, aims to provide a medium for acquisitions librarians and others to exchange information, ideas, and to find solutions to common problems. The editor, assisted by a five-member editorial board, receives all potential postings and organizes, edits and summarizes them for distribution. *ACQNET* combines many features of a newsletter with some characteristics of a bulletin board.

INDEXED: Index available via anonymous FTP

EDITOR: Christian M. Boissonnas

MANUSCRIPT ADDRESS: Central Technical Services, Cornell University Library, 107A Olin Library, Ithaca, NY 14853-5301, BITNET: CRI@CORNELLC.BITNET

EDITORIAL POLICY:

Student Papers Accepted: Yes	**Abstract Required:** No
Publication Lag Time: Up to 3 days	**Proofs Corrected By:** Editor
Reprints: Not applicable	**Payment:** No
Authorship Restrictions: None	

THE MANUSCRIPT:

Number of Copies: 1 electronic copy	**Length:** 150-400 words
Acknowledgment: No	**Critique Provided:** No
Acceptance Lag Time: Not applicable	**Style:** Plain clear English preferred

Format: Submit items by E-mail. If this is not feasible, submit items as an ASCII file on a floppy disk, limited to no more than 190 lines of 75 characters per line.

REVIEW POLICY:

Refereed: No	**Acceptance Rate:** 95-99%
Reviewed By: Editor	

COPYRIGHT HELD BY:

First Publication: Author	**Republication:** Author

SUBSCRIPTION ADDRESS: BITNET: CRI@CORNELLC. SUBSCRIBE
ACQNET your-first-name your-last name

Frequency: Irregular   **Circulation:** 715
Cost: Free to computer network users

TELECOMMUNICATIONS: BITNET: CRI@CORNELLC.

ALCTS NETWORK NEWS

AFFILIATION: Association for Library Collections & Technical Services, a division of the American Library Association

SCOPE & CONTENT: *ALCTS NETWORK NEWS* was established in May 1991, and is published by the Association for Library Collections & Technical Services with the goal of distributing news and information to its membership. A recent issue described two ALCTS awards, their sponsors, and the recipients. It reviewed three new Spec Kits published by the Office of Management Services. Lastly, it gave a brief overview of reports from a recent American Library Association meeting, and outlined the procedure for obtaining the reports electronically from ALCTS files.

INDEXED: Index available through the list server

EDITOR: Karen Muller

MANUSCRIPT ADDRESS: BITNET: U34261@UICVM

EDITORIAL POLICY:
Student Papers Accepted: No   **Abstract Required:** No
Publication Lag Time: Varies   **Proofs Corrected By:** Editor
Reprints: Not applicable   **Payment:** No
Authorship Restrictions: none

THE MANUSCRIPT:
Number of copies: 1 electronic copy   **Length:** Varies
Acknowledgment: No   **Critique Provided:** No
Acceptance Lag Time: Varies   **Style:** Not given

Format: News items should be sent to the editor in electronic format.

REVIEW POLICY:
Refereed: No   **Acceptance Rate:** Not given
Reviewed By: Editor and editorial board

COPYRIGHT HELD BY:
First Publication: Author/ALA   **Republication:** Author, with notification to ALA

SUBSCRIPTION ADDRESS: LISTSERV@UICVM.BITNET. SUB ALCTS your-first name your-last-name

Frequency: Irregular   **Circulation:** Not given
Cost: Free to computer network users

TELECOMMUNICATIONS: Editor: Phone: (800) 545-5031

ARACHNET ELECTRONIC JOURNAL ON VIRTUAL CULTURE

AFFILIATION: None

SCOPE & CONTENT: The *Arachnet Electronic Journal on Virtual Culture* (EJVC) is a scholarly journal that fosters, encourages, advances and communicates scholarly thought on virtual culture. Virtual culture is computer-mediated experience, behavior, action, interaction and thought, including electronic conferences, electronic journals, networked information systems, the construction and visualization of models of reality, and global connectivity. It includes unrefereed comments, reviews, and letters.

INDEXED: Index available via anonymous FTP or through the list server

EDITOR: Ermel Stepp

MANUSCRIPT ADDRESS: BITNET: MO34050@MARSHALL or, Internet: mo34050@marshall.wvnet.edu

EDITORIAL POLICY:

Student Papers Accepted: Yes   **Abstract Required:** Yes
Publication Lag Time: 1 month   **Proofs Corrected By:** Not given
Reprints: Not applicable   **Payment:** No
Authorship Restrictions: None

THE MANUSCRIPT:

Number of Copies: 1 electronic copy   **Length:** 1,000 lines or less
Acknowledgment: Yes   **Critique Provided:** Yes
Acceptance Lat Time: Almost   **Style:** APA preferred
    immediately

Format: Send all submissions by electronic mail. Any recognized standard of style is acceptable, with APA, modified for ASCII, the preferred style.

REVIEW POLICY:

Refereed: Yes   **Acceptance Rate:** Not specified
Reviewed By: Blind reviewers,
    at least three

COPYRIGHT HELD BY:

First Publication: Author   **Republication:** Author

SUBSCRIPTION ADDRESS: Internet: listserv@kentvm.kent.edu SUBSCRIBE EJVC-L your-first-name your-last name

Frequency: Monthly   **Circulation:** About 1,300
Cost: Free to computer network users

TELECOMMUNICATIONS: Co-editor: Diane Kovacs BITNET:DKOVACS@KENTVM or Internet: dkovacs@kentvm.kent.edu

ISSUES IN SCIENCE AND TECHNOLOGY LIBRARIANSHIP

AFFILIATION: Science and Technology Section of the Association of College and Research Libraries, a division of the American Library Association

SCOPE & CONTENT: Known unofficially as ISTL, this journal publishes concise but substantial articles of interest to science and technology librarians. It covers a variety of issues from scientific literacy to document delivery to European online databases. It attempts to include articles on current "hot" topics in the form of letters. "From The Director's Chair" is a column for library directors to address issues in an editorial format. ISTL editors encourage reports on conference workshops and training sessions. Announcements, press releases and general news are also included.

INDEXED: Citations to Serials Literature, Internet: sercites@mitvma.mit.edu. Back issues are available from the editor.

EDITOR: Harry Llull

MANUSCRIPT ADDRESS: Internet: acrlsts@hal.unm.edu

EDITORIAL POLICY:

Student Papers Accepted: Yes
Publication Lag Time: Very rapid
Reprints: Not applicable
Authorship Restrictions: None

Abstract Required: No
Proofs Corrected By: Editor
Payment: No

THE MANUSCRIPT:

Number of Copies: 1 electronic copy
Acknowledgment: Yes
Acceptance Lag Time: Quickly

Length: 200-300 electronic lines
Critique Provided: Yes
Style: Not specified

Format: Submit material electronically. No format requirements. Bibliographies are encouraged when appropriate.

REVIEW POLICY:

Refereed: Yes
Reviewed By: Editor and/or editorial board

Acceptance Rate: High

COPYRIGHT HELD BY:

First Publication: Author, when requested

Republication: Author with acknowledgment to ISTL

SUBSCRIPTION ADDRESS: arclsts@hal.unm.edu SUBSCRIBE ISTL with a message to subscribe to ISTL followed by your name

Frequency: Quarterly, with irregular updates
Cost: Free to computer network users

Circulation: 700

TELECOMMUNICATIONS: Gregg Sapp: BITNET: ALIGS@MTSUNIXI.
for access service topics; John Saylor john_saylor@qmrelay.mail.cornell.e-
du for virtual librarianship; Lynn Kaczor lkaczor@hal.unm.edu for workshop and conference reports

LIBRES: LIBRARY AND INFORMATION SCIENCE RESEARCH

AFFILIATION: None

SCOPE & CONTENT: *LIBRES* aims to facilitate and foster research in library and information science. It serves as a platform for initiating, developing, and refining research projects and ideas useful for both librarians and other information professionals. In 1993, *LIBRES* expanded its scope and reorganized with the goal of becoming a peer-reviewed, scholarly journal. It also includes sections for news, discussion and reviews, and applications and essays.

INDEXED: Index available via anonymous FTP or through the list server

EDITOR: Diane Kovacs

MANUSCRIPT ADDRESS: Internet: Libres@Kentvm.kent.edu or, BIT-NET: LIBRES@KENTVM

EDITORIAL POLICY:
Student Papers Accepted: Yes   **Abstract Required:** Yes
Publication Lag Time: 2 weeks to   **Proofs Corrected By:** Author/
  2 months   Editor
Reprints: Not applicable   **Payment:** No
Authorship Restrictions: None

THE MANUSCRIPT:
Number of Copies: 1 electronic copy   **Length:** Varies
Acknowledgment: Yes   **Critique Provided:** Yes
Acceptance Lat Time: Almost   **Style:** Standard
  immediately

Format: Send all submissions by electronic mail.

REVIEW POLICY:
Refereed: Yes   **Acceptance Rate:** Not given
Reviewed By: Editors or peer reviewed

COPYRIGHT HELD BY:
First Publication: Author   **Republication:** Author, with
                      permission from publisher

SUBSCRIPTION ADDRESS: BITNET: LIBRES@KENTVM or Internet: Libres@kentvm.kent.edu SUBSCRIBE LIBRES your-first-name your-last name

Frequency: Monthly   **Circulation:** About 2,000
Cost: Free to computer network users

TELECOMMUNICATIONS: Editor: E-mail: Internet: dkovacs@kentvm.kent.edu

MC JOURNAL: THE JOURNAL OF ACADEMIC MEDIA LIBRARIANSHIP

AFFILIATION: None

SCOPE & CONTENT: The primary mission of this journal is to provide both practical and scholarly information on topics and issues concerning academic media librarianship. Its scope encompasses technologies that include audiovisuals as the primary, but not necessarily the exclusive modes of communication. Examples of topics as they relate to audiovisual librarianship include: a/v production, collection development, cataloging, storage and preservation of materials, media center management, and copyright and emerging technologies. Articles pertaining to the profession of academic media librarianship and library education are also acceptable as are conference reports, literature reviews, and reviews of hardware and software.

INDEXED: No

EDITOR: Lori Widzinski or Terrence McCormack

MANUSCRIPT ADDRESS: Internet: mcjrnl@ubvm.cc.buffalo.edu or, MCJ RNL@UBVM.BITNET

EDITORIAL POLICY:
Student Papers Accepted: No   **Abstract Required:** 10-12 lines
Publication Lag Time: 2-3 months   **Proofs Corrected By:** Author
Reprints: Not applicable   **Payment:** No
Authorship Restrictions: None

THE MANUSCRIPT:
Number of Copies: 1 electronic copy   **Length:** 2,300 words
Acknowledgment: Yes   **Critique Provided:** Upon request
Acceptance Lag Time: 4-6 weeks   **Style:** *Chicago Manual of Style*

Format: Submit in ASCII format via E-mail. You may also send your file saved in ASCII on a 3 1/2" diskette to Lori Widzinski, Media Resources Center, Health Sciences Library, Abbott Hall, South Campus, State University of New York at Buffalo, NY 14214.

REVIEW POLICY:
Refereed: Yes   **Acceptance Rate:** Not given
Reviewed By: Blind refereed

COPYRIGHT HELD BY:
First Publication: Author   **Republication:** Author, with
                                          notification to journal

SUBSCRIPTION ADDRESS: Internet: listserv@ubvm.cc.edu or LIST-SERV@UBVM.BITNET. SUBSCRIBE MCJRNL your-first-name your-last name.

Frequency: Irregular   **Circulation:** 359
Cost: Free to computer network users
TELECOMMUNICATIONS: No given

MECKJOURNAL

AFFILIATION: None

SCOPE & CONTENT: *MeckJournal* addresses electronic publishing issues as they affect library and academic research. Contributors are generally librarians and academic researchers, and the types of articles most frequently published are theoretical or empirical research, or case studies. *MeckJournal* includes commentaries, special "theme" issues, news items, new products, and reports on conferences and workshops. It does not publish reviews. The intended audience is international.

INDEXED: No

EDITOR: Tony Abbott

MANUSCRIPT ADDRESS: Internet: meckler@jvnc.net

EDITORIAL POLICY:

Student Papers Accepted: No	**Abstract Required:** No
Publication Lag Time: 4 weeks	**Proofs Corrected By:** Editor
Reprints: Not applicable	**Payment:** No
Authorship Restrictions: None	

THE MANUSCRIPT:

Number of Copies: 1 electronic copy	**Length:** 7-10 pages
Acknowledgment: Yes	**Critique Provided:** Never
Acceptance Lag Time: 2 weeks	**Style:** MLA preferred

Format: Submit material electronically.

REVIEW POLICY:

Refereed: No	**Acceptance Rate:** 25%
Reviewed By: Editor	

COPYRIGHT HELD BY:

First Publication: Author	**Republication:** Author

SUBSCRIPTION ADDRESS: Internet:meckler@jvnc.net. Subscribe Meck-Journal your-first-name your-last name

Frequency: Monthly	**Circulation:** 1,000
Cost: Free to computer network users	

TELECOMMUNICATIONS: Editor: Phone: (203) 226-6967; Fax: (203) 454-5840; E-mail: Internet: meckler@jvnc.net

NEWSLETTER ON SERIALS PRICING ISSUES

AFFILIATION: None

SCOPE & CONTENT: This newsletter focuses on pricing/costs of library serials publications, especially journals. It includes items on related topics such as electronic publishing, conferences and workshops, and publisher/vendor activities. It is published by the editor through the Office of Information Technology at the University of North Carolina at Chapel Hill as news is available.

INDEXED: Index available through the list server or through Citations to Serials Literature, Internet: sercites@mitvma.mit.edu

EDITOR: Marcia Tuttle

MANUSCRIPT ADDRESS: Serials Dept., CB #3938 Davis Library, University of North Carolina at Chapel Hill, Chapel Hill, NC 27599-3938, Internet: tuttle@gibbs.oit.unc.edu

EDITORIAL POLICY:
Student Papers Accepted: Yes   **Abstract Required:** No
Publication Lag Time: 1 to 2 weeks   **Proofs Corrected By:** Editor
Reprints: Not applicable   **Payment:** No
Authorship Restrictions: None

THE MANUSCRIPT:
Number of Copies: 1 electronic copy   **Length:** 100-1,000 words
Acknowledgment: Yes, sent   **Critique Provided:** Not applicable
electronically   **Style:** No requirements
Acceptance Lag Time: Almost
immediately

Format: Submit news articles or items by E-mail.

REVIEW POLICY:
Refereed: No   **Acceptance Rate:** About 80%
Reviewed By: Editor and occasionally
the editorial board.

COPYRIGHT HELD BY:
First Publication: Author   **Republication:** Author

SUBSCRIPTION ADDRESS: Internet:listserv@gibbs.oit.unc.edu. SUBSCRIBE PRICES your-first-name your-last name

Frequency: Irregular   **Circulation:** About 1,300
Cost: Free to computer network users

TELECOMMUNICATIONS: Editor: Phone: (919) 962-1067; Fax: (919) 962-0484; E-mail: Internet: tuttle@gibbs.oit.unc.edu

PUBLIC ACCESS COMPUTER SYSTEMS REVIEW

AFFILIATION: None

SCOPE & CONTENT: Known by the acronym, PACS Review, it is associated with the PACS-L and PACS-P lists, and is distributed via BITNET, Internet, and other computer networks. The journal deals with end-user computer systems in libraries, covering topics such as campus-wide information systems, CD-ROM LANs, document delivery systems, electronic publishing, expert systems, hypermedia and multimedia systems, locally mounted databases, microcomputer labs, network-based information resources, and online catalogs. It was established in September 1989 and became refereed in November 1991. The journal has a sixteen-member editorial board.

INDEXED: Index available via anonymous FTP, or through the list server

EDITOR: Charles W. Bailey, Jr.

MANUSCRIPT ADDRESS: Assistant Director For Library Systems, University Libraries, University of Houston, Houston, TX 77204-2091, Internet: lib3@uhupvm1.uh.edu, BITNET: LIB3@UHUPVM1

EDITORIAL POLICY:

Student Papers Accepted: Yes	**Abstract Required:** Yes
Publication Lag Time: 1-3 months	**Proofs Corrected By:** Editor
Reprints: Not applicable	**Payment:** No
Authorship Restrictions: None	

THE MANUSCRIPT:

Number of Copies: 1 electronic copy	**Length:** 2,000 words
Acknowledgment: Not applicable	**Critique Provided:** Sometimes
Acceptance Lag Time: 2-4 weeks	**Style:** *Chicago Manual of Style*

Format: Keep format of the manuscript as simple as possible. Manuscripts should be single-spaced with a line length of 65 characters. Do not underline or italicize text. Minimize use of illustrations and tables. Submit manuscripts by E-mail or file transfer. If this is not feasible, submit manuscript as an ASCII file or a WordPerfect file on a 1.2 MB or a 1.44 MB IBM floppy disk.

REVIEW POLICY:

Refereed: Yes	**Acceptance Rate:** Not applicable
Reviewed By: Editors or peer reviewed	

COPYRIGHT HELD BY:

First Publication: Author	**Republication:** Author

SUBSCRIPTION ADDRESS: Internet: listserv@uhupvm1.uh.edu OR LISTSERV@UHUPVM1 SUBSCRIBE PAC-L your-first-name your-last-name

Frequency: Irregular	**Circulation:** About 6,400
Cost: Free to computer network users	

TELECOMMUNICATIONS: Phone: (713) 743-9804; Fax: (713) 743-9748

Additional Periodicals

The following is a listing of additional publications for which detailed information was unavailable.

Art Libraries Journal
ARLIS/UK and Eire
18 College Rd.
Bromsgrove, Worcestershire B60
   2NE
England

Australian & New Zealand Journal of Serials Librarianship: The Serials
Journal of Australasia
The Haworth Press, Inc.
10 Alice St.
Binghamton, NY 13904

Document Image Automation
Meckler Publishing Corporation
11 Ferry Lane W.,
Westport, CT 06880

The Electronic Library: The International Journal for Minicomputer, Microcomputer, and Software Applications in Libraries
Learned Information, Ltd.
143 Old Marlton Pike
Medford, NJ 08055

Federal Librarian
American Library Association
Federal Librarians Round Table
110 Maryland Ave., N.E.
Washington DC 20002

Health Libraries Review
Blackwell Scientific Publications,
   Ltd.
Osney Mead
Oxford, OX2 OEL
England

Information Development: The International Journal for Librarians, Archivists and Information Specialists
Mansell Publishing Ltd.
Villiers House
41-47 Strand
London WC2N 5JE
England

Information Processing and Management: An International Journal
Pergamon Press, Inc.
Journals Division
Maxwell House
Fairview Park
Elmsford, NY 10523

International Classification: A Journal Devoted to Concept Theory, Organization of Knowledge and Data, and to Systematic Terminology
Indeks Verlag
Woogstr. 36a
6000 Frankfurt 50
Germany

International Journal of Legal Information
International Institute for Legal Information
Box 5709
Washington DC 20016-1309

International Library Review
Academic Press Ltd.
24-28 Oval Rd.
London NW1 7DX
England

Library
Oxford University Press
Oxford Journals
Pinkhill House
Southfield Rd.
Eynsham, Oxford OX8 1JJ
England

Library & Information Science Research: An International Journal
Ablex Publishing Corporation
355 Chestnut St.
Norwood, NJ 07648

LIBRI; International Library Review
Munksgaard International Publishers Ltd.
Journals Division
35 Noerre Soegade
P.O. Box 2148
DK-1016 Copenhagan K
Denmark

The New Library Scene
Library Binding Inst.
8013 Centre Park Dr.
Austin, TX 78754

State Library Associations

The publications of state library associations provide many opportunities for the writer. Typically, these publications focus on state-wide issues of concern to libraries. Articles that publicize and critique regional library events and update the membership on finance, legislation, and education are frequent topics in state association bulletins and newsletters. Some state publications also address subjects that are of a more general interest to librarians.

Alabama Library Association
Deborah J. Grimes
Shelton State Community
College Library
202 Skyland Blvd.
Tuscaloosa, AL 35405
(205) 391-2233

Alaska Library Association
Maurine Canarsky, President
1009 Pedro Street
Fairbanks, AK 99701
(907) 459-1020
FAX: (907) 459-1024

Arizona State Library Association
Carol Hammond, President
Arizona State University
West Campus Library
P.O. Box 37100
Phoenix, AZ 85069-7100
(602) 542-8504
FAX: (602) 543-8521

Arkansas Library Association
Alice Coleman, President
Texarkana Public Library
600 West 3rd Street

Texarkana, AR 75501
(501) 794-2149

California Library Association
Joy Thomas, President
California State Univ.-Long Beach
University Library
Long Beach, CA 90840
(301) 985-7817

Colorado Library Association
Stephany Liptak, President
University of Southern Colorado
2200 Bonforte Blvd.
Pueblo, CO 81001-4901
(719) 549-2361
FAX: (719) 549-2738

Connecticut Library Association
Peter Chase, President
Plainville Public Library
56 East Main Street
Plainville, CT 06062
(203) 793-1446
FAX: (203) 793-2285

Delaware Library Association
Verlie Gaither, President
Delaware Tech & Community
    College
Wilmington Campus
3333 Shipley Street
Wilmington, DE 19801
(302) 573-5432

District of Columbia Library
    Association
Sue Uebelacker, President
4102 Canterbury Way
Tempo Hills, MD 20748
(301) 390-7458

Florida Library Association
Dr. Susan Anderson
St. Petersburg Junior College
8580 66th Street N
Pinnellas Park, FL 34665-1299
(813) 341-3600

Georgia Library Association
Donna D. Mancini, President
Dekalb County Public Library
Administration
215 Sycamore Street
Decatur, GA 30030
(404) 370-8450
FAX: (404) 370-8469

Guam Library Association
Chih Wang, President
Dean, Learning Resources
University of Guam
Mangilao, GU 96923
(671) 734-2482
FAX: (671) 734-6882

Hawaii Library Association
Kenneth Herrick, President

University of Hawaii at Hilo
50-I Malaai Road
Hilo, HI 96720
(808) 933-3507
FAX: (808) 933-3329

Idaho Library Association
Randy Simmons, President
Northwest Nazarene
College Library
623 Holly Street
Nampa, ID 83686
(208) 467-8609

Illinois Library Association
Barbara Aron, President
Blue Island Public Library
2433 York Street
Blue Island, IL 60406
(708) 388-1078
FAX: (708) 388-1143

Indiana Library Federation
Sandy Sawyer, President
Fulton County Public Library
RR 6, Box 162
Rochester, IN 46975
(219) 223-2008
FAX: (317) 738-9635

Iowa Library Association
Ricardo Suaro, President
Tipon Public Library
206 Cedar Street
Tipton, IA 52272
(319) 886-6266

Kansas Library Association
Kay Bradt, President
606 8th Street
Baldwin, KS 66066
(913) 594-6451 x414
FAX: (913) 594-6721

Kentucky Library Association
Janet Stith, President
226 Jesselin Drive
Lexington, KY 40503
(606) 233-5727

Louisiana Library Association
Grace G. Moore, President
Recorder of Documents
State Library of Louisiana
P.O. Box 131
Baton Rouge, LA 70808
(504) 342-4929
FAX: (504) 342-3547

Maine Library Association
Barbara Rice, President
Bangor Public Library
145 Harlow Street
Bangor, ME 04401
(207) 947-8336

Maryland Library Association
Dr. Shirley Peck, President
Dir. Library & Media Services
Essex Community College
7201 Rossville Blvd.
Baltimore, MD 21237
(410) 522-1321

Massachusetts Library Association
Ellen Rainville, President
J. V. Fletcher Library
50 Main Street
Westford, MA 01886
(508) 692-5555

Michigan Library Association
Sandra Yee, President
4657 Kingswood Drive
Brighton, MI 48116
(313) 487-0020

Middle Atlantic Regional
   Library Federation (MARLF)
Katharine C. Hurrey, President
Southern Maryland Regional
   Library Association
P.O. Box 459
Charlotte Hall, MD 20622
(410) 934-9442
FAX: (410) 884-0438

Midwest Federation of Library
   Associations (MFLA)
Patricia Llerandi, President
Schaumburg Township Library
32 West Library Lane
Schaumburg, IL 60194
(708) 885-3373, ext. 150
FAX: (708) 885-8271

Minnesota Library Association
Linda DeBeau-Melting
2824 43rd Ave. South
Minneapolis, MN 55406
(612) 625-5050

Mississippi Library Association
Sherry Laughlin, President
University of Southern Mississippi
Cook Memorial Library
Hattiesburg, MS 39404-5053
(601) 266-4270

Missouri Library Association
Julie Schneider, President
Learning Resources Center
Missouri Western State College
4525 Downs Drive
St. Joseph, MO 64507
(816) 271-4369

Montana Library Association
Jane Howell, President
Eastern Montana College
1500 North 30th Street
Billings, MT 59101-0298
(406) 657-1662
FAX: (406) 657-2037

Mountain Plains Library Association (MPLA)
Ronelle Thompson, President
Mikkelsen Library
Augustana College
Sioux Falls, SD 57197
(605) 336-4921

Nebraska Library Association
Carol Connor, President
Lincoln City Library
136 S. 14th
Lincoln, NE 68508
(402) 471-8510
FAX: (402) 471-8586

Nevada Library Association
Gary Avent, President
Elko County Public Library
720 Court Street
Elko, NV 89801
(702) 738-3066
FAX: (702) 738-8262

New England Library Association (NELA)
Carol K. DiPrete, President
Roger Williams College Library
1 Old Ferry Road
Bristol, RI 02809
(401) 254-3063
FAX: (401) 254-0818

New Hampshire Library Association
Ann Trementozzi, President
R.R. 2, Box 112
Norwich, VT 05055
(802) 649-3351

New Jersey Library Association
Norma Blake, President
Burlington County Library
West Woodlane Road
Mt. Holly, NJ 08060
(609) 267-9660

New Mexico Library Association
Allison E. Almquist, President
Wherry Elementary School
Inez Elementary School
Albuquerque, NM 87116
(505) 268-2434

New York Library Association
Sandra Miranda, President
White Plains Public Library
100 Martine Ave.
White Plains, NY 10601
(914) 422-1406

North Carolina Library Association
Gwendolyn Jackson, President
Southeastern Tech. Assistant Cir.
2013 Lejeune Blvd.
Jacksonville, NC 28546
(919) 577-8920
FAX: (919) 577-1427

North Dakota Library Association
Jan Hendrickson, President
Hazen Public Library
P.O. Box 471
Hazen, SD 58545
(701) 748-2977

Ohio Library Association
James Bouchard, President
Lima Public Library
650 W. Market Street
Lima, OH 45801
(419) 224-2669

Oklahoma Library Association
Jan Keene, President
Tulsa City-County Library
400 Civic Center
Tulsa, OK 74103
(918) 596-7880

Oregon Library Association
Patrick Grace, President
Kerr Library
Oregon State University
Corvallis, OR 97331
(503) 737-7265
FAX: (503) 737-3453

Pacific North West Library Association (PNLA)
Audrey Kolb, President
2471 NW Williams Loop
Redmond, OR 97756
(503) 548-0381

Pennsylvania Library Association
Cynthia K. Richey, President
439 Austin Ave.
Pittsburgh, PA 15240
(412) 531-1912
(412) 531-1161

Rhode Island Library Association
Florence Kell Dokansky, President
Box 1
Brown University
Providence, RI 02912

(401) 863-2162
FAX: (401) 863-2753

South Carolina Library Association
Debbie Coleman, President
Rt. 2, Box 139F
Denmark, SC 29042
(803) 793-5836

South Dakota Library Association
Glenda Oakely, President
1241 Frank
Huron, SD 57350
(605) 352-9818

Southeastern Library Association (SELA)
Gail Lazenby, President
Cobb County Public Library
266 Roswell Street
Marietta, GA 30060
(404) 528-2324
FAX (404) 528-2349

Tennessee Library Association
Carolyn Daniel, President
McGavock High School Library
3150 McGavock Pike
Nashville, TN 37214
(615) 885-8881

Texas Library Association
E. Dale Cluff, President
Texas Tech University Libraries
Lubbock, TX 79409-0002
(806) 742-1920

Utah Library Association
Peter J. Giacoma
365 Emery
Salt Lake City, UT 84104
(801) 451-2322

Vermont Library Association
Laurel Stanley, President
Lyndon State College Library
Lyndonville, VT 05851
(802) 626-9371

Virgin Islands Library Association
St. Croix Lib. Assn.
Virginia Wilder
P.O. Box 3017
Christiansted
St. Croix, VI 00820
(809) 778-1600

Virginia Library Association
John Stewart, President
Dept. of Pub. Lib. Municipal Ctr.
Virginia Beach, VA 23456
(804) 427-4321
FAX: (804) 427-4220

Washington Library Association
Randall Hensley, President
University of Washington Libs.

OUGL, DF-10
Seattle, WA 98195
(206) 543-1968
FAX: (206) 685-8049

West Virginia Library Association
J. D. Waggoner, President
WV Library Commission
Science & Cultural Center
1900 Kanawha Blvd. E.
Charleston, WV 25305-0627
(304) 558-2531

Wisconsin Library Association
Ethel Himmel, President
8427 W. Hawthorne
Wauwatosa, WI 53226-4635
(414) 453-2126

Wyoming Library Association
Helen Higby, President
Sweetwater County Library
P.O. Box 550
Green River, WY 82935
(307) 875-3615

Source: Chapter Relations Office of the American Library Association

Refereed Journals

For this book, a refereed journal is defined as one in which submitted manuscripts are evaluated by an independent expert or a panel of experts. The reviewers evaluating the manuscript may be members of the journal's editorial board, or external reviewers, or a combination of both.

Acquisitions Librarian
Advances in Librarianship
Advances in Library Administration and Organization
African Journal of Academic Librarianship
Against the Grain
American Society for Information Science Journal
Arachnet Electronic Journal on Virtual Culture
Archivum
Art Documentation
Art Reference Services Quarterly
Asian Libraries
ASLIB Information
ASLIB Proceedings
Australian Library Review
Behavioral and Social Sciences Librarian
British Journal of Academic Librarianship
British Library Journal
Canadian Library Journal
Cataloging & Classification Quarterly
CD-ROM Librarian
CD-ROM Professional
Church and Synagogue Libraries
Collection Building

Collection Management
College and Research Libraries
Concepts in Communication Informatics and Librarianship
Education for Information
Education for Library and Information Services: Australia
Emergency Librarian
FID News Bulletin
Free State Libraries
Government Information Quarterly
Government Publications Review
IFLA Journal
Illinois Libraries
Indian Archives
Information Reports & Bibliographies
Information Services and Use
Information Systems Management
Information Technology and Libraries
Interlending and Document Supply
International Journal of Information and Library Research
International Review of Children's Literature and Librarianship
Internet Research: Electronic Networking, Applications and Policy
Issues in Science and Technology Librarianship
Journal of Academic Librarianship
Journal of Business & Finance Librarianship
Journal of Documentation
Journal of Education for Library and Information Science
Journal of Information Science
Journal of Interlibrary Loan & Information Supply
Journal of Librarianship and Information Science
Journal of Library Administration
Journal of the Rutgers University Library
Journal of Youth Services in Libraries
Judaica Librarianship

Legal Reference Services Quarterly

Libraries & Culture

Library Acquisitions: Practice & Theory

Library Administration & Management

Library & Archival Security

Library & Information Science Research: An International Journal

Library History

Library History Review

Library Hi Tech

Library Journal

Library Management

Library Quarterly

Library Resources & Technical Services

Library Review

Library Times International

Library Trends

LIBRES: Library and Information Science

Lucknow Librarian

MC Journal: The Journal of Academic Media Librarianship

Medical Library Association. Bulletin

Medical Reference Services Quarterly

Microcomputers for Information Management

Music Reference Services Quarterly

North Carolina Libraries

Ohio Media Spectrum

Orana: Journal of School and Children's Librarianship

Pakistan Library Bulletin

Popular Culture in Libraries

Primary Sources & Original Works

Program: Automated Library & Information Systems

Public Access Computer Systems Review

Public Libraries

Public Library Quarterly

Public Services Quarterly
Rare Books and Manuscripts Librarianship
Reference Librarian
Reference Services Review
Research Strategies
Resource Sharing and Information Networks
RQ
School Library Journal: The Magazine of Children's, Young Adult
    and School Librarians
School Library Media Activities Monthly
School Library Media Quarterly
Science & Technology Libraries
Serials Librarian
Serials Review
Special Libraries
Technical Services Quarterly
Urban Academic Librarian

Index